The Ultimate
World Wrestling
Entertainment™
Trivia Book

The Ultimate

World Wrestling Entertainment™ Trivia Book

Aaron Feigenbaum

Kevin Kelly

Seth Mates

Brian Solomon

Phil Speer

World Wrestling Entertainment™ BOOKS

This book is a publication of Pocket Books, a division of Simon & Schuster, Inc., under exclusive license from World Wrestling Entertainment, Inc.

All rights reserved, including the right to reproduce this book or portions thereof in any form whatsoever. For information address Pocket Books, 1230 Avenue of the Americas, New York, NY 10020

ISBN: 0-7434-5756-0

First Pocket Books printing November 2002

POCKET and colophon are registerd trademarks of Simon & Schuster, Inc.

Designed by Laura Lindgren and Celia Fuller

Visit us on the World Wide Web

http://simonsays.com

http://www.wwe.com

Printed in the U.S.A.

For information regarding special discounts for bulk purchases, please contact Simon & Schuster Special Sales at 1-800-456-6798 or business@simonandschuster.com

CONTENTS

WRESTLEMANIA

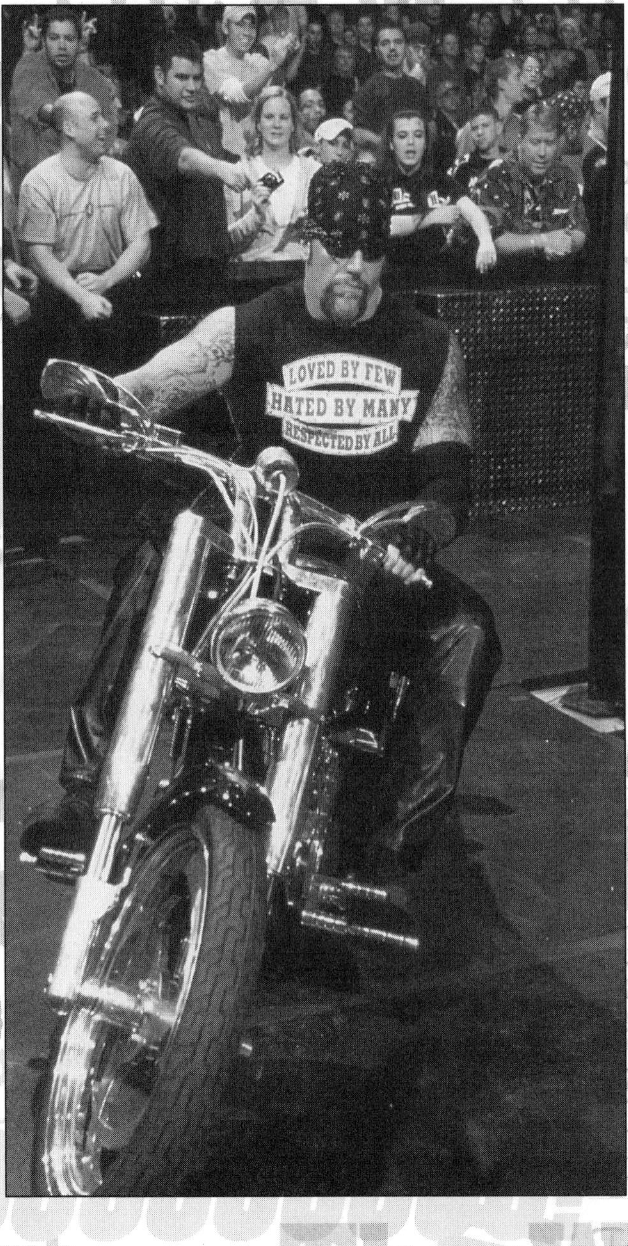
LOVED BY FEW
HATED BY MANY
RESPECTED BY ALL

WrestleMania

1. What was the date of the first *WrestleMania*?
a) March 17, 1985   b) March 23, 1986
c) March 31, 1985   d) April 4, 1990

2. True or false: The inaugural *WrestleMania* was seen on Pay-Per-View.

3. Which of these stars was NOT a part of the first *WrestleMania*:
a) Liberace   b) Morton Downey Jr.
c) Muhammad Ali   d) Billy Martin

4. What was the first match in *WrestleMania* history?
a) King Kong Bundy vs. S. D. Jones
b) Tito Santana vs. the Executioner
c) Ricky Steamboat vs. Ted DiBiase
d) Randy Savage vs. Hulk Hogan

5. The first title to change hands at *WrestleMania* was the...
a) Tag Team Championship
b) Women's Championship
c) Light Heavyweight Championship
d) Intercontinental Championship

6. Which pop music star accompanied Wendi Richter to the ring for her match at the first *WrestleMania* against Leilani Kai?
a) Alice Cooper   b) Mick Jagger
c) Cyndi Lauper   d) Dexy's Midnight Runners

7. How much money did Andre the Giant win in the Bodyslam Challenge against Big John Studd?
a) $5,000   b) $15,000   c) $1 million   d) $1,000

8. Who were the two referees for the main event at the premiere *WrestleMania*?
a) **Jersey Joe Walcott and Pat Patterson**
b) **Mike Tyson and Earl Hebner**
c) **Muhammad Ali and Pat Patterson**
d) **Alan Thicke and Robert Goulet**

9. The first *WrestleMania* was held at ...
a) **Rosemont Horizon**
b) **Los Angeles Memorial Sports Arena**
c) **Arrowhead Pond**
d) **Madison Square Garden**

10. How long did it take King Kong Bundy to beat S.D. Jones at the inaugural *WrestleMania*?
a) **1 minute**
b) **9 seconds**
c) **37 seconds**
d) **14 minutes and 59 seconds**

11. Who was Roddy Piper's tag-team partner for the first *WrestleMania*?
a) **Mr. T**
b) **Bam Bam Bigelow**
c) **Cowboy Bob Orton**
d) **Paul Orndorff**

WrestleMania 2

12. Which two Superstars made their *WrestleMania* debut at *WrestleMania 2*?
a) Jake Roberts   b) Mick Foley
c) Bret Hart   d) Vader

13. *WrestleMania 2* emanated from how many cities?
a) 1   b) 3   c) 5   d) 2

14. Which celebrity was a guest judge for the boxing match between Roddy Piper and Mr. T at *WrestleMania 2*?
a) Joan Rivers   b) Mary Hart
c) Cab Calloway   d) Ozzy Osbourne

15. What was the outcome of the Paul Orndorff vs. Don Muraco match at *WrestleMania 2*?
a) Muraco won by pinfall.
b) Orndorff won by pinfall.
c) Muraco won by submission.
d) It was a double countout.

16. Who defeated Nikolai Volkoff at *WrestleMania 2*?
a) Barry Windham   b) Cpl. Kirschner
c) Mike Rotundo   d) Iron Sheik

17. Who was NOT a part of the Open Invitational 20-Man Battle Royal at *WrestleMania 2*?
a) Bill Fralic
b) Lawrence Taylor
c) William "Refrigerator" Perry
d) Harvey Martin

18. Which was NOT a host city for *WrestleMania 2*?
a) Los Angeles   b) Chicago
c) Detroit   d) New York

19. Who did Hulk Hogan face at *WrestleMania 2*?
a) **King Kong Bundy**   b) **Andre the Giant**
c) **Ted DiBiase**   d) **Randy Savage**

20. The Los Angeles Memorial Sports Arena was one of
the venues for *WrestleMania 2*. Which rock 'n' roll
star has performed at the historic site seventeen
times?
a) **Elvis Presley**   b) **Ricky Martin**
c) **Bruce Springsteen**   d) **Sting**

21. Who did the British Bulldogs beat to win the Tag
Team Championships at *WrestleMania 2*?
a) **the Moondogs**
b) **The Hart Foundation**
c) **Brutus Beefcake & Greg Valentine**
d) **Jack and Gerry Brisco**

22. *I critique celebrity fashion on the E! Network and
I was a guest ring announcer at* WrestleMania 2.
Who am I?
a) **Susan St. James**   b) **Joan Rivers**
c) **Martha Stewart**   d) **Mr. Blackwell**

23. Who was King Kong Bundy's manager for his match
against Hulk Hogan at *WrestleMania 2*?
a) **Bobby "The Brain" Heenan**
b) **The Grand Wizard**
c) **"Classy" Freddie Blassie**
d) **Captain Lou Albano**

24. Who was the ring announcer for the Los Angeles
Memorial Sports Arena portion of *WrestleMania 2*?
a) **Howard Finkel**
b) **Michael Buffer**
c) **Gorilla Monsoon**
d) **Lee Marshall**

WrestleMania III

25. Which of the following previously held the indoor attendance record that was broken at *WrestleMania III?*
a) The Pope   b) Super Bowl
c) The Rolling Stones   d) The Beach Boys

26. *WrestleMania III* was held at...
a) Madison Square Garden
b) Pontiac Silverdome
c) L.A. Coliseum
d) Soldier Field

27. What was unique about the *WrestleMania III* match between Ricky Steamboat and Randy Savage?
a) It went to a one-hour draw.
b) It was the first time the Intercontinental Championship changed hands at *WrestleMania*.
c) It was a retirement match.
d) It took place inside a steel cage.

28. Who were Hillbilly Jim's partners in the six-man Tag Team match at *WrestleMania III?*
a) Little Beaver & Haiti Kid
b) Phineas & Henry Godwinn
c) Little Tokyo & Cowboy Lang
d) The Conquistadors

29. What was the prematch stipulation in the *WrestleMania III* battle between the Junkyard Dog and Harley Race?
a) The loser had to retire.
b) The loser had to eat a snake.
c) The loser had his head shaved.
d) The loser had to bow down to the winner.

30. Who sang "America the Beautiful" at *WrestleMania III*?
  a) **Willie Nelson**   b) **Salt-n-Pepa**
  c) **Aretha Franklin**   d) **INXS**

31. Which major sports event has the Pontiac Silverdome NOT hosted?
  a) **World Cup Finals**   b) **NCAA Final Four**
  c) ***WrestleMania***   d) **Super Bowl**

32. Who defeated Adrian Adonis at *WrestleMania III*?
  a) **Roddy Piper**   b) **Mr. T**
  c) **Outback Jack**   d) **Pepper Gomez**

33. Koko B. Ware lost to Butch Reed at *WrestleMania III*. What was the name of Koko's bird?
  a) **Harvey**   b) **Bruno**
  c) **Brawler**   d) **Frankie**

34. After turning on his tag-team partner, Brutus Beefcake, who did Greg Valentine align himself with?
  a) **Ricky Steamboat**   b) **Danny Davis**
  c) **Dino Bravo**   d) **Dr. Tom Prichard**

35. Who was the referee for the *WrestleMania III* main event featuring Hulk Hogan and Andre the Giant?
  a) **Joey Morella**   b) **Earl Hebner**
  c) **Dave Hebner**   d) **Mike Chioda**

36. Who did Billy Jack Haynes wrestle at *WrestleMania III*?
  a) **Dusty Rhodes**   b) **Hercules**
  c) **Jake Roberts**   d) **Bret Hart**

WrestleMania IV

37. What was the subtitle of *WrestleMania IV*?
a) The New Generation
b) The Ragin' Climax
c) What the World Is Watching
d) Four on the Floor

38. Who had decided that there would be a championship tournament at *WrestleMania IV*?
a) Hulk Hogan   b) Jack Tunney
c) Gorilla Monsoon   d) Ric Flair

39. How many Superstars were in the tournament?
a) 8   b) 12   c) 16   d) 14

40. Who won a 20-Man Battle Royal at *WrestleMania IV*?
a) Bad News Brown   b) Bret Hart
c) Big John Studd   d) Earthquake

41. Who did Randy Savage defeat in the first round of the championship tournament?
a) One Man Gang   b) Greg Valentine
c) Red Rooster   d) Butch Reed

42. What was the outcome of the Andre the Giant vs. Hulk Hogan match at *WrestleMania IV*?
a) Andre won by pinfall.
b) It was a double disqualification.
c) It was a time-limit draw.
d) Hogan won by pinfall.

43. Brutus Beefcake defeated Intercontinental Champion Honky Tonk Man, but Brutus didn't win the title. Why not?

a) **The title wasn't on the line.**

b) **Brutus cheated.**

c) **Brutus won by disqualification.**

d) **The referee's decision was reversed.**

44. Who was the Islanders's tag-team partner for their match at *WrestleMania IV*?

a) **Rikishi**   b) **Haku**

c) **Afa**   d) **Bobby Heenan**

45. *I introduced the championship tournament at* WrestleMania IV *and I enjoy caviar and champagne. Who am I?*

a) **Donald Trump**

b) **Robin Leach**

c) **Ted Lange ("Isaac" from *The Love Boat*)**

d) **Bernie Kopell ("Doc" from *The Love Boat*)**

46. How many matches took place at *WrestleMania IV*?

a) **15**   b) **16**   c) **12**   d) **11**

47. Who did Randy Savage defeat to win the championship tournament at *WrestleMania IV*?

a) **Ricky Steamboat**   b) **Andre the Giant**

c) **Ted DiBiase**   d) **Jake Roberts**

48. The World Championship was up for grabs at *WrestleMania IV*'s tournament. When was the next WWE Championship tournament after *WrestleMania IV*?

a) ***WrestleMania X***

b) ***Survivor Series 1998***

c) **The first *SmackDown!* show**

d) ***SummerSlam 1997***

WrestleMania V

49. Who did Mr. Perfect defeat at *WrestleMania V*?
a) Bret Hart   b) Bad News Brown
c) Blue Blazer   d) Honky Tonk Man

50. The Brain Busters defeated Strike Force at *WrestleMania V*. Who were the two members of the Brain Busters?
a) Hawk & Animal
b) Tully Blanchard & Arn Anderson
c) Ricky Morton & Robert Gibson
d) Stan Lane & Steve Keirn

51. Who did Rick Rude defeat for the Intercontinental Championship at *WrestleMania V*?
a) Ultimate Warrior   b) Ricky Steamboat
c) Honky Tonk Man   d) Tito Santana

52. Which celebrity got "smoked out" on *Piper's Pit* at *WrestleMania V*?
a) Fire Marshall Bill
b) Smokey the Bear
c) Lisa "Left Eye" Lopes
d) Morton Downey, Jr.

53. Who was the guest referee for the *WrestleMania V* match between Andre the Giant and Jake Roberts?
a) Alice Cooper   b) Donald Trump
c) Big John Studd   d) Brother Love

54. What was the team of Randy Savage and Hulk Hogan collectively known as prior to their battle at *WrestleMania V*?
a) the Mega Powers   b) Hogan & Savage
c) Liz's Boys   d) the Main Event

55. Which rap group performed a special *WrestleMania* rap at *WrestleMania V*?
a) Salt-n-Pepa b) Run-DMC
c) Beastie Boys d) Wu-Tang Clan

56. Who did the Red Rooster defeat at *WrestleMania V*?
a) Brooklyn Brawler b) King Haku
c) Bobby Heenan d) Sean Mooney

57. Which main eventer from the inaugural *WrestleMania* made a special guest appearance at *WrestleMania V*?
a) Mr. T
b) Cowboy Bob Orton
c) Paul Orndorff
d) "Superfly" Jimmy Snuka

58. Which lovely lady was at the center of the Hulk Hogan vs. Randy Savage match at *WrestleMania V*?
a) Cyndi Lauper b) Miss Elizabeth
c) Wendi Richter d) the Fabulous Moolah

59. Which future World Champion made his *WrestleMania* debut in the opening match at *WrestleMania V*?
a) Shawn Michaels
b) Diesel
c) Stone Cold Steve Austin
d) Bret Hart

60. Who were the members of the Twin Towers, who met The Rockers in the opening match at *WrestleMania V*?
a) Afa & Sika
b) Sid Vicious & Danny Spivey
c) Big Boss Man & Akeem
d) Earthquake & Typhoon

WrestleMania VI

61. Who was Dusty Rhodes's tag-team partner at *WrestleMania VI*?
a) Dustin Rhodes   b) Sapphire
c) Blackjack Mulligan   d) Dick Murdoch

62. Where was *WrestleMania VI* held?
a) Chicago, IL
b) Los Angeles, CA
c) New York City
d) Toronto, Ontario, Canada

63. Which title did the Ultimate Warrior hold going into the main event match at *WrestleMania VI*?
a) European Championship
b) Warrior's Championship
c) Intercontinental Championship
d) World Championship

64. Which future Intercontinental Champion attended *WrestleMania VI* as a fan?
a) Christian   b) Edge
c) Billy Gunn   d) Eddie Guerrero

65. How many fans attended *WrestleMania VI*?
a) 61,275   b) 63,424   c) 67,678   d) 66,251

66. Who sang "O Canada" at *WrestleMania VI*?
a) Celine Dion   b) Roberta Flack
c) Anne Murray   d) Robert Goulet

67. Which talk show host interviewed Miss Elizabeth before Liz's surprise *WrestleMania VI* appearance?
a) Rona Barrett   b) Oprah Winfrey
c) Jay Leno   d) David Letterman

68. Which team defeated The Rockers by countout at
WrestleMania VI?
**a) the Colossal Connection   b) the Bolsheviks
c) the Hart Foundation   d) the Orient Express**

69. Brutus Beefcake pinned which Superstar at
WrestleMania VI?
**a) Koko B. Ware   b) Mr. Perfect
c) Bret Hart   d) Tito Santana**

70. Which team won the Tag Team Championship for the
third time at *WrestleMania VI*?
**a) Iron Sheik & Nikolai Volkoff
b) The Brain Busters
c) Demolition
d) The Hart Foundation**

71. *"Oh Rob!"* Which TV star sat ringside at
WrestleMania VI?
**a) Dick Van Dyke   b) Mary Tyler Moore
c) Valerie Harper   d) Betty White**

72. Jim Duggan beat Dino Bravo at *WrestleMania VI*.
What was Duggan's nickname?
**a) "Dirty"   b) "Gigolo"
c) "Hacksaw"   d) "Blackjack"**

73. In his first ten *WrestleMania* matches, how many
times was Hulk Hogan pinned?
a) 1   b) 2   c) 3   d) 4

74. Who won the opening match at *WrestleMania VI*?
**a) Koko B. Ware   b) Rick Martel
c) Jake Roberts   d) Undertaker**

75. What was the subtitle of *WrestleMania VI*?
**a) When Worlds Collide   b) A Canadian Collision
c) The Ultimate Challenge   d) Toronto Tornado**

WrestleMania VII

76. Which "cool" Hollywood star gave a "thumbs-up"
to *WrestleMania VII* from ringside?
a) Vanna White   b) Steve Allen
c) Ron Howard   d) Henry Winkler

77. Which Superstar competed in the opening match at
WrestleMania VII, the first of three consecutive
WrestleMania opening-match appearances?
a) Owen Hart   b) Shawn Michaels
c) Haku   d) Big Boss Man

78. Which legendary Superstar made his final
WrestleMania appearance at *WrestleMania VII*?
a) Big John Studd   b) Bruno Sammartino
c) Andre the Giant   d) Harley Race

79. Which team captured the Tag Team Championships
at *WrestleMania VII*?
a) the Nasty Boys   b) Demolition
c) Legion of Doom   d) Dynamic Dudes

80. What were the stipulations for the Jake Roberts vs.
Rick Martel match at *WrestleMania VII*?
a) No-Holds-Barred
b) Bullrope match
c) Blindfold match
d) Human Dartboard match

81. Which Japanese duo defeated Demolition at
WrestleMania VII?
a) Great Muta & Kenta Kobashi
b) The Jumping Bomb Angels
c) Kaientai
d) Genichiro Tenryu & and Koji Kitao

82. What country did Sgt. Slaughter represent at
WrestleMania VII?
a) **Germany**   b) **Iran**
c) **Iraq**   d) **Russia**

83. Power & Glory lost a tag-team match at *WrestleMania
VII*. Who made up Power & Glory?
a) **Paul Roma & Hercules**
b) **Tito Santana & Rick Martel**
c) **Tom Prichard & Jimmy Del Rey**
d) **Animal & Hawk**

84. What was on the line in the *WrestleMania VII* match
between Hulk Hogan and Sgt. Slaughter?
a) **Hogan's hair**   b) **the World Championship**
c) **ownership of the company**   d) **an American flag**

85. Which Superstar hailing from "Death Valley" made
his *WrestleMania* debut at *WrestleMania VII*?
a) **Tommy Dreamer**   b) **The Godfather**
c) **Undertaker**   d) **"Superstar" Billy Graham**

86. Which company personality has had an on-camera
role at every *WrestleMania*?
a) **Vince McMahon**   b) **Jim Ross**
c) **Jerry Lawler**   d) **Howard Finkel**

87. Which Canadian was a guest interviewer at
WrestleMania VII?
a) **Michael J. Fox**   b) **Celine Dion**
c) **Anne Murray**   d) **Alex Trebek**

88. These two personalities debated the use of instant
replay at events during *WrestleMania VII*:
a) **Joe Frazier and Larry Holmes**
b) **George Steinbrenner and Paul Maguire**
c) **Paul Tagliabue and Pete Rozelle**
d) **Bud Selig and David Stern**

89. Which tag team won the opening match at
WrestleMania VII?
a) The Rockers   b) The Hart Foundation
c) Legion of Doom   d) Power & Glory

90. Which music superstar sang "America the Beautiful"
at *WrestleMania VII*?
a) Whitney Houston   b) Aretha Franklin
c) Willie Nelson   d) Billy Idol

91. This former duo faced each other for the first time at
WrestleMania VII:
a) Shawn Michaels & Marty Jannetty
b) Ted DiBiase & Virgil
c) Gorilla Monsoon & Bobby Heenan
d) Tony Garea & Dean Ho

92. Which *Live* host was a guest announcer for the main
event at *WrestleMania VII*?
a) Kelly Ripa   b) Kathie Lee Gifford
c) Regis Philbin   d) Joy Philbin

93. This *Home Alone* star saw *WrestleMania VII* from a
ringside seat:
a) Macaulay Culkin   b) Joe Pesci
c) Daniel Stern   d) Catherine O'Hara

94. Who lost a retirement match at *WrestleMania VII*?
a) Ric Flair   b) Ultimate Warrior
c) Sensational Sherri   d) Randy Savage

WrestleMania VIII

95. This Midwest venue hosted *WrestleMania VIII*:
a) **Rosemont Horizon**   b) **Hoosier Dome**
c) **Pontiac Silverdome**   d) **the Astrodome**

96. This TV game show host introduced an eight-man Tag Team Match at *WrestleMania VIII*:
a) **Richard Dawson**   b) **Louie Anderson**
c) **Ray Combs**   d) **Pat Sajak**

97. Which Superstar returned to the organization at *WrestleMania VIII*, after an eight-month absence?
a) **Hulk Hogan**   b) **Randy Savage**
c) **Bret Hart**   d) **Ultimate Warrior**

98. Who defeated Jake Roberts at *WrestleMania VIII*?
a) **Undertaker**   b) **Bret Hart**
c) **Ric Flair**   d) **Hulk Hogan**

99. This Native American defeated Rick Martel at *WrestleMania VIII*:
a) **Chief Jay Strongbow**   b) **Wahoo McDaniel**
c) **Tatanka**   d) **Billy White Wolf**

100. The Intercontinental Championship changed hands at *WrestleMania VIII* as Roddy Piper faced whom?
a) **Ricky Steamboat**   b) **Bret Hart**
c) **Honky Tonk Man**   d) **Greg Valentine**

101. Skinner lost to Owen Hart at *WrestleMania VIII*. What did Skinner carry to the ring?
a) **rattlesnake**   b) **buffalo**
c) **spittoon**   d) **shark teeth**

102. Randy Savage won the World Championship at
WrestleMania VIII for the _____ time.
a) **first**   b) **second**   c) **third**   d) **fourth**

103. The Repo Man was part of the eight-man Tag Team
Match at *WrestleMania VIII*. Before he was the Repo
Man, what was he known as?
a) **the Mountie**   b) **Smash of Demolition**
c) **Bushwacker Luke**   d) **the Blue Blazer**

104. What nickname did Tito Santana go by at
WrestleMania VIII?
a) **the Kid**   b) **El Bandito**
c) **El Matador**   d) **Raging Bull**

105. What do the Hoosier Dome, now called the RCA
Dome, and the Pontiac Silverdome have in common?
a) **They are both air-supported roofed stadiums.**
b) **They both have hosted *WrestleManias*.**
c) **They both are home to NFL teams.**
d) **All of the above.**

106. What country singer opened *WrestleMania VIII* with a
stirring rendition of "America the Beautiful"?
a) **Dolly Parton**   b) **Reba McEntire**
c) **Tanya Tucker**   d) **Loretta Lynn**

107. Who interfered on Sid Justice's behalf in his match
against Hulk Hogan in the main event at
WrestleMania VIII?
a) **Ultimate Warrior**   b) **Undertaker**
c) **Papa Shango**   d) **The Warlord**

108. What is Shawn Michaels's finishing move?
a) **the Piledriver**   b) **the Brain Buster**
c) **Sweet Chin Music**   d) **Figure-Four Leglock**

WrestleMania IX

109. What former WWE Champion did Razor Ramon
defeat at *WrestleMania IX*?
a) "Superstar" Billy Graham   b) Bob Backlund
c) Bruno Sammartino   d) Buddy Rogers

110. Tatanka won a match over Shawn Michaels at
WrestleMania IX. What title was at stake?
a) World Championship
b) European Championship
c) Intercontinental Championship
d) TV Championship

111. The Steiner Brothers competed at *WrestleMania IX*.
What are the Steiner Brothers' names?
a) Al & Steve   b) Sam & Ray
c) Rick & Ray   d) Rick & Scott

112. *WrestleMania IX* was held at Caesars Palace in Las
Vegas, and the night had a Roman flavor. What was
ring announcer Howard Finkel's "Roman" name?
a) Howard Roman   b) Roman Moronie
c) Finkus Stinkus   d) Finkus Maximus

113. How many times did the World Championship
change hands at *WrestleMania IX*?
a) 2   b) 1   c) 0
d) It was not defended at *WrestleMania IX.*

114. What announcer made his debut with the company at
WrestleMania IX?
a) Todd Pettingill   b) Jim Ross
c) Jerry Lawler   d) Michael Cole

115. Headshrinker Fatu teamed with brother Samu at *WrestleMania IX*. What name is Fatu better known by?
a) **The Rock**   b) **Afa the Wild Samoan**
c) **Rikishi**   d) **Shrinky Dinky Finky**

116. What was unique about *WrestleMania IX*?
a) **It was the first *WrestleMania* held outdoors.**
b) **It was Hulk Hogan's final *WrestleMania* appearance.**
c) **Bret Hart denounced Canada during the event.**
d) **Bobby Heenan cheered for Hulk Hogan on commentary.**

117. Crush lost to Doink at *WrestleMania IX*. Where was Crush from?
a) **Detroit, MI**   b) **Kona, HI**
c) **Phoenix, AZ**   d) **Orange County, CA**

118. Tag Team Champions Money Inc. retained the Tag Team titles at *WrestleMania IX*. Who were the members of Money Inc.?
a) **Richie Rich & Mr. Moneybags**
b) **Ted DiBiase & Diesel**
c) **Ted DiBiase & Irwin R. Schyster**
d) **Hulk Hogan & Brutus Beefcake**

119. What was Lex Luger's nickname at *WrestleMania IX*?
a) **"the Bus"**   b) **"the Narcissist"**
c) **"Sexy Lexy"**   d) **"Crowbar"**

120. Which manager seconded Giant Gonzales during his match with Undertaker?
a) **Bobby Heenan**   b) **Freddie Blassie**
c) **Harvey Whippleman**   d) **Jim Cornette**

121. This special guest gave Howard Finkel a special hairpiece at *WrestleMania IX:*
a) Telly Savalas   b) Sy Sperling
c) Frank Sinatra   d) Vince McMahon

122. This man was the special guest referee for Bret Hart's *WrestleMania IX* match against Yokozuna:
a) Mr. Perfect   b) Mr. Fuji
c) Jim Cornette   d) Roddy Piper

WrestleMania X

123. Who defeated his "loving brother Bret" at *WrestleMania X?*
a) Bruce Hart   b) British Bulldog
c) Jim Neidhart   d) Owen Hart

124. These two men competed at the first nine *WrestleMania's* but neither competed at *WrestleMania X:*
a) Brooklyn Brawler and Tito Santana
b) Hulk Hogan and Brutus Beefcake
c) Hulk Hogan and Tito Santana
d) Brooklyn Brawler and Brutus Beefcake

125. What team met Bam Bam Bigelow & Luna at *WrestleMania X?*
a) Doink & Dink
b) King Kong Bundy & Little Beaver
c) Marc Mero & Sable
d) Alundra Blayze & Ricky Steamboat

126. This team entered *WrestleMania X* as Tag Team Champions:
a) **Men on a Mission**   b) **The Quebecers**
c) **The Heavenly Bodies**   d) **The Smokin' Gunns**

127. The match between Shawn Michaels and Razor Ramon at *WrestleMania X* was one of the greatest matches ever. What kind of match was it?
a) **cage match**   b) **bullrope match**
c) **ladder match**   d) **hell in the cell match**

128. At *WrestleMania X*, Men on a Mission faced the Quebecers. Who was NOT a member of Men on a Mission?
a) **Oscar**   b) **Marvin**
c) **Mable**   d) **Mo**

129. Which manager accompanied the Quebecers to the ring for their match at *WrestleMania X*?
a) **Captain Lou Albano**   b) **Jim Cornette**
c) **Johnny Polo**   d) **Mr. Fuji**

130. Who was the special guest referee for the Yokozuna vs. Lex Luger match at *WrestleMania X*?
a) **Mr. Perfect**   b) **British Bulldog**
c) **Bobby Heenan**   d) **Roddy Piper**

131. Which pop singer was the guest ring announcer for the Yokozuna vs. Lex Luger match at *WrestleMania X*?
a) **Corey Hart**   b) **Jon Bon Jovi**
c) **Donnie Wahlberg**   d) **Marky Mark**

132. Madison Square Garden hosted *WrestleMania X*. In what year did the Garden open on that site?
a) **1971**   b) **1968**   c) **1973**   d) **1943**

133. Adam Bomb lost to Earthquake at *WrestleMania X*. Where was Adam Bomb from?
a) Harrisburg   b) Fire Island
c) Three Mile Island   d) the nuclear wastelands

134. Who was the guest timekeeper for the Bret Hart vs. Yokozuna match at *WrestleMania X*?
a) Rhonda Shear   b) Donnie Wahlberg
c) Burt Reynolds   d) Jennie Garth

WrestleMania XI

135. What city hosted *WrestleMania XI*?
a) New York, NY   b) Boston, MA
c) Hartford, CT   d) Anaheim, CA

136. What sport was on strike at the time of *WrestleMania XI*?
a) baseball   b) football
c) basketball   d) hockey

137. What Hall of Fame linebacker wrestled Bam Bam Bigelow at *WrestleMania XI*?
a) Jack Lambert   b) Lawrence Taylor
c) Dick Butkus   d) Randy White

138. Which brother tag team lost the opening match at *WrestleMania XI*?
a) The Smokin' Gunns   b) Bart & Brad Batten
c) Jacob & Eli Blu   d) The Rougeaus

139. Who was Owen Hart's surprise partner for the tag team title match at *WrestleMania XI*?
a) Bret Hart   b) Yokozuna
c) Blue Blazer   d) Jeff Jarrett

140. Who did Undertaker defeat at *WrestleMania XI*?
a) Diesel   b) Shawn Michaels
c) Bret Hart   d) King Kong Bundy

141. What was unique about the Bret Hart vs. Bob Backlund match at *WrestleMania XI*?
a) It was a retirement match.
b) It was an "I Quit" match.
c) It was a "Kiss My Foot" match.
d) It was a submission match.

142. The British Bulldog's tag team partner in the Allied Powers team that competed at *WrestleMania XI* was...
a) Tito Santana   b) Dynamite Kid
c) Lex Luger   d) Sycho Sid

143. Which celebrity accompanied Shawn Michaels to the ring for the Heartbreak Kid's match at *WrestleMania XI*?
a) Pam Anderson   b) Jenny McCarthy
c) Jennie Garth   d) Joan Rivers

144. What game did *Home Improvement* star Jonathan Taylor-Thomas play with Bob Backlund at *WrestleMania XI*?
a) checkers   b) dodge ball
c) chess   d) Twister

145. Which *NYPD Blue* star did backstage interviews at *WrestleMania XI*?
a) Dennis Franz   b) Kim Delaney
c) David Caruso   d) Nicholas Turturro

WrestleMania XII

146. What was the Roddy Piper vs. Goldust match at WrestleMania XII called?
a) A Shattered Dreams Street Fight
b) A Golden Cage Match
c) A Hollywood Backlot Brawl
d) A Bra and Panties Match

147. Who did Ultimate Warrior defeat at *WrestleMania XII*?
a) Stone Cold Steve Austin
b) the Ringmaster
c) Hunter Hearst-Helmsley
d) King Kong Bundy

148. What city hosted *WrestleMania XII*?
a) Los Angeles, CA   b) Anaheim, CA
c) New York, NY   d) Boston, MA

149. What official called for sudden-death overtime when sixty minutes expired in the Iron Man match between Shawn Michaels and Bret Hart at *WrestleMania XII*?
a) Vince McMahon   b) Jack Tunney
c) Sgt. Slaughter   d) Gorilla Monsoon

150. What Hollywood celebrity played a role at *WrestleMania XII*?
a) Burt Reynolds   b) Regis Philbin
c) Kathie Lee Gifford   d) None of the above

151. What Undertaker move defeated Diesel at *WrestleMania XII*?
a) Chokeslam
b) Last Ride
c) Tombstone Piledriver
d) Dragon Sleeper

WrestleMania 13

152. Who did Undertaker defeat at *WrestleMania 13* to win the WWE Championship?
a) Sycho Sid   b) Shawn Michaels
c) Bret Hart   d) Triple H

153. Who won the submission match between Bret Hart and Stone Cold Steve Austin at *WrestleMania 13*?
a) Stone Cold Steve Austin
b) Bret Hart
c) Both men were disqualified.
d) Ken Shamrock

154. Who was Legion of Doom's tag-team partner for the Chicago Street Fight at *WrestleMania 13*?
a) the British Bulldog   b) Crush
c) Ahmed Johnson   d) Faarooq

155. Who suffered broken ribs during the Chicago Street Fight at *WrestleMania 13*?
a) Crush   b) Savio Vega
c) Ahmed Johnson   d) Faarooq

156. Who won the Four-Team Elimination Tag match that kicked off *WrestleMania 13*?
a) the Headbangers   b) Furnas & LaFon
c) the Blackjacks   d) the Godwinns

WrestleMania XIV

157. Which lady linked romantically at one time to Bill Clinton interviewed The Rock at *WrestleMania XIV*?
a) **Hillary Clinton**   b) **Gennifer Flowers**
c) **Paula Jones**   d) **Monica Lewinsky**

158. Who won the fifteen-team Battle Royal that opened *WrestleMania XIV*?
a) **the Headbangers**   b) **the New Midnight Express**
c) **LOD 2000**   d) **Test & D'Lo Brown**

159. Taka Michinoku defeated Aguila in a Light-Heavyweight Championship match at *WrestleMania XIV*. What name was Aguila later known by?
a) **Frenchy Martin**   b) **Papi Chulo**
c) **Funaki**   d) **Kaientai**

160. At *WrestleMania XIV*, Cactus Jack & Chainsaw Charlie won the Tag Team Championships from the New Age Outlaws in a Dumpster match. What was Chainsaw Charlie's real name?
a) **Mick Foley**   b) **John Tenta**
c) **Terry Funk**   d) **Pete Rose**

161. What is/was the relationship between Paul Bearer and Kane?
a) **They were fraternity brothers.**
b) **They are father and son.**
c) **They are cousins.**
d) **They were business partners.**

162. How many Tombstone Piledrivers did it take Undertaker to beat Kane at *WrestleMania XIV*?
a) **1**   b) **2**   c) **3**   d) **4**

163. Which of these was a first at *WrestleMania XIV*?
a) A Mixed Tag Team Match.
b) A meeting between Shawn Michaels and Stone Cold Steve Austin.
c) A defense of the European Championship at a *WrestleMania*.
d) The only appearance ever at a *WrestleMania* by Pete Rose.

164. What city hosted *WrestleMania XIV*?
a) Philadelphia, PA b) Boston, MA
c) Detroit, MI d) New York, NY

165. Who assaulted Pete Rose at *WrestleMania XIV*?
a) Bill Buckner b) the San Diego Chicken
c) Larry Bird d) Kane

WrestleMania XV

166. What was the subtitle for *WrestleMania XV*?
a) Championship Collision
b) The Ragin' Climax
c) Dark Daze
d) A Flair for the Gold

167. Which boxer knocked out Bart Gunn in the finals of the Brawl-For-All?
a) Bobby Czyz b) Ray Mancini
c) Butterbean d) Mike Tyson

168. Who won the Hardcore Championship at *WrestleMania XV*?
a) Billy Gunn b) Al Snow
c) Hardcore Holly d) Road Dogg

169. What treacherous trio helped Shane McMahon defeat X-Pac at *WrestleMania XV*?
a) the Good Fellas
b) the J.O.B. Squad
c) the Nation of Domination
d) the Mean Street Posse

170. Who counted the pinfall as Stone Cold Steve Austin defeated The Rock at *WrestleMania XV*?
a) Mick Foley   b) Vince McMahon
c) Earl Hebner   d) Mike Tyson

171. Who turned his back on D-Generation X at *WrestleMania XV*?
a) Billy Gunn   b) Road Dogg
c) X-Pac   d) Triple H

WrestleMania XVI

172. What was the main event match at *WrestleMania XVI*?
a) Triple-Threat Match   b) Fatal Four-Way
c) Hell in the Cell   d) Six-Pack Challenge

173. Which member of the McMahon family was in the corner of The Rock at *WrestleMania XVI*?
a) Linda McMahon   b) Shane McMahon
c) Stephanie McMahon   d) Vince McMahon

174. Which title did Kurt Angle lose to Chris Jericho at *WrestleMania XVI*?
a) Intercontinental Championship
b) European Championship
c) Light-Heavyweight Championship
d) Hardcore Championship

175. Who rapped The Godfather and D'Lo Brown to the ring at *WrestleMania XVI*?

a) Ice Cube   b) DMX

c) Ja Rule   d) Ice-T

176. What team defeated X-Pac & Road Dogg at *WrestleMania XVI*?

a) Kane & Rikishi

b) Kane & Undertaker

c) Too Cool

d) The Radicalz

177. Who managed the team of Test & Albert at *WrestleMania XVI*?

a) Terri   b) Ivory

c) Trish Stratus   d) Jacqueline

178. Who won the Tables, Ladders & Chairs match at *WrestleMania XVI*?

a) the Dudley Boyz   b) Edge & Christian

c) the Hardy Boyz   d) Too Cool

179. What city hosted *WrestleMania XVI*?

a) Houston, TX

b) Toronto, Ontario, Canada

c) Anaheim, CA

d) New York, NY

180. Who won the Hardcore Battle Royal at *WrestleMania XVI*?

a) Tazz   b) Crash Holly

c) Raven   d) Hardcore Holly

WrestleMania X-Seven

181. What was the name of the fan festival that took place the weekend of *WrestleMania X-Seven*?
a) the *Fan Expo*   b) *Axxess*
c) *Slam Jam*   d) *Fandemonium*

182. Who won the opening match at *WrestleMania X-Seven*?
a) Chris Jericho   b) William Regal
c) Chris Benoit   d) Kurt Angle

183. Who won the Gimmick Battle Royal at *WrestleMania X-Seven*?
a) Sgt. Slaughter   b) Hillbilly Jim
c) Iron Sheik   d) Jim Cornette

184. Who was NOT a part of the Triple-Threat match for the Hardcore Championship at *WrestleMania X-Seven*?
a) Kane   b) Tazz
c) Big Show   d) Raven

185. Who played Triple H's entrance music at *WrestleMania X-Seven*?
a) Saliva   b) Creed
c) Motörhead   d) Metallica

186. How many different championships changed hands at *WrestleMania X-Seven*?
a) 3   b) 4   c) 5   d) 6

187. Who sat in a wheelchair watching the Street Fight between Vince and Shane McMahon at *WrestleMania X-Seven*?
a) Trish Stratus   b) Linda McMahon
c) Stephanie McMahon   d) Howard Finkel

188. The Astrodome hosted *WrestleMania X-Seven.* What nickname does that building go by?
a) the Eighth Wonder of the World
b) the Mega Dome
c) the House that Ruth Built
d) the Texasplex

189. With his win at *WrestleMania X-Seven*, Stone Cold Steve Austin improved his *WrestleMania* main event record to ...
a) 1–1   b) 2–1   c) 3–0   d) 4–2

190. Which team did Tazz & the APA defeat at *WrestleMania X-Seven*?
a) D-Generation X
b) Right to Censor
c) the Nation of Domination
d) the Alliance

WrestleMania X8

191. With his win at *WrestleMania X8*, Undertaker improved his *WrestleMania* record to ...
a) 5–3   b) 9–0   c) 10–0   d) 6–1

192. Who did Edge defeat at *WrestleMania X8*?
a) Christian   b) Test
c) Kane   d) Booker T

193. What move did Triple H give to Stephanie McMahon at *WrestleMania X8*?
a) a Spin-a-roonie   b) Rock Bottom
c) Pedigree   d) Walls of Jericho

194. Who attacked Hollywood Hulk Hogan after his match with The Rock at *WrestleMania X8*?
a) Triple H   b) Nash and Hall
c) Stone Cold Steve Austin   d) Kurt Angle

195. Rob Van Dam won what title at *WrestleMania X8*?
a) European Championship
b) Intercontinental Championship
c) Hardcore Championship
d) None

196. Who interfered on behalf of Ric Flair in his match against Undertaker at *WrestleMania X8*?
a) David Flair   b) Shawn Michaels
c) Arn Anderson   d) Tom Prichard

197. Who refereed the Ric Flair vs. Undertaker match at *WrestleMania X8*?
a) Nick Patrick   b) Charles Robinson
c) Earl Hebner   d) Tim White

198. Who did Goldust face for the Hardcore Championship at *WrestleMania X8*?
a) Raven   b) Mr. Perfect
c) Maven   d) Rico

199. Who did NOT win the Hardcore Championship at *WrestleMania X8*?
a) Christian   b) Molly Holly
c) Trish Stratus   d) Maven

200. Who won the Triple-Threat match for the Women's Championship at *WrestleMania X8*?
a) Jazz   b) Lita
c) Trish Stratus   d) Ivory

RAW

he Game and I am
amn good.
Banzai Dr
Twist Of Fate

n Bomb
The Walls Of Jericho
The Worm

1993

1. From what New York-area venue did *Raw* emanate for much of 1993?
   a) **Madison Square Garden**
   b) **Nassau Coliseum**
   c) **Manhattan Center**
   d) **Broome County Arena**

2. What was the first match on the first episode of *Raw* in January 1993?

3. Who were the three ringside commentators for that first episode of *Raw*?

4. Who tried to sneak into the arena that day dressed in drag?

5. What Superstar lost a "Loser Leaves WWE" match to Mr. Perfect on *Raw* in January 1993?

6. The first title change in *Raw* history saw _____ defeat _____ for the _____ Championship.

7. The June 7, 1993 episode of *Raw* marked the TV debut of Shawn Michaels's new bodyguard. Who was that bodyguard, who would eventually go on to capture the World Championship a year and a half later?

8. What was the name of Lex Luger's cross-country bus tour during the summer of 1993, which was featured on *Raw*?

9. On September 13, 1993, the Quebecers defeated the Steiner Brothers for the Tag Team Championship in a _____ match.

10. On October 4, 1993, Razor Ramon was one of the final two competitors in a Battle Royal match. The following week, he would defeat the other competitor to capture the vacant Intercontinental Championship. Who was that other Superstar?

1994

11. The January 10, 1994 episode of *Raw* was called *Raw*'s "One-Year Anniversary show." On that show, the Quebecers lost the Tag Team Championship to what duo?

12. On the January 31, 1994 episode of *Raw,* Marty Jannetty pinned the Quebecers's manager. Currently known as Raven, what was that Superstar's name when the 1994 match took place?

13. Hardcore Holly made his first *Raw* appearance on the February 7, 1994 episode. Under what name did he compete?

14. What future host of "Byte This!" on WWE.com lost a hard-fought twenty-minute bout to Bret Hart on the February 21, 1994 episode of *Raw*?

15. The May 16, 1994 episode of *Raw* featured a Sumo Match between what two behemoths?

16. What future Tag Team, Hardcore and European Champion lost to Nikolai Volkoff via submission on the May 23, 1994 episode of *Raw*?

17. Volkoff competed again on the June 20, 1994 episode of *Raw,* losing to what future D-Generate?

18. What "imposter" made his *Raw* debut on July 4, 1994?
a) **Fake Razor Ramon**   b) **Fake Diesel**
c) **Fake Undertaker**   d) **Fake Bret Hart**

19. The November 7, 1994 episode of *Raw* featured a tag bout with four members of the Hart family. Which of these Hart Foundation members was NOT involved in the bout?
a) **Bret Hart**   b) **Owen Hart**
c) **British Bulldog**   d) **Brian Pillman**

20. Who won the last *Raw* match of 1994?
a) **Undertaker**   b) **Triple H**
c) **Stone Cold**   d) **Randy Savage**

1995

21. The January 2, 1995 episode of *Raw* featured two matches pitting Lex Luger and Davey Boy Smith against Bam Bam Bigelow and Tatanka. What was the name of the Luger-Smith tag team?

22. What two Superstars clashed in a tuxedo match the following week?

23. The 1-2-3 Kid and Bob Holly won a tournament final at the 1995 *Royal Rumble* to capture the vacant Tag Team Championship. Just one night later—on the January 23, 1995 episode of *Raw*—they lost those titles. To whom?

24. What monster made his *Raw* debut on February 6, 1995?
a) **Kane**   b) **Mantaur**
c) **King Kong Bundy**   d) **Giant Gonzalez**

25. On the April 3, 1995 episode of *Raw* (just one night after *WrestleMania XI*), who launched a brutal attack on Shawn Michaels, repeatedly powerbombing the Heartbreak Kid and sending him to the injured list for a few months with a back injury?

26. What future World Champion made his *Raw* in-ring debut on May 22, 1995?

27. Although *Raw* was preempted on September 4, 1995, that was still an important night in sports entertainment history, as it marked the first episode of *WCW Monday Nitro*. From where did *Nitro's* premier episode emanate?

28. The same team that defeated the 1-2-3 Kid & Bob Holly on the January 23, 1995 episode of *Raw* would again capture the Tag Team Championship on the September 25, 1995 episode of *Raw*. Who did they defeat on that night?

29. What was the name of the demented dentist that Bret Hart defeated in a Cage match on the October 16, 1995 episode of *Raw*?

30. Shawn Michaels collapsed in the ring during a match on the November 20, 1995 episode of *Raw*. Who was he fighting at the time?

1996

31. The January 1, 1996 episode of *Raw* featured a unique match called the "*Raw* Bowl." What pro sport was the *Raw* Bowl based on?

32. Who won the *Raw* Bowl?

33. The January 1, 1996 episode of *Raw* also featured the debut of a skit that poked fun at WCW. The skit featured such characters as Billionaire Ted, the Huckster, Nacho Man and Scheme Gene. What was the name of the skit?

34. On the January 8, 1996 episode of *Raw*, "The Million Dollar Man" Ted DiBiase introduced his new protégé to the world. Who was he?

35. What title did DiBiase present to that protégé?

36. And what was the name of the interview segment on which DiBiase and his protégé appeared?

37. What Superstar made his debut on the January 29, 1996 episode of *Raw*, teaming with his cousin, Henry O. Godwinn, to defeat the Bodydonnas?

38. What future World Champion made his *Raw* debut on the April 1, 1996 episode of *Raw*—the day after *WrestleMania XII*?

39. What former WCW Champion made his WWE debut on the July 22, 1996 episode of *Raw*, attacking Ahmed Johnson?

40. Who won the finals of an Intercontinental Championship tournament on the September 23, 1996 episode of *Raw*, upending Faarooq in the finals?

41. What former champion returned to *Raw* on October 21, 1996?

42. On that same episode, who used outside interference from Mr. Perfect to capture his first Intercontinental Championship?

43. The November 4, 1996 episode of *Raw* featured Stone Cold Steve Austin breaking in to what former tag-team partner's Cincinnati home?

44. What announcer was trying to interview that Superstar when Austin broke in?

1997

45. For the first time in *Raw* history, the World Championship changed hands on the show on February 17, 1997. Who defeated whom?

46. The February 24, 1997 episode of *Raw* featured a number of Extreme Championship Wrestling (ECW) stars competing in the ring. Which of these ECW stars did NOT compete on *Raw* that night?
a) D-Von Dudley   b) Little Guido
c) Steve Corino   d) Tommy Dreamer

47. What Superstar did Owen Hart serve with a restraining order on the September 15, 1997 episode?

48. The September 22, 1997 episode of *Raw* was the first episode of *Raw* to air from what world-famous arena?
a) Madison Square Garden   b) Tokyo Dome
c) SkyDome   d) Hoosier Dome

49. Which of the three faces of Mick Foley made his debut on the September 22, 1997 episode of *Raw*?

50. Who did Stone Cold give the Stunner to for the first time ever on that episode?

51. Who made his *Raw* debut on October 6, 1997, destroying the Hardy Boyz?

52. What faction saw its locker room vandalized on the October 20, 1997 episode of *Raw*, with things written on their wall such as "Uncle Tom" and "KFC"?

53. What Superstar walked out on his wife during a sit-down interview on the November 3, 1997 episode of *Raw*?

54. "Marvelous" Marc Mero challenged what portly boxer to a fight on the November 10, 1997 episode of *Raw*?

55. Which of Mr. McMahon's famous quotes was born on the November 17, 1997 episode of *Raw*?
a) "I'm Vince McMahon, damnit!"
b) "No Chance in hell!"
c) "Bret screwed Bret!"
d) "Screw you—you're fired!"

56. What legendary tag team won their first Tag Team Championship on the November 24, 1997 episode of *Raw*?

57. What playful nickname did D-Generation X give to Owen Hart on the December 8, 1997 episode of *Raw*?

58. On that episode, DX didn't want to leave the ring. In fact, they decided to remain in the ring and play what card game?

59. Stone Cold Steve Austin forfeited the Intercontinental Championship to what Superstar on the December 8, 1997 episode of *Raw*?

60. One week later, what did the Rattlesnake do with the Intercontinental Championship?

61. On the December 15, 1997 episode of *Raw,* Vince McMahon made what earthshaking announcement?
a) Stone Cold was suspended indefinitely.
b) He was stripping Shawn Michaels of the WWE Championship.
c) WWE would be moving in a more adult direction.
d) Undertaker was fired.

62. A special Christmas-themed episode of *Raw* aired on December 22, 1997. What three Superstars mooned the crowd at the beginning of the show, revealing thongs that spelled out "Merry X-Mas"?

63. Who did Stone Cold give a Stunner to on that episode of *Raw*?

64. To whom did Shawn Michaels lose his European Championship that night?

65. What Superstar dressed up as Baby New Year on the December 29, 1997 episode of *Raw*?

66. On that same episode, Terry Funk returned to WWE, but he wasn't known as "Terry Funk." What moniker did the former NWA Champion assume?

1998

67. What Superstar won the NWA title on the January 5, 1998 episode of *Raw*—the first time the NWA title had ever been contested on that program?

68. On the January 19, 1998 episode of *Raw,* boxer Mike Tyson got into a shoving match with which Superstar?

69. Owen Hart defeated Triple H to win the European title on the January 26, 1998 episode of *Raw*—sort of. You see, it wasn't actually Triple H he defeated, but was actually _____ dressed up as Triple H. Still, the title victory stood.

70. On March 30, 1998, D-Generation X was re-formed, as Triple H, X-Pac, Road Dogg, Mr. Ass and Chyna got together. What tag team did Road Dogg & Mr. Ass defeat for the Tag Team Championship as the show went off the air?

71. The following week on *Raw,* what was Stone Cold Steve Austin wearing as he headed to the ring?
**a) lumberjack outfit   b) suit and tie
c) combat gear   d) a tuxedo**

72. For the first time in eighty-three weeks, *Raw* won the ratings battle against *WCW Monday Nitro* on April 13, 1998. What was the main event of that show?

73. On April 27, 1998, D-Generation X invaded a WCW event at what arena?

74. What was unique about the No. 1 Contenders match on the May 4, 1998, episode of *Raw*?
   a) It was the first time Mick Foley had ever competed under his real name.
   b) He took on his best friend, Terry Funk.
   c) The bout saw Mick's opponent do a moonsault off a balcony.
   d) All of the above.

75. On May 11, 1998, D-Generation X invaded the WCW offices in Smyrna, GA. At first, the fivesome didn't even recognize the building—in fact, Mr. Ass commented that it actually looked like a _____!

76. On that same night, Al Snow made his return to *Raw*. Which of the following was NOT one of Snow's former WWE personas?
   a) Zip   b) Leif Cassidy
   c) Shinobi   d) Avatar

77. Stone Cold Steve Austin challenged Mr. McMahon, Pat Patterson and Gerald Brisco to a one-on-three Handicap match on the May 18, 1998 episode of *Raw*. But he only wound up facing two of those men. Which two did he face?

78. What group—which included Golga, Kurggan and Giant Silva—did Jackyl debut on the May 25, 1998 episode of *Raw*?

79. The June 15, 1998 episode of *Raw* featured the first-ever Tag Team *Royal Rumble*. What unlikely duo won that bout, and went on to defeat the New Age Outlaws for the Tag Team Championship a few weeks later?

80. What future Tag Team, U.S. and Intercontinental Champion made his WWE in-ring debut on the June 22, 1998 episode of *Raw* defeating Jose Estrada via countout?

81. What unique tournament started on *Raw* in June 1998, combining boxing and wrestling?

82. After defeating Hardcore Holly in the first round of that tournament, Bart Gunn defeated who in the second round, in what was considered a major upset?

83. Who did Gunn knock out in the finals of that tournament?

84. The June 29, 1998 episode of *Raw* featured a "King of Kings" match, with Ken Shamrock (1998 King), Owen Hart (1994 King) and Triple H (1997 King) battling it out. Who won that match?

85. On that same night, Stone Cold Steve Austin regained the WWE Championship he had lost just one night earlier at *King of the Ring*. Who did he defeat?

86. Kane won a No. 1 Contender's match on the July 6, 1998 episode of *Raw*—or so fans thought. After pinning Mankind to win the bout, Kane removed his mask to actually reveal who?

87. That same episode saw D-Generation X do an infamous parody of the Nation of Domination. What did Triple H christen his version of The Rock?

88. What did X-Pac call his version of Mark Henry?

89. And what did Road Dogg entitle his version of D'Lo Brown?

90. What former WWE Champion—who had last appeared on WWE programming at *WrestleMania XIV*—made his return to *Raw* on July 13, 1998?

91. Yamaguchi-san "choppy-choppied" whose "pee-pee" on the August 17, 1998 episode of *Raw*?

92. After nearly three years of dormancy, the Women's Championship was reborn on the September 21, 1998 episode of *Raw,* when _____ defeated _____ to win the title.

93. The September 28, 1998, episode of *Raw* featured a special ceremony, as Mr. McMahon was to present the WWE Championship to either Undertaker or Kane, both of whom had pinned Stone Cold Steve Austin in a Triple Threat match the night before to win the title. But before Mr. McMahon could present the title, Austin invaded the arena driving what type of vehicle?

94. After Austin's invasion, Undertaker and Kane laid a hurting on Mr. McMahon, breaking his right ankle using what ringside weapon?
a) a ring bell   b) ring steps
c) a hammer   d) a steel chair

95. The following week, as Mr. McMahon recovered in a hospital, Mankind paid him a visit and cheered him up with the debut of what piece of foot apparel?

96. One week after that, Stone Cold drove a cement truck to the Nassau Coliseum and filled Mr. McMahon's car with cement! What kind of car was Mr. McMahon driving that night?

97. In October 1998, Triple H was forced to vacate the Intercontinental Championship due to a knee injury. The October 12, 1998 episode of *Raw* featured a one-night tournament for that vacant title. Who defeated Steve Blackman, Val Venis and X-Pac to win the championship?

98. Which of the following did NOT happen on the October 19, 1998 episode of *Raw*?
a) The Rock won the Intercontinental Championship.
b) Stone Cold took Mr. McMahon hostage with a toy gun.
c) Undertaker fought Kane in a Casket match.
d) Mr. McMahon urinated on himself.

99. The _____ Championship was born on the November 2, 1998 episode of *Raw*.

100. The Rock was forced to defend the WWE Championship against Stone Cold Steve Austin on the November 16, 1998 episode of *Raw*, per an edict from what infamous boxing official and judge?

101. What unlikely Superstar pinned Christian to win the Light-Heavyweight Championship the following week?
a) "Iron" Mike Sharpe
b) Red Tyler
c) Duane Gill
d) Barry Hardy

102. Also on that episode, who was named the new commissioner of WWE?

103. The December 14, 1998 episode of *Raw* was highlighted by a WWE Championship match pitting The Rock against Triple H. What future Intercontinental, Tag Team, European and Hardcore Champion made his WWE debut during that match, joining the Corporation and helping Rock to a successful title defense?

104. On the December 21, 1998 episode of *Raw,* Shane McMahon competed in his first official WWE match. Who was his opponent?

1999

105. Mankind accomplished a lifelong dream on the January 4, 1999 episode of *Raw,* defeating The Rock to win the WWE Championship. But Mankind actually had another match before his bout with the People's Champion. Who did Mankind face in his first match that night?

106. The following week, who won the "Corporate *Royal Rumble*"?

107. The February 8, 1999 episode of *Raw* featured Stone Cold Steve Austin in a Gauntlet Match against every member of the Corporation. Which Corporate member was finally able to pin the Rattlesnake?

108. On the February 15, 1999 episode of *Raw,* Shane McMahon teamed up with Kane to take on X-Pac and Triple H. What happened when Shane pinned X-Pac to win the bout?

109. On that same episode of *Raw,* The Rock regained the WWE Championship from Mankind in what kind of match?

110. Stone Cold is well known for his "road rage" on *Raw.* What was his vehicle of choice on the March 22, 1999 episode of *Raw*—the Monday before *WrestleMania XV*?

111. Who defeated Goldust to win the Intercontinental Championship on the April 12, 1999 episode of *Raw*?

112. Who was Goldust originally scheduled to defend the title against that night?

113. After adbucting Stephanie McMahon one night earlier, Undertaker tried to marry her in a black wedding on the April 26, 1999 episode of *Raw,* only for Stephanie to be eventually saved by Stone Cold Steve Austin. Before Austin, what two Superstars tried unsuccessfully to save Stephanie?

114. What was history-making about the six-man main event on the May 10, 1999 episode of *Raw,* pitting Stone Cold, The Rock and Mr. McMahon against Undertaker, Triple H and Shane McMahon?
  a) It was the most-watched match in the history of Monday night wrestling at the time.
  b) It marked the WWE debut of Big Show.
  c) Thanks to a unique pre-match stipulation, Undertaker won the WWE Championship.
  d) None of the above.

115. Who was the Greater Power?

116. _____ became the Chief Executive Officer of WWE on the June 7, 1999 episode of *Raw.*

117. Which of the following did NOT happen on the June
7, 1999 episode of *Raw*?
   **a) Mr. McMahon defeated Ken Shamrock in a Lion's
   Den match.**
   b) Road Dogg won the Intercontinental Championship.
   c) Test asked out Stephanie McMahon.
   **d) Big Show chokeslammed Undertaker through the
   ring.**

118. The new WWE CEO took over Titan Tower on the
June 14, 1999 episode of *Raw*. Whose salary did he
turn into the new beer budget?

119. Stone Cold Steve Austin won his fourth WWE
Championship on the June 28, 1999 episode of *Raw*,
defeating whom?

120. One week later, what tandem won their first WWE
Tag Team Championship just minutes from their
hometown of Cameron, NC?

121. Who was the team's manager when they won the
titles that week?

122. What Hollywood actor was attacked by Jeff Jarrett on
the July 26, 1999 episode of *Raw*, only to be saved by
D'Lo Brown?

123. Brown pinned Jarrett the following week on *Raw*,
unifying what two championships for the first time
ever?

124. The "millennium countdown" ended on the August
9, 1999 episode of *Raw*. What monumental event
happened that night as the countdown reached zero?

125. What former WWE Superstar and current political giant appeared on that same episode, promoting his upcoming appearance at *SummerSlam 1999* to referee the main event?

126. In a huge upset, what Superstar defeated Triple H and Undertaker in a Triple-Threat Street Fight that same night to become the No. 1 contender to the WWE Championship?

127. After missing three months of action due to a knee injury, what Superstar returned to WWE on the August 16, 1999 episode of *Raw,* earning a spot in the main event of *SummerSlam*?

128. ____ won the WWE Championship for the first time on August 23, 1999 in a match that had ____ as the special guest referee.

129. The Rock & Mankind won the first of their three WWE Tag Team Championships on the August 30, 1999 episode of *Raw,* defeating Undertaker & Big Show. What was the official name of The Rock/Mankind tandem?

130. The September 13, 1999 episode of *Raw* featured a bout pitting Chris Jericho against a masked wrestler named "Gotch Gracie." Who was he?

131. Stephanie McMahon competed in her first match on the September 20, 1999 episode of *Raw,* teaming with her then-fiancé Test in mixed-tag action. Whom did Stephanie pin that night?

132. A segment featuring The Rock and Mankind aired on the September 27, 1999 episode of *Raw,* and drew an incredible 8.4 rating. What was the name of the segment?

133. The Rock and Mankind had their problems on the October 18, 1999 episode of *Raw,* as Mankind thought that The Rock had thrown a copy of his autobiography into the trash. But The Rock was not the culprit; who did it turn out to be?

134. What renegade faction officially re-formed on the October 25, 1999 episode of *Raw*?

135. Test and Stephanie McMahon were set to be married on the November 29, 1999 episode of *Raw*. But before the wedding, Test had a match. Who did he take on?

136. _____ and _____ McMahon left WWE on the December 13, 1999 episode of *Raw,* after _____ McMahon revealed an alliance with Triple H.

137. Who lost a "Pink Slip on a Pole" match on the December 27, 1999 episode of *Raw,* and was thereby fired by Triple H and Stephanie?

2000

138. _____ regained the WWE Championship from _____ on the January 3, 2000 episode of *Raw.*

139. What controversial foursome made their WWE debut on the January 31, 2000 episode of *Raw,* live in Pittsburgh?

140. That same night, Kurt Angle suffered his first WWE pinfall loss to whom?

141. Also on that night, history was made when which wrestler defeated The Kat to become the first man ever to win the WWE Women's Championship?

142. The February 7, 2000 episode of *Raw* was highlighted by an electric ten-man tag match, as Triple H, X-Pac and the Radicalz took on The Rock, Cactus Jack, Too Cool and Rikishi. After the bout, what Superstar made his return to WWE, led down the aisle by his father, Paul Bearer?

143. Who returned to WWE television on the March 13, 2000 episode of *Raw,* helping The Rock defeat Big Show and thereby win a spot in the main event of *WrestleMania XVI*?

144. The following week, the *WrestleMania* main event changed again when Linda McMahon added whom to the mix?

145. Eddie Guerrero captured the WWE European Championship on the April 3, 2000 episode of *Raw,* when which wrestler turned on Jericho to become Eddie's "*mamacita*"?

146. The April 17, 2000 episode of *Raw* opened with a lot of excitement, as someone defeated Triple H to win the WWE Championship—or so he thought. Thanks to political maneuvering on "The Game"'s part, referee Earl Hebner reversed the decision just minutes later. Who almost became WWE Champion that night?

147. Chris Jericho was forced to defend the Intercontinental Championship three times on the May 8, 2000 episode of *Raw*. Who were his three opponents?

148. With some help from Joe C of Kid Rock fame, what tandem defeated Edge & Christian on the May 29, 2000 episode of *Raw* to win the WWE Tag Team Championship?

149. The Rock, Kane and Undertaker were all forced into Handicap matches on the June 19, 2000, episode of *Raw*. Match each Superstar with the tandem he faced:

a) The Rock   1) Hardy Boyz
b) Kane   2) T&A
c) Undertaker   3) Bull Buchanan & Big Boss Man

150. Lita defeated Stephanie McMahon-Helmsley for the Women's Championship on the August 22, 2000 episode of *Raw*. What multitime WWE Champion served as guest referee for that bout?

151. Stephanie wasn't the only McMahon involved in a title match on the August 22, 2000 episode of *Raw*. Also on that show, Shane McMahon defeated _____ to win the _____ Championship.

152. _____ made his first *Raw* appearance in nearly a year on the September 25, 2000 episode of *Raw*.

153. The September 25, 2000 episode of *Raw*—the first episode of *Raw* on TNN—featured a special _____ match for the Tag Team Championship, as _____ defended against _____.

154. Who joined the Right to Censor on the October 23, 2000 episode of *Raw*?

155. After observing Kurt Angle and his family singing Christmas carols on the December 25, 2000 episode of *Raw,* what Superstar commented, "Man, talk about a white Christmas!"

2001

156. What happened after Lita defeated Dean Malenko on the February 19, 2001 episode of *Raw*?
a) **Malenko attacked her.**
b) **Lita joined the Radicalz.**
c) **Chris Benoit made his WWE debut.**
d) **Matt Hardy and Lita had their first kiss.**

157. Which of the following did Vince McMahon NOT force Trish Status to do on the March 5, 2001 episode of *Raw*?
a) **Kiss him.**
b) **Take off her skirt.**
c) **Bark like a dog.**
d) **Take off her blouse.**

158. After six months away from WWE, what Superstar returned on the March 12, 2001 episode of *Raw* to attack his own father?

159. The Tag Team Championship changed hands twice on the March 19, 2001 episode of *Raw*. What team wound up with the titles when the night was through?

160. **True or false:** The March 26, 2001 episode of *Raw* featured the first-ever simulcast between *Raw* and *WCW Monday Nitro*.

161. _____ and _____ teamed up to form the Two-Man Power Trip on the April 2, 2001 episode of *Raw*.

162. Which of these memorable moments did NOT take place on the May 21, 2001 episode of *Raw*?
   a) Chris Jericho & Chris Benoit won the Tag Team Championship.
   b) Kurt Angle held a medal ceremony.
   c) Val Venis won the Intercontinental Championship.
   d) Triple H tore his quadriceps muscle in the middle of a match.

163. What mat legend was sitting at ringside for the May 28, 2001 episode of *Raw*—which aired live from Calgary, Alberta, Canada?

164. Also on May 28, 2001, a WCW Superstar invaded *Raw* for the first time, superkicking Perry Saturn, and then fleeing from the arena with WCW owner Shane McMahon in a limo. Who was that superstar?

165. The June 4, 2001 episode of *Raw* featured a WWE Championship match between Stone Cold Steve Austin and Chris Jericho. What powerful Minnesotan put that match together, even though Vince McMahon tried to fight it?

166. The following week, Chris Benoit and Kurt Angle met in a cage match on *Raw*. Each of the men did a maneuver from the top of the cage—what maneuver did each perform?

167. WCW invaded Madison Square Garden for the first time on the June 25, 2001 episode of *Raw*. Who was the first WCW Superstar to appear on the show, winning the Hardcore Championship from Rhyno?

168. The following week's episode featured the first-ever WCW match in *Raw* history. What two Superstars met for the WCW Championship that night?

169. What renegade organization re-formed on the July 9, 2001 episode of *Raw*?

170. After a four-month suspension, what Superstar returned to *Raw* on July 30, 2001, later culminating his comeback by beating Booker T for the WCW Championship at *SummerSlam* the following month?

171. Whose breast enhancements did Chris Jericho point out on the August 13, 2001 episode of *Raw*?

172. What special name did the Alliance give to the August 20, 2001, episode of *Raw*?

173. During a special in-ring ceremony that night, Stephanie McMahon-Helmsley sang a song to the Rattlesnake. What was the name of that song?

174. During that ceremony, all of the members of the Alliance were wearing Stone Cold shirts—except one. Who was that one?

175. Kurt Angle interrupted the ceremony driving what kind of vehicle?

176. After years together, Christian finally turned on his brother Edge on the September 3, 2001 episode of *Raw.* From what city did that show emanate?

177. _____ regained the WWE Championship from _____ on the October 8, 2001 episode of *Raw,* when WWE Commissioner _____ turned on the champion.

178. The October 22, 2001 episode of *Raw* saw four WWE
Superstars defeat four Alliance Superstars to win
championships. Match the Superstar with the title he
won.

a) Bradshaw   1) Cruiserweight
b) Tajiri   2) U.S.
c) Kurt Angle   3) European
d) The Rock   4) Tag Team Championship
                      (with Chris Jericho)

179. As the October 29, 2001 episode of *Raw* kicked off,
Vince McMahon named his five members of Team
WWE for the *Survivor Series.* But by the end of the
night, one of those five Superstars had jumped to the
Alliance. Which one?

a) The Rock   b) Kurt Angle
c) Chris Jericho   d) Kane

180. Also on that night, Vince took on his son, Shane, in
what kind of match?

181. The November 4, 2001 episode of *Raw* featured two
title changes. In the first, The Rock defeated Chris
Jericho to win the _____ Championship.

182. The other title change on November 4, 2001 saw Test
defeat Edge for a championship. As a result of that
win, Test held the _____ and the _____
Championships simultaneously.

183. _____ and _____ returned to WWE on the November
19, 2001 episode of *Raw,* which emanated live from
Charlotte, NC, the day after the *Survivor Series.*

184. On that same night, who resigned as WWE
Commissioner?

185. Also on that evening, Mr. McMahon welcomed the very first member of the "Vince McMahon Kiss My Ass Club." Who was that first member?

186. One week later, Mr. McMahon welcomed a second member to the club. Who was it?

2002

187. After nine months of rehab for a quadriceps injury, what Superstar returned to WWE on the January 7, 2002 episode of *Raw,* live from Madison Square Garden?

188. The January 21, 2002 episode of *Raw* saw Stone Cold Steve Austin interfere in a match pitting Val Venis against Mr. Perfect. After cleaning house, the Rattlesnake recited the theme song of what TV show?
a) *Gilligan's Island*   b) *The Beverly Hillbillies*
c) *All in the Family*   d) *The Jeffersons*

189. What blockbuster announcement did Stephanie McMahon-Helmsley make on the February 4, 2002 episode of *Raw?*
a) She had bought ECW.
b) She was bringing in the nWo.
c) She was pregnant.
d) She was going to try to regain the Women's Championship.

190. Triple H and Stephanie renewed their wedding vows one week later on *Raw.* Before Stephanie went out to the ring, someone tried to warn her that Triple H knew she had lied to him. Who tried to warn her?

191. Which of the following took place on the February 18, 2002 episode of *Raw*?
   a) **Stone Cold Steve Austin was arrested.**
   b) **Triple H won the No. 1 contenders spot for the WWE Championship at *WrestleMania*.**
   c) **The nWo trapped The Rock in an ambulance and tried to run him down with a truck.**
   d) **All of the above.**

192. Led by Paul Heyman, what self-professed "Next Big Thing" made his first WWE appearance on the March 18, 2002 episode of *Raw*—just one day after *WrestleMania X8*?

193. On the March 25, 2002 episode of *Raw*, a draft was held for WWE's brand extension. Who did then *Raw* owner Ric Flair select as the No. 1 draft pick for the *Raw* brand?

194. Which of the following did NOT happen on the April 1, 2002 episode of *Raw*?
   a) **Triple H won the WWE Championship.**
   b) **Stone Cold signed an exclusive contract with the *Raw* brand.**
   c) **Bubba Ray Dudley won the Hardcore Championship.**
   d) ***Raw* debuted a new set, new logo and new theme music.**

195. X-Pac won a Falls Count Anywhere match on the April 8, 2002 episode of *Raw*, and sent his opponent to the sidelines for months. X-Pac would mock his opponent by wearing a piece of the Superstar's ring attire. Who was his opponent?

196. Who joined the nWo on the April 22, 2002 episode of *Raw*—the third time the Superstar had joined the renegade faction?

197. What campaign made its debut on the May 6, 2002 episode of *Raw*?
a) Attitude
b) The New Generation
c) Get the "F" out
d) What the World is Watching

198. After nearly a full year away from the WWE spotlight, what Superstar returned on the May 27, 2002 episode of *Raw,* in his hometown of Edmonton, Alberta, Canada?

199. On that same episode, who defeated Eddie Guerrero in a thrilling Ladder match to capture his second Intercontinental Championship?

200. Who was named the general manager of *Raw* on the July 15, 2002 episode?

SUMMERSLAM®

he Game and I am
lamn good.
Banzai Dr
Twist Of Fate
Hulkamani
what The Rock is cookin
What?
And that's the bottom li

Spit A Room
Twist Of Fat
plex
LATINO HEAT
plash
Baldo Bom
Shooting Star Press
Wussup wit da
Woooooooo!
on Bomb
The Wor
The Walls Of Jericho

1. *SummerSlam* has traditionally been held in which month?

2. The Intercontinental Championship changed hands at the first ____ *SummerSlams.*

3. Out of the first fourteen *SummerSlams,* how many times did the Intercontinental Champion successfully defend his title?

4. *SummerSlam 2002* took place at Nassau Coliseum in Long Island, New York. What was the last WWE Pay-Per-View to take place there?

5. Out of the first fifteen, which *SummerSlam* was the most attended?

6. Who was Sable's mystery partner for her mixed Tag Team match at *SummerSlam '98*?

7. How long did it take Ultimate Warrior to defeat the Honky Tonk Man at *SummerSlam '88*?
   **a) 28 seconds   b) 2 minutes
   c) 3 minutes   d) 1 hour**

8. Who was scheduled to be Honky Tonk Man's opponent at *SummerSlam '88*?

9. Honky Tonk Man's scheduled opponent at *SummerSlam '88* could not compete due to an injury. Who injured him?

10. Who accompanied Honky Tonk Man to the ring at *SummerSlam '88*?

11. When Ultimate Warrior defeated Honky Tonk Man at *SummerSlam '88*, it ended Honky's record-setting reign as Intercontinental Champion. How long was Honky's reign?
   a) 6 months   b) 6 years   c)18 months   d) 36 months

12. Who joined Shane McMahon and Jim Ross for commentary during the *Sunday Night Heat* preceding *SummerSlam '98*?
a) Vince McMahon   b) Gorilla Monsoon
c) Shawn Michaels   d) Savio Vega

13. What two celebrities, best known for their roles in the *Naked Gun* movies, tried to solve the Undertaker mystery leading up to *SummerSlam '94*?

14. At *SummerSlam '94* Undertaker took on Underfaker. Undertaker was managed by Paul Bearer. Who seconded Underfaker?

15. Hulk Hogan and Randy "Macho Man" Savage teamed up in the main event of *SummerSlam '88*. They were collectively known as what?

16. What was the subtitle of *SummerSlam '88*?

17. Which morning talk show host was in attendance at *SummerSlam '88*?

18. Ted DiBiase wrestled Razor Ramon at *SummerSlam '88* in what would turn out to be the last match for the "Million-Dollar Man." What year was it?

19. Who were the announcers for *SummerSlam '88*?
a) Vince McMahon and Jerry "the King" Lawler
b) Tony Schiavone and Jesse "the Body" Venture
c) Vince McMahon and "Rowdy" Roddy Piper
d) Gorilla Monsoon and "Superstar" Billy Graham

20. What did Miss Elizabeth do to distract the Mega-Bucks during the main event at *SummerSlam '88*?

21. Who was the manager of the Mega-Bucks?
a) **Mr. Fuji**
b) **Slick**
c) **"Mouth of the South" Jimmy Hart**
d) **Bobby "The Brain" Heenan**

22. Who managed the Powers of Pain to a victory over the Bolsheviks at *SummerSlam '88*?

23. Who did Big Boss Man defeat at *SummerSlam '88*?

24. Who did Ludvig Borga defeat at *SummerSlam '88*?
a) **Irwin R. Schyster**   b) **Owen Hart**
c) **Marty Jannetty**   d) **1-2-3 Kid**

25. Who was the special referee for the main event of *SummerSlam '88*?

26. Who ran into the ring during the "Ravishing" Rick Rude vs. Junkyard Dog match at *SummerSlam '88*, causing JYD to be disqualified?

27. What was the name of the finishing maneuver that Bad News Brown used to defeat Ken Patera at *SummerSlam '88*?

28. Who did Brother Love interview at *SummerSlam '88*?

29. How did the very first *SummerSlam* match end?
a) **British Bulldogs defeated the Rougeau Brothers.**
b) **Rougeau Brothers defeated the British Bulldogs.**
c) **Both teams were counted out.**
d) **A time-limit draw.**

30. What was the subtitle of *SummerSlam '89*?

31. Who were the announcers for *SummerSlam '89*?
a) Vince McMahon and Jerry "the King" Lawler
b) Tony Schiavone and Jesse "the Body" Ventura
c) Vince McMahon and "Rowdy" Roddy Piper
d) Gorilla Monsoon and "Superstar" Billy Graham

32. Who was the referee for the Brain Busters vs. Hart Foundation match at *SummerSlam '89*?

33. Who pinned whom in the Brain Busters vs. Hart Foundation match?
a) Arn Anderson pinned Bret Hart
b) Tully Blanchard pinned Jim Neidhart
c) Hart pinned Blanchard
d) Neidhart pinned Anderson

34. In an interview after losing to Dusty Rhodes at *SummerSlam '89,* who did the wobbly-kneed Honky Tonk Man seem to think he was?

35. What kind of match did Bret Hart and Owen Hart have at *SummerSlam '94*?
a) ladder match   b) cage match
c) hell in the cell   d) best-of-three falls

36. Who teamed up with The Rockers to take on the Rougeau Brothers and Rick Martel at *SummerSlam '89*?

37. Who came to the ring and distracted "Ravishing" Rick Rude during Rude's Intercontinental title match with Ultimate Warrior at *SummerSlam '89*?

38. What "perennial preliminary competitor" actually won a match, against Skip, at *SummerSlam '95*?

39. Who was the guest ring announcer for the Hercules vs. Greg Valentine match at *SummerSlam '89*?

40. Jimmy "Superfly" Snuka wrestled Ted DiBiase at *SummerSlam '89,* but who did "Superfly" end up giving the big splash to?

41. How did Ted DiBiase defeat Jimmy "Superfly" Snuka at *SummerSlam '89*?
a) pinfall   b) submission
c) he put him to sleep   d) countout

42. Which two women were at ringside for the main event at *SummerSlam '89*?

43. Which two men did Hulk Hogan and Brutus "The Barber" Beefcake defeat in the main event of *SummerSlam '89*?

44. Who read a poem before the main event of *SummerSlam '89*?

45. Who did Mr. Perfect pin at *SummerSlam '89*?

46. Which team did "Hacksaw" Jim Duggan partner with to defeat Andre the Giant and the Twin Towers at *SummerSlam '89*?

47. Who were the announcers for *SummerSlam '90*?
a) Vince McMahon and Jerry "the King" Lawler
b) Tony Schiavone and Jesse "the Body" Ventura
c) Vince McMahon and "Rowdy" Roddy Piper
d) Gorilla Monsoon and "Superstar" Billy Graham

48. What was the subtitle of *SummerSlam '90*?

49. What European city was D'Lo Brown announced from at *SummerSlam '98*?
a) Helsinki, Finland   b) Milan, Italy
c) Cologne, Germany   d) Madrid, Spain

50. When Brutus Beefcake was injured in a boating accident, who challenged and defeated Mr. Perfect for the Intercontinental title at *SummerSlam '90*?

51. Who was the referee for the Intercontinental title match at *SummerSlam '90*?
**a) Earl Hebner   b) Tim White
c) Joey Marella   d) Mike Chioda**

52. Who did Brother Love interview at *SummerSlam '90*?

53. In addition to the Intercontinental title, which other title changed hands at *SummerSlam '90*?

54. Ultimate Warrior defeated "Ravishing" Rick Rude in a _____ match at *SummerSlam '90*.

55. How did the Warlord defeat Tito Santana at *SummerSlam '90*?
**a) pinfall   b) submission
c) countout   d) disqualification**

56. Who did Hulk Hogan defeat at *SummerSlam '90*?

57. Who accompanied Hulk Hogan to the ring at *SummerSlam '90*?
**a) Tugboat   b) Jimmy Hart
c) Miss Elizabeth   d) Big Boss Man**

58. What song did "Hacksaw" Jim Duggan and Nikolai Volkoff sing before their match with the Orient Express at *SummerSlam '90*?

59. Power & Glory defeated The Rockers at *SummerSlam '90*. Which two men comprised the team of Power & Glory?

60. Who was the special referee for the Jake "The Snake" Roberts vs. Bad News Brown match at *SummerSlam '90*?

61. What did Bad News Brown have at ringside with him for his match with Jake Roberts at *SummerSlam '90*?
a) a cage full of sewer rats
b) a large "ghetto blaster"
c) his manager
d) a venom antidote

62. Who revealed at *SummerSlam '90* that he had "bought" Sapphire?

63. Who defeated Barry Horowitz in a nontelevised match just before *SummerSlam '93*?
a) Kwang   b) 1-2-3 Kid
c) the Warlord   d) Owen Hart

64. What was the nontelevised "dark match" at *SummerSlam '91*?

65. What was the subtitle of *SummerSlam '91*?

66. Who got married at *SummerSlam '91*?

67. Who were the three announcers for *SummerSlam '91*?

68. In one of the all-time best *SummerSlam* matches, Bret "Hit Man" Hart defeated _____ to win the Intercontinental Championship at the 1991 event. It was Bret's _____ singles title.

69. What maneuver did Bret Hart use to win the Intercontinental title at *SummerSlam '91*?

70. What two Superstars were responsible for the horrifying attack on Macho Man and Miss Elizabeth at *SummerSlam '91*?

71. Who came to the ring during the Disciples of Apocalypse vs. Los Boricuas match at *SummerSlam '97*?

72. Which championship did Virgil win by defeating the "Million-Dollar Man" Ted DiBiase at *SummerSlam '91*?

73. In 1994, many fans suspected that Lex Luger was secretly working with Ted DiBiase's "Million-Dollar Corporation." What happened during the Luger vs. Tatanka match *SummerSlam '94*?
   a) Luger beat up DiBiase to put the rumors to rest.
   b) Luger actually joined the Corporation.
   c) Tatanka joined the Corporation.
   d) DiBiase attacked both men.

74. How many championships changed hands at *SummerSlam '91*?

75. Which two Superstars defeated Sgt. Slaughter, Col. Mustafa and Gen. Adnan in the main event at *SummerSlam '91*?

76. What was Col. Mustafa known as for most of his time in WWE?

77. Who was the special referee in the main event of *SummerSlam '91*?

78. Irwin R. Schyster pinned which former Intercontinental Champion at *SummerSlam '91*?
   a) Greg "The Hammer" Valentine
   b) Tito Santana
   c) Pedro Morales
   d) Pat Patterson

79. Who defeated Yokozuna in the "Free For All" before *SummerSlam '96*?

80. Who were the three announcers for *SummerSlam '96*?

81. Who attacked Savio Vega after his loss to Owen Hart at *SummerSlam '96*?

82. Who came to ringside to proposition Sable during the Marc Mero vs. Goldust match at *SummerSlam '96*?

83. Who defeated Davey Boy Smith at *SummerSlam '96*?
a) Sycho Sid   b) Aldo Montoya
c) Bret Hart   d) Kane

84. Who provided guest commentary during the Jake "The Snake" Roberts vs. Jerry "the King" Lawler match at *SummerSlam '96*?

85. Which tag team "hosted" *SummerSlam 2000* from WWE's entertainment complex in Times Square?

86. Undertaker told *WWE Magazine* that, as a result of his match at *SummerSlam '96,* he almost lost his _____ due to a staph infection.

87. Who turned his back on Undertaker, costing the "Deadman" his match at *SummerSlam '96*?

88. Who did Undertaker defeat in a Casket match at *SummerSlam '95*?
a) Kama   b) Isaac Yankem, D.D.S.
c) Kane   d) Bret Hart

89. Who was Shawn Michaels's opponent in the WWE Championship match at *SummerSlam '96*?

90. At the insistence of Jim Cornette, how many times was the WWE Championship match at *SummerSlam '96* restarted?
a) once   b) twice   c) three times   d) six times

91. Which two men battled for the WWE Championship at *SummerSlam '95*?

92. What was the subtitle of *SummerSlam '96*?

93. How did Chris Jericho defeat Rhyno at *SummerSlam 2001*?
a) pinfall   b) submission
c) countout   d) disqualification

94. Who sang the national anthem just before the main event at *SummerSlam '93*?
a) Aaron Neville   b) Boyz II Men
c) Aretha Franklin   d) Regis Philbin

95. How many people attended *SummerSlam '92*?
a) 67,925   b) 68,923
c) 80,355   d) 93,173

96. How many championships changed hands at *SummerSlam '96*?

97. What was the subtitle of *SummerSlam '97*?

98. What three men were the announcers for *SummerSlam '97*?

99. During the cage match at *SummerSlam '97,* what did Chyna do to Mankind that, he said in interviews after the match, caused "unbearable" pain?

100. What was supposed to be painted on Mankind's chest when he ripped open his shirt near the end of the cage match at *SummerSlam '97*?

101. Mankind won the cage match at *SummerSlam '97* after imitating which of his idols?
a) Iron Sheik
b) Dominic DeNucci
c) Jimmy "Superfly" Snuka
d) Hulk Hogan

102. Which persona did Mankind "transform" into after the cage match at *SummerSlam '97*?

103. Which member of the Hart family hadn't been seen on WWE television in more than two years when he appeared at *SummerSlam '94*?

104. What was Brian Pillman forced to do after losing to Goldust at *SummerSlam '97*?

105. Who was Owen Hart's trainer/manager for the Lion's Den match at *SummerSlam '98*?

106. What kind of food came into play during the Davey Boy Smith vs. Ken Shamrock match at *SummerSlam '97*?

107. How did Davey Boy Smith defeat Ken Shamrock at *SummerSlam '97*?
a) pinfall   b) submission
c) countout   d) disqualification

108. What was The Mountie forced to do after losing to Big Boss Man at *SummerSlam '91*?
a) Kiss Boss Man's feet.
b) Leave the WWE.
c) Spend the night in jail.
d) Have his head shaved.

109. What kind of injury did Stone Cold Steve Austin sustain during his match with Owen Hart at *SummerSlam '97*?

110. What would Stone Cold Steve Austin have been forced to do if he had lost the Intercontinental title match at *SummerSlam '97*?

111. What was the name of the bus in which Lex Luger rode around the country to generate support leading up to *SummerSlam '93*?

112. Bret Hart defeated _____ in the main event of
SummerSlam '97 to become the WWE Champion for
the _____ time.

113. What did Bret Hart promise he would never do again
if he lost in the main event of *SummerSlam '97*?

114. What song did Bret Hart insist be played before his
match at *SummerSlam '97*?

115. What three men appeared at ringside during the
course of the main event at *SummerSlam '97*?

116. Who was the special guest referee during the main
event of *SummerSlam '97*?
**a) Sycho Sid   b) Vince McMahon
c) Triple H   d) Shawn Michaels**

117. What state politician was named honorary WWE
Champion during *SummerSlam '97*?

118. Who had his head shaved by Jeff Jarrett and Southern
Justice prior to *SummerSlam '98*?

119. What AC/DC classic was the theme song (and
subtitle) for *SummerSlam '98*?
**a) "Highway to Hell"
b) "Back in Black"
c) "T.N.T."
d) "Dirty Deeds Done Dirt Cheap"**

120. What Chicago legend accompanied Razor Ramon to
the ring at *SummerSlam '94*?

121. Which rap group accompanied the Oddities to the
ring at *SummerSlam '98*?

122. Who did the Oddities defeat at *SummerSlam '98*?
a) **Disciples of Apocalypse**
b) **Nation of Domination**
c) **Kaientai**
d) **D-Generation X**

123. Which competitor had his head shaved after losing a Hair vs. Hair match at *SummerSlam '98*?
a) **X-Pac** b) **Kurt Angle**
c) **Edge** d) **Jeff Jarrett**

124. Who was the first Superstar to successfully defend the Intercontinental Championship at a *SummerSlam*?

125. Among Road Dogg, Billy Gunn, Mankind and Kane, which competitor did not show up for the Tag Team title match at *SummerSlam '98,* forcing the match to become a two-on-one affair?

126. Who did the Legion of Doom defeat at *SummerSlam '97*?
a) **the Godwinns** b) **the Headbangers**
c) **New Rockers** d) **New Age Outlaws**

127. What kind of match did Triple H and The Rock have at *SummerSlam '98*?
a) **ladder match** b) **cage match**
c) **hell in the cell** d) **best-of-three falls**

128. Who left *SummerSlam '98* as Intercontinental Champion?

129. In several interviews, Triple H has mentioned that a body part was giving him problems going into his match at *SummerSlam '98*. He subsequently had surgery to correct the problem. Which part was it?
a) **left quadriceps** b) **right biceps**
c) **back** d) **right knee**

130. What injury did Undertaker sustain while driving Stone Cold Steve Austin through the Spanish announcers' table at *SummerSlam '98*?
a) broken coccyx
b) sprained ankle
c) severe concussion
d) torn ACL in right knee

131. Who came to the ring during Undertaker vs. Stone Cold Steve Austin match at *SummerSlam '98*, but was told to return to the locker room area by Undertaker?

132. What highly anticipated match at *SummerSlam '95* was a rematch from *WrestleMania X*?

133. Which two men were the announcers for *SummerSlam* in 1998, 1999, and 2000?

134. *SummerSlam '99* was the first time in WWE history that which five titles changed hands on the same night?

135. What was the subtitle of *SummerSlam '99*?

136. Which then-Minnesota Viking received a Rock T-shirt from the "Great One" himself on the *Sunday Night Heat* prior to *SummerSlam '99*?
a) John Randle   b) Cris Carter
c) Robert Smith   d) Randy Moss

137. Jeff Jarrett defeated "Euro-Continental" Champion D'Lo Brown at *SummerSlam '99* to win the Intercontinental Championship for the _____ time and the European Championship for the _____ time.

138. Which two Superstars helped Jeff Jarrett win his match at *SummerSlam '99*?

139. _____ defeated _____ in a nontelevised match just before *SummerSlam '94.*

140. At *SummerSlam '99*, Ken Shamrock battled Steve Blackman in a _____ match.

141. What type of match did Shane McMahon and Test battle in at *SummerSlam '99*?

142. Because Test defeated Shane McMahon at *SummerSlam '99*, Shane was forced to do what?

143. Which two competitors battled for the Hardcore title at *SummerSlam '99*?

144. Who came out to interrupt Road Dogg's interview at *SummerSlam '99*?
a) Mr. Ass   b) Al Snow
b) Big Boss Man   d) Chris Jericho

145. What type of match did The Rock and Mr. Ass battle in at *SummerSlam '99*?

146. Which team won the Tag Team Turmoil match at *SummerSlam '99*?
a) Acolytes
b) Crash & Hardcore Holly
c) Edge & Christian
d) Hardy Boyz

147. Who did Ivory defeat at *SummerSlam '99* to retain the Women's Championship?
a) Jacqueline   b) Terri
c) Tori   d) Trish Stratus

148. Who made her WWE return by attacking Ivory after Ivory's match at *SummerSlam '99*?

149. Which duo won the Tag Team Championship at *SummerSlam '99*?

150. Which three Superstars battled for the WWE Championship at *SummerSlam '99*?

151. Who was the special guest referee for the Triple Threat WWE title match at *SummerSlam '99*?

152. Who walked out of *SummerSlam '99* as the WWE Champion?

153. According to his article in *WWE Magazine,* which match at *SummerSlam 2000* inspired Tommy Dreamer to remain as an active competitor?
   a) Chris Benoit vs. Chris Jericho
   b) Tables, Ladders & Chairs
   c) Shane McMahon vs. Steve Blackman Hardcore title match
   d) The Rock vs. Triple H vs. Kurt Angle

154. Which Superstar's prematch interview kicked off *SummerSlam 2000*?

155. Who pinned whom in the six-man tag team match that kicked off *SummerSlam 2000*?

156. Who won the Road Dogg vs. X-Pac match at *SummerSlam 2000*?

157. Which match at *SummerSlam '92* was actually a battle between former members of Demolition?

158. How did Lex Luger defeat Yokozuna at *SummerSlam '93*?
   a) pinfall   b) submission
   c) countout   d) disqualification

159. Who won the Intercontinental Championship at *SummerSlam 2000*?
   a) Eddie Guerrero   b) Chyna
   c) Trish Stratus   d) Jeff Hardy

160. What did Jim Ross break over Tazz's head at
SummerSlam 2000, helping Jerry Lawler win the
match?

161. Which two men tried unsuccessfully to help Shane
McMahon beat Steve Blackman in the Hardcore title
match at *SummerSlam 2000?*

162. What kind of match did Chris Benoit and Chris Jericho
have at *SummerSlam 2000?*
a) ladder match   b) cage match
c) hell in the cell   d) best-of-three falls

163. Who interfered during the Tables, Ladders & Chairs
Match at *SummerSlam 2000?*
a) Lita   b) Spike Dudley
c) Rhyno   d) All of the above

164. Who walked out of *SummerSlam 2000* as the Tag
Team Champions?
a) Billy & Chuck
b) Edge & Christian
c) Hardy Boyz
d) Dudley Boyz

165. What kind of match did Terri and The Kat battle in
at *SummerSlam 2000?*
a) Lingerie match
b) Paddle-on-a-Pole match
c) Snow Bunny match
d) Thong Stinkface match

166. Who were the announcers for *SummerSlam '94*
and '95?
a) Vince McMahon and Jerry "the King" Lawler
b) Tony Schiavone and Jesse "the Body" Ventura
c) Vince McMahon and "Rowdy" Roddy Piper
d) Gorilla Monsoon and "Superstar" Billy Graham

167. Who accompanied The Kat to the ring at *SummerSlam 2000*?

168. Who accompanied Terri to the ring at *SummerSlam 2000*?

169. Which Hart family member sat ringside for the Davey Boy Smith vs. Bret Hart Intercontinental title match at *SummerSlam '92*?

170. Which match at *SummerSlam '96* did Undertaker say was the most physically brutal match he's ever been in?

171. What did Undertaker take from Kane during their encounter at *SummerSlam 2000*?
a) his urn   b) his manager
c) his mask   d) his girlfriend

172. What injury did Kurt Angle suffer at *SummerSlam 2000* when Triple H gave him a Pedigree through the Spanish announcers' table?
a) broken coccyx
b) sprained ankle
c) severe concussion
d) torn ACL in right knee

173. *SummerSlam '94* was the first-ever event in which arena?

174. What was the result of the main event of *SummerSlam 2000*?
a) The Rock retained the WWE Championship.
b) Triple H won the title.
c) Kurt Angle won the title.
d) Stephanie McMahon won the title.

175. Who were the announcers for *SummerSlam 2001*?

176. Which of the following women was NOT involved in the six-person Tag Team match on the *Sunday Night Heat* preceding *SummerSlam 2001*?
a) Jazz   b) Lita
c) Molly Holly   d) Torrie Wilson

177. At *SummerSlam 2001*, Edge won the _____ Championship for the _____ time.

178. Which two Superstars battled in a Hardcore Ladder match at *SummerSlam 2001*?

179. Name the four teams that were involved in the Tag Team Elimination match at *SummerSlam '96*.

180. How did Kurt Angle defeat Stone Cold Steve Austin at *SummerSlam 2001*?
a) pinfall   b) submission
c) countout   d) disqualification

181. Which year did Sean Waltman (1-2-3 Kid/X-Pac) make his *SummerSlam* debut?
a) 1993   b) 1994   c) 1996   d) 1998

182. Who were the announcers for *SummerSlam '92* and '93?

183. Who won The Rock vs. Booker T WCW title match at *SummerSlam 2001*?

184. Which two former members of D-Generation X squared off at *SummerSlam 2002*?

185. Undertaker battled Giant Gonzales in what kind of match at *SummerSlam '93*?

186. Who did Undertaker defeat at *SummerSlam 2002*?

187. How did Ultimate Warrior defeat Randy Savage at *SummerSlam '92*?
a) pinfall   b) submission
c) countout   d) disqualification

188. Which two men battled for the Undisputed Championship at *SummerSlam 2002*?

189. Which cruiserweight did Kurt Angle face at *SummerSlam 2002*?

190. *SummerSlams* in 1988, 1991 and 1998 took place at which "world famous" arena?

191. In what city did the *SummerSlams* in 1989 and 1997 take place?

192. Where did *SummerSlam '90* take place?

193. Where did *SummerSlam '92* take place?

194. Where did *SummerSlam '93* take place?

195. Where did *SummerSlam '94* take place?

196. Where did *SummerSlam '95* take place?

197. Where did *SummerSlam '96* take place?

198. Where did *SummerSlam '99* take place?

199. Where did *SummerSlam 2000* take place?

200. Where did *SummerSlam 2001* take place?

ROYAL RUMBLE

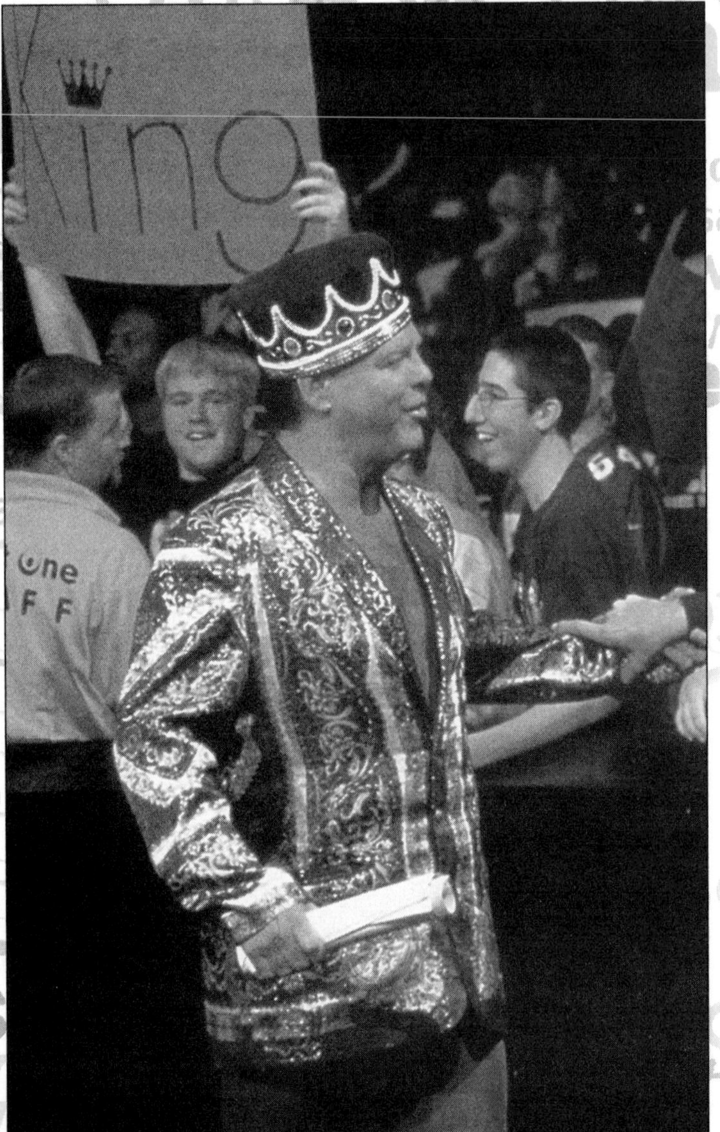

1. Who did Ricky Steamboat defeat at the 1988 *Royal Rumble*?
   a) "Hacksaw" Jim Duggan   b) Junkyard Dog
   c) "Ravishing" Rick Rude   d) Randy Savage

2. Which WWE Hall of Famer came up with the concept of the *Royal Rumble*?
   a) Captain Lou Albano   b) Pat Patterson
   c) James Dudley   d) Johnny Rodz

3. **True or false:** The first *Royal Rumble* was on Pay-Per-View.

4. Who was the first man to enter the 1988 *Royal Rumble*?
   a) Junkyard Dog   b) Dino Bravo
   c) Hulk Hogan   d) Bret Hart

5. How many competitors did the 1988 *Royal Rumble* have?
   a) 20   b) 25   c) 30   d) 1

6. Who won the first *Royal Rumble* match?
   a) Bret Hart   b) Hercules
   c) "Hacksaw" Jim Duggan   d) Iron Sheik

7. Who was the final entrant into the first *Royal Rumble* match?
   a) One Man Gang   b) Junkyard Dog
   c) "Hacksaw" Jim Duggan   d) Ron Bass

8. Who was the first man eliminated at the first *Royal Rumble* match?
   a) Harley Race   b) Butch Reed
   c) Tito Santana   d) Jake Roberts

9. How much weight did Dino Bravo attempt to bench-press at the first *Royal Rumble*?
   a) 500 pounds   b) 715 pounds
   c) 600 pounds   d) 835 pounds

10. Who provided a "spot" and may have helped Bravo
lift the massive weight at the 1988 *Royal Rumble*?
a) "Mean" Gene Okerlund   b) Frenchy Martin
c) Greg Valentine   d) Jesse Ventura

11. Who were the first two entrants into the 1989 *Royal Rumble*?
a) Bret Hart and Jim Neidhart
b) Butch Reed and Koko B. Ware
c) Ax and Smash
d) B. Brian Blair and Jim Brunzell

12. Who was the winner of the 1989 *Royal Rumble* match?
a) Ted DiBiase   b) Big John Studd
c) Andre the Giant   d) Hulk Hogan

13. Who successfully defended the Women's
Championship at the 1989 *Royal Rumble*?
a) Wendi Richter   b) Fabulous Moolah
c) Judy Martin   d) Rockin' Robin

14. Who became "King" at the 1989 *Royal Rumble*?
a) Haku   b) Harley Race
c) Jerry Lawler   d) Bret Hart

15. Who did The Hart Foundation team with in their
match against the Rougeau Brothers and Dino Bravo
at the 1989 *Royal Rumble*?
a) Jimmy Hart   b) "Hacksaw" Jim Duggan
c) British Bulldog   d) Randy Savage

16. Who was the final entrant into the 1989 *Royal Rumble*
match?
a) Virgil   b) Greg Valentine
c) Ted DiBiase   d) Honky Tonk Man

17. Who was the final man eliminated in the 1989 *Royal Rumble* Match?
a) Ted DiBiase   b) Andre the Giant
c) Bret Hart   d) Hercules

18. How was Andre the Giant eliminated in the 1989 *Royal Rumble* match?
a) Hulk Hogan bodyslammed Andre out.
b) Jake Roberts's snake, Damian, spooked Andre.
c) The ring broke and Andre fell out.
d) Andre was thrown out by Bret Hart.

19. How many *Royal Rumbles* did Big John Studd win?
a) 0   b) 1   c) 2   d) 3

20. What tag-team partners were eliminated at No. 16 and 17 in the 1989 *Royal Rumble*?
a) Ax & Smash
b) Bret Hart & Jim Neidhart
c) Tully Blanchard & Arn Anderson
d) Shawn Michaels & Marty Jannetty

21. Who won the 1990 *Royal Rumble*?
a) Andre the Giant   b) Hulk Hogan
c) Ted DiBiase   d) Randy Savage

22. Who was the final entrant into the 1990 *Royal Rumble*?
a) Ted DiBiase   b) Virgil
c) Mr. Perfect   d) Hercules

23. Who defeated the Rougeau Brothers in the opening match of the 1990 *Royal Rumble* event?
a) The Hart Foundation
b) The Rhythm & Blues
c) The Killer Bees
d) The Bushwackers

24. How many Superstars did Hulk Hogan eliminate in the 1990 *Royal Rumble*?
a) 3   b) 5   c) 6   d) 8

25. Who was the first man eliminated from the 1990 *Royal Rumble* match?
a) Koko B. Ware   b) Earthquake
c) Ax   d) Jimmy Snuka

26. Brutus Beefcake wrestled Lanny Poffo at the 1990 *Royal Rumble* event. What was Poffo's "brainy" nickname?
a) Mr. Smart   b) the Genius
c) the Brain   d) Serious Cerebellum!

27. What Superstar in the 1990 *Royal Rumble* was also known as One Man Gang and returned at *WrestleMania X8* in the Gimmick Battle Royal?
a) Iron Sheik   b) Brother Love
c) Akeem   d) Terry Taylor

28. What Superstar clucked his way to the ring for the 1990 *Royal Rumble* match?
a) Brooklyn Brawler   b) Bad News Brown
c) Chicken George   d) Red Rooster

29. Ronnie Garvin defeated Greg Valentine at the 1990 *Royal Rumble*. What was Valentine's nickname?
a) Hands of Stone   b) Heart of Glass
c) The Hammer   d) The Mallet

30. **True or false:** The 1990 *Royal Rumble* was the first time the WWE Champion won the *Royal Rumble* match.

31. Who broke a glass scepter over Ultimate Warrior's head at the 1991 *Royal Rumble*?
a) Sgt. Slaughter   b) General Adnan
c) Randy Savage   d) Sherri Martel

32. Where was the 1991 *Royal Rumble* event held?
a) Utica, NY   b) Richmond, VA
c) Nashville, TN   d) Miami, FL

33. Who defeated the Orient Express in the opening
match at the 1991 *Royal Rumble*?
a) The Hart Foundation   b) The Rockers
c) The Bushwackers   d) Demolition

34. What father and son team did Ted DiBiase and Virgil
defeat at the 1991 *Royal Rumble*?
a) Greg & Verne Gagne
b) Eddie & Mike Graham
c) Vince & Shane McMahon
d) Dusty & Dustin Rhodes

35. What African name did former Tag Team Champion
Tony Atlas take for the 1991 *Royal Rumble*?
a) Akeem   b) Kamala
c) Saba Simba   d) Lion King

36. Who was the first man to enter the ring for the 1991
Royal Rumble match?
a) Warlord   b) Bret Hart
c) Honky Tonk Man   d) Hulk Hogan

37. Who was the lucky No. 30 entrant in the 1991 *Royal
Rumble* match?
a) Earthquake   b) Skinner
c) Bushwacker Luke   d) Tugboat

38. What was a *Royal Rumble* first from the 1991 event?
a) Bret Hart was the No. 1 entrant.
b) The WWE Championship changed hands at a *Royal
Rumble* event.
c) Mr. Perfect made his *Royal Rumble* debut.
d) Superstars had to be thrown over the top rope to be
eliminated from the *Royal Rumble* match.

39. What two "law and order" Superstars appeared in the 1991 *Royal Rumble* event?
a) Sgt. Slaughter and Cpl. Kirschner
b) Big Boss Man and Bert the Cop
c) Big Boss Man and The Mountie
d) The Mountie and Bull Buchanan

40. Who was the manager of The Orient Express?
a) Mr. Fuji   b) Jim Cornette
c) The Coach   d) Afa the Wild Samoan

41. What did the winner of the 1992 *Royal Rumble* win?
a) a brand new car
b) WWE Championship
c) a shot at the WWE Champion at *WrestleMania*
d) a trip to Hawaii

42. Who defeated the Orient Express in the opening match for the 1992 *Royal Rumble* event?
a) The Rockers   b) The Bushwackers
c) The New Foundation   d) Demolition

43. What was on the line for the 1992 *Royal Rumble* event match between Roddy Piper and The Mountie?
a) the WWE Championship
b) the Intercontinental Championship
c) a night in jail
d) Jimmy Hart's megaphone

44. Who won the 1992 *Royal Rumble* match?
a) Hulk Hogan   b) Sid Justice
c) Ric Flair   d) Bret Hart

45. How long was Ric Flair in the ring for the 1992 *Royal Rumble* match?
a) 15 minutes   b) over an hour
c) 30 seconds   d) 2 minutes

46. Who was the No. 1 entrant in the 1992 *Royal Rumble* match?
a) Ted DiBiase   b) Uncle Elmer
c) British Bulldog   d) Ric Flair

47. Kerry Von Erich was in the 1992 *Royal Rumble* match. What nickname was he called?
a) Phenom   b) Texas Tornado
c) Hot Stuff   d) Sensational

48. Who was the final man to enter the ring for the 1992 *Royal Rumble* match?
a) Repo Man   b) Berzerker
c) Randy Savage   d) Warlord

49. Who was the first man eliminated from the 1992 *Royal Rumble* match?
a) Haku   b) Ted DiBiase
c) Randy Savage   d) British Bulldog

50. Who was the manager of the Beverly Brothers at the 1992 *Royal Rumble*?
a) Captain Lou Albano   b) the Genius
c) Mr. Fuji   d) Chief Jay Strongbow

51. Earthquake & Typhoon, the Natural Disasters, faced the Legion of Doom at the 1992 *Royal Rumble.* What was Typhoon's former name?
a) Hillbilly Jim   b) Dusty Rhodes
c) Tugboat   d) Uncle Elmer

52. How many titles did Roddy Piper hold during his WWE career?
a) 1   b) 2   c) 3   d) 4

53. How is a WWE Superstar eliminated from a *Royal Rumble* match?

a) pinfall

b) submission

c) over the top rope and both feet must hit the floor

d) through the ropes and onto the apron

54. What month is the *Royal Rumble* traditionally held?

a) April   b) June   c) January   d) September

55. Who was the final man eliminated from the 1992 *Royal Rumble* match?

a) Hulk Hogan   b) Sid Justice

c) Ted DiBiase   d) Repo Man

56. Which former Rocker challenged Shawn Michaels for the Intercontinental Championship at the 1993 *Royal Rumble*?

a) Diesel   b) Triple H

c) Marty Jannetty   d) Rockin' Robin

57. Who won the 1993 *Royal Rumble* match?

a) Randy Savage   b) Yokozuna

c) Hulk Hogan   d) Sid Justice

58. What brother team beat the Beverly Brothers at the 1993 *Royal Rumble*?

a) The Hart Foundation

b) The Orient Express

c) Edge & Christian

d) The Steiner Brothers

59. Who was the No. 1 entrant in the 1993 *Royal Rumble* match?

a) Max Moon   b) Papa Shango

c) Ric Flair   d) Sid Justice

60. What "Double D" was an entrant in the 1993 *Royal Rumble* match?
   a) Danny Davis   b) Damian Demento
   c) Dirty Dick Slater   d) Max Moon

61. What Puerto Rican legend competed in the 1993 *Royal Rumble* match?
   a) Savio Vega   b) Victor Jovica
   c) Carlos Colon   d) Miguelito Perez

62. Who did Bret Hart defeat at the 1993 *Royal Rumble* event?
   a) Razor Ramon   b) Owen Hart
   c) Bob Backlund   d) Jerry Lawler

63. Who lasted over an hour in the 1993 *Royal Rumble* match?
   a) Ric Flair   b) Owen Hart
   c) Headshrinker Fatu   d) Bob Backlund

64. What new special stipulation was added to the 1993 *Royal Rumble* match?
   a) Winner gets a crown.
   b) Winner faces the WWE Champion at *WrestleMania*.
   c) Winner gets a brand new car.
   d) Winner gets an island in the Pacific.

65. Which was the year that Bob Backlund didn't compete at a *Royal Rumble*?
   a) 1999   b) 2000   c) 1993   d) 1994

66. Of the Superstars in this group, who was eliminated first in the 1993 *Royal Rumble* match?
   a) Mr. Perfect   b) Samu
   c) Tenryu   d) Terry Taylor

67. What other character did 1993 *Royal Rumble* match entrant Max Moon portray in WWE?
a) Shinobi
b) Avatar
c) Kato of The Orient Express
d) former WWE announcer Todd Pettingill

68. What mystical weapon did Papa Shango use on opponents?
a) voodoo   b) levitation
c) "The Force"   d) a steel chair

69. What were the first names of the Beverly Brothers?
a) Bob & Buff   b) Beau & Blake
c) Benny & Bobby   d) Ron & Fez

70. How many Superstars did Yokozuna eliminate in the 1993 *Royal Rumble*?
a) 5   b) 6   c) 7   d) 8

71. Who clipped Bret Hart's leg out from under him, causing the referee to stop the Tag Team title match against the Quebecers at the 1994 *Royal Rumble* event?
a) Jacques Rougeau   b) Owen Hart
c) Bob Backlund   d) Johnny Polo

72. What specialty match did Yokozuna and Undertaker have at the 1994 *Royal Rumble* event?
a) Ladder match
b) No-Holds-Barred match
c) Casket match
d) Inferno match

73. Who eliminated Shawn Michaels from the 1994 *Royal Rumble* match?
a) Bret Hart   b) Lex Luger
c) Scott Steiner   d) Diesel

74. How many times did Razor Ramon defend the
Intercontinental Championship at *Royal Rumble*
events?
a) 1   b) 2   c) 3   d) 4

75. Diesel made a name for himself at the 1994 *Royal
Rumble* by...
a) breaking the ring
b) eliminating seven Superstars in a row
c) winning the event
**d) being the fastest man eliminated in *Royal Rumble*
history**

76. Who entered at the No. 25 position in the 1994 *Royal
Rumble* match?
a) Tenryu   b) Scott Steiner
c) no one   d) Lex Luger

77. Who was the first man eliminated from the 1994
Royal Rumble match?
a) Headshrinker Samu   b) Headshrinker Fatu
c) Rick Steiner   d) Bart Gunn

78. Who did Razor Ramon defeat in the Intercontinental
Championship match at the 1994 *Royal Rumble*?
a) Ted DiBiase   b) Irwin R. Schyster
c) Jeff Jarrett   d) 1-2-3 Kid

79. Sparky Plugg made his debut in the 1994 *Royal
Rumble* match. What was Sparky's first name?
a) Bob   b) Harold
c) Howard   d) Thurman

80. What Japanese masked Superstar that blew green mist
was in the 1994 *Royal Rumble* match?
a) Tenryu   b) Tajiri
c) Great Kabuki   d) Kwang

81. Which member of Men on a Mission was NOT in the 1994 *Royal Rumble* match?
a) Mo b) Oscar
c) Mabel d) All three were in the match.

82. Who won the 1994 *Royal Rumble* match?
a) Bret Hart b) Lex Luger
c) Both Bret and Lex d) Hulk Hogan

83. What did Bam Bam Bigelow have tattooed on his head?
a) Hair b) Flames c) Skulls d) Blood

84. Who shoved Lawrence Taylor at the 1995 *Royal Rumble*?
a) Shawn Michaels b) British Bulldog
c) Jeff Jarrett d) Bam Bam Bigelow

85. Who won the Intercontinental Championship at the 1995 *Royal Rumble*?
a) Jeff Jarrett b) Razor Ramon
c) 1-2-3 Kid d) Bob Holly

86. What was the outcome of the WWE Championship match between Diesel and Bret Hart at the 1995 *Royal Rumble*?
a) Bret won by pinfall. b) Diesel lost by DQ.
c) draw d) double countout

87. Who entered the 1995 *Royal Rumble* match in the No. 1 position?
a) British Bulldog b) Shawn Michaels
c) Jacob Blu d) Duke Droese

88. True or false: Both members of The Heavenly Bodies and Well Dunn were in the 1995 *Royal Rumble* match.

89. What "Half Man, Half Bull" was in the 1995 *Royal Rumble* match?
a) Dick Murdoch b) Bart Gunn
c) Eli Blu d) Mantaur

90. Who was the No. 30 entrant in the 1995 *Royal Rumble* match?
a) Crush b) Crash Holly
c) Mabel d) Mo

91. What team captured the WWE Tag Team Championship at the 1995 *Royal Rumble*?
a) Bam Bam Bigelow & Tatanka
b) 1-2-3 Kid & Bob Holly
c) Smokin' Gunns
d) Heavenly Bodies

92. True or false: The first two men in the 1995 *Royal Rumble* match were also the last two men remaining.

93. Through 2002, Shawn Michaels had won how many *Royal Rumble*s?
a) 1 b) 2 c) 3 d) 4

94. Who did NOT make their *Royal Rumble* debut at the 1996 event?
a) the Ringmaster
b) Vader
c) Hunter Hearst-Helmsley
d) Jerry Lawler

95. Why was Jeff Jarrett disqualified in his 1996 *Royal Rumble* match against Ahmed Johnson?
a) Jeff threw Ahmed over the top rope.
b) Jeff slugged the referee.
c) Jeff hit Ahmed with a guitar.
d) Jeff hit Ahmed with a low blow.

96. What future WWE Champion was the No. 1 entrant in the 1996 *Royal Rumble* match?
a) Stone Cold Steve Austin b) Triple H
c) Shawn Michaels d) Undertaker

97. The Bodydonnas were managed by whom?
a) **Jim Cornette** b) **Mr. Fuji**
c) **Sable** d) **Sunny**

98. What Hollywood outcast defeated Razor Ramon for
the Intercontinental Championship at the 1996 *Royal
Rumble*?
a) **Goldust** b) **Jeff Jarrett**
c) **1-2-3 Kid** d) **Shawn Michaels**

99. The Smokin' Gunns consisted of...
a) **Billy & Batty** b) **Billy & Bart**
c) **Sam & Dave** d) **Chuck & Billy**

100. Duke Droese was the No. 30 entrant in the 1996 *Royal
Rumble* match because...
a) **He won a coin toss.**
b) **He won a match against Triple H.**
c) **He had friends in high places.**
d) **He was a garbage man and smelled like curdled milk.**

101. Who caused the disqualification in the WWE
Championship match between Undertaker and
Bret Hart?
a) **Jeff Jarrett** b) **Yokozuna**
c) **Diesel** d) **Shawn Michaels**

102. Which member of the medical community was in the
1996 *Royal Rumble* match?
a) **Dr. Vinnie Boombots**
b) **Isaac Yankem, D.D.S.**
c) **Dr. Jack DiTeodoro**
d) **Dr. Laura**

103. Who was the last man eliminated from the 1996 *Royal
Rumble* match?
a) **Kama** b) **British Bulldog**
c) **Diesel** d) **Bob Holly**

104. What former NWA World Heavyweight Champion
was in the 1996 *Royal Rumble* match?
a) Dory Funk, Jr.   b) Ric Flair
c) Lou Thesz   d) Jack Brisco

105. Where was the 1997 *Royal Rumble* held?
a) Jacksonville, FL   b) Tampa, FL
c) Dallas, TX   d) San Antonio, TX

106. What militant group felt the wrath of Ahmed Johnson
at the 1997 *Royal Rumble*?
a) Ministry of Defense
b) Alliance of Defiance
c) Nation of Domination
d) Ministry of Darkness

107. What furry boot-wearing star competed in the 1997
Royal Rumble match?
a) Perro Aguayo   b) Aldo Montoya
c) El Kabong   d) Phineas I. Godwinn

108. Who won the 1997 *Royal Rumble* match?
a) Bret Hart   b) Jake Roberts
c) Vader   d) Stone Cold Steve Austin

109. What instrument did Shawn Michaels use on Sycho
Sid to win the WWE Championship?
a) a steel chair   b) a TV camera
c) a table   d) a towel soaked in ether

110. What was unique about the participants in the
opening match at the 1997 *Royal Rumble*?
a) They were all women.
b) They were Minis.
c) They were all former WWE Champions.
d) They all wore white masks.

111. What female was at ringside for the Intercontinental
Championship match at the 1997 *Royal Rumble*?
a) Marlena b) Trish Stratus
c) Sable d) Sunny

112. "What time is it?" Who defeated Undertaker at the
1997 *Royal Rumble*?
a) Marc Mero b) Bret Hart
c) Vader d) Kane

113. What massive arena hosted the 1997 *Royal Rumble*?
a) the Astrodome b) the Alamodome
c) Reunion Arena d) Freeman Coliseum

114. Sycho Sid came into the 1997 *Royal Rumble* as WWE
Champion. Where did Sid win the title in 1996?
a) *WrestleMania XII* b) *In Your House*
c) *SummerSlam* d) *Survivor Series*

115. Who was fighting on the floor and distracted the
referees, allowing the previously eliminated Stone
Cold Steve Austin to sneak back in and eliminate
Bret Hart?
a) Ahmed Johnson and Faarooq
b) Crush and Savio Vega
c) Terry Funk and Mankind
d) Triple H and Goldust

116. Where is Shawn Michaels from?
a) Dallas, TX b) San Antonio, TX
c) Las Vegas, NV d) Houston, TX

117. What was the name of the annoying duo that led the
Nation of Domination to the ring?
a) PG-13 b) the Ministry
c) Bow-Tie Brigade d) Mason's Masons

118. Which boxer watched the 1998 *Royal Rumble* from a skybox?
a) Lennox Lewis   b) Mike Tyson
c) Muhammad Ali   d) Larry Holmes

119. What city hosted the 1998 *Royal Rumble*?
a) Sacramento, CA   b) Fresno, CA
c) San Jose, CA   d) Bakersfield, CA

120. Who won the 1998 *Royal Rumble* match?
a) Bret Hart   b) Shawn Michaels
c) Undertaker   d) Stone Cold Steve Austin

121. What kind of match did Shawn Michaels win against Undertaker at the 1998 *Royal Rumble*?
a) Hell in the Cell   b) Casket match
c) Inferno match   d) No Holds Barred match

122. What Hollywood movie star was the Intercontinental Champion at the 1998 *Royal Rumble*?
a) Goldust   b) The Rock
c) Chuck Norris   d) David Arquette

123. How many times did Mick Foley enter the 1998 *Royal Rumble* match?
a) 2   b) 1   c) 3   d) 0

124. Who were the last two men remaining in the 1998 *Royal Rumble* match?
a) Stone Cold Steve Austin and The Rock
b) Stone Cold Steve Austin and Triple H
c) Triple H and The Rock
d) The Rock and Ken Shamrock

125. This "World's Strongest Man" was in the 1998 *Royal Rumble* match.
a) Ted Arcidi   b) Dino Bravo
c) Mark Henry   d) Headbanger Mosh

126. Who defeated Goldust in the opening match of the 1998 *Royal Rumble*?
a) Kane   b) Vader
c) Marc Mero   d) Savio Vega

127. Who were the members of the New Age Outlaws?
a) Triple H & X-Pac
b) Shane McMahon & Test
c) Billy Gunn & Road Dogg
d) Triple H & Shawn Michaels

128. Tom Brandi was in the 1998 *Royal Rumble* match. What other name did Tom use to compete in the WWE?
a) the Patriot   b) Salvatore Sincere
c) Kwang   d) Blue Blazer

129. Chainz and 8-Ball competed in the 1998 *Royal Rumble* match. What was their collective name?
a) Nation of Domination   b) D.O.A.
c) Ministry   d) Mean Street Posse

130. What was Mike Tyson's reaction when Stone Cold Steve Austin won the 1998 *Royal Rumble*?
a) He booed.
b) He cheered wildly.
c) He threw a fit.
d) He bit someone on their ear.

131. What was the subtitle of the 1999 *Royal Rumble*?
a) "The End is Here"
b) "Dark Daze"
c) "Happy Daze are Here Again"
d) "No Chance in Hell"

132. How much was the bounty placed on Stone Cold Steve Austin's head by Mr. McMahon for the Rattlesnake's elimination from the 1999 *Royal Rumble* match?
a) $50   b) $1,000   c) $100,000   d) $1 million

133. Who was the No. 2 entrant in the 1999 *Royal Rumble* match?

a) **Stone Cold Steve Austin** b) **Vince McMahon**
c) **Test** d) **Triple H**

134. Who made the seatings for the No. 1 and 2 positions in the 1999 *Royal Rumble* match?

a) **Vince McMahon**
b) **Pat Patterson and Gerald Brisco**
c) **Shane McMahon**
d) **Shawn Michaels**

135. How many chairshots did The Rock hit Mankind with during their WWE Championship match at the 1999 *Royal Rumble*?

a) **1** b) **5** c) **11** d) **8**

136. What submission move did Ken Shamrock use on Billy Gunn to retain the Intercontinental Championship at the 1999 *Royal Rumble*?

a) **abdominal stretch**
b) **ankle lock**
c) **figure-four leglock**
d) **torture rack**

137. What kind of match did Sable beat Luna in at the 1999 *Royal Rumble*?

a) **Bra & Panties match**
b) **Lingerie match**
c) **Strap match**
d) **Inferno match**

138. Who was the No. 30 entrant in the 1999 *Royal Rumble* match?

a) **Golga** b) **Droz**
c) **Owen Hart** d) **Chyna**

139. What kind of match did The Rock and Mankind have at the 1999 *Royal Rumble*?
a) **Street Fight**
b) **No Disqualification match**
c) **"I Quit" match**
d) **Hair vs. Eyebrow match**

140. Gangrel faced X-Pac at the 1999 *Royal Rumble.* What group was Gangrel a part of?
a) **D-Generation X   b) The Brood**
c) **The Ministry   d) The Nation**

141. Who won the 1999 *Royal Rumble* match?
a) **Stone Cold Steve Austin   b) The Rock**
c) **Vince McMahon   d) Triple H**

142. How did Stone Cold Steve Austin win a spot in the 1999 *Royal Rumble*?
a) **Luck of the draw.**
b) **Winning the Corporate *Royal Rumble* on *Raw*.**
c) **Shawn Michaels put him in.**
d) **Defeating Undertaker in a Buried Alive match in December 1998.**

143. What former NWA Champion was in the 1999 *Royal Rumble* match?
a) **Dan Severn   b) Chris Candido**
c) **Jack Brisco   d) Dusty Rhodes**

144. Golga and Kurrgan were in the 1999 *Royal Rumble* match. What was the name of the bizarre group these men were a part of?
a) **Happy Dancing Giants   b) The Oddities**
c) **The Odd Squad   d) Bumps and Grinds**

145. What unnamed mystery opponent met Kurt Angle at the 2000 *Royal Rumble*?
a) **Shawn Stasiak**   b) **Meat**
c) **Tazz**   d) **Raven**

146. What was unique about the Dudley Boyz vs. Hardy Boyz match at the 2000 *Royal Rumble*?
a) **It was a No. 1 Contender's match.**
b) **It was a Tables match.**
c) **It was for the Tag Team Championship.**
d) **It was a Loser Leave Town match.**

147. Who won the *Miss Royal Rumble* Pageant at the 2000 *Royal Rumble*?
a) **Ivory**   b) **Jackie**
c) **Mae Young**   d) **The Kat**

148. Who won the Intercontinental Championship in the Triple-Threat match at the 2000 *Royal Rumble*?
a) **Chyna**   b) **Bob Holly**
c) **Mark Henry**   d) **Chris Jericho**

149. Whose interference helped the New Age Outlaws defeat the Acolytes at the 2000 *Royal Rumble*?
a) **Triple H**   b) **Chyna**
c) **X-Pac**   d) **Kevin Nash**

150. What office supply did Triple H use against Cactus Jack in their Street Fight at the 2000 *Royal Rumble*?
a) **pencils**   b) **thumbtacks**
c) **paperclips**   d) **staplers**

151. Who won the 2000 *Royal Rumble* match?
a) **Stone Cold Steve Austin**   b) **Big Show**
c) **Triple H**   d) **The Rock**

152. Who was the last man eliminated from the 2000 *Royal Rumble* match?
a) The Rock   b) Big Show
c) Stone Cold Steve Austin   d) Undertaker

153. What did Too Cool do in the 2000 *Royal Rumble* match when Rikishi, Grandmaster Sexay and Scotty 2 Hotty were all in the ring at the same time?
a) Dance
b) Fight
c) Give each other Stinkfaces.
d) Grandmaster Sexay begged for mercy.

154. Who was the No. 1 entrant in the 2000 *Royal Rumble* match?
a) Tiger Ali Singh   b) Kurt Angle
c) D'Lo Brown   d) Viscera

155. Who was the No. 30 entrant in the 2000 *Royal Rumble* match?
a) Bradshaw   b) X-Pac
c) Kane   d) The Godfather

156. What famous fighting Diva was a part of the 2000 *Royal Rumble* match?
a) Lita   b) Mae Young
c) Chyna   d) Ivory

157. What name has Rikishi NOT competed under in a *Royal Rumble* match?
a) Fatu   b) the Sultan
c) Mr. Ass   d) Rikishi

158. True or false: Kurt Angle tapped out to Tazz in their match at the 2000 *Royal Rumble*.

159. What did The Rock earn with his win in the 2000 *Royal Rumble* match?
   a) A shot at the WWE Champion at *WrestleMania*.
   b) A match with Vince McMahon the next night on *Raw*.
   c) A Street Fight with Triple H on *SmackDown!*
   d) A bouquet of flowers.

160. What Japanese duo attempted to enter the 2000 *Royal Rumble* match even though they weren't a part of the field of thirty?
   a) Great Kabuki & Great Sasuke
   b) Kaientai
   c) Tajiri & Kwang
   d) The Great Muta & Keiji Muto

161. What team captured the WWE Tag Team Championship at the 2001 *Royal Rumble*?
   a) Edge & Christian   b) the Hardy Boyz
   c) the Dudley Boyz   d) Too Cool

162. What kind of match was fought for the Intercontinental Championship at the 2001 *Royal Rumble*?
   a) Chain match   b) Ladder match
   c) Cage match   d) Hell in the Cell match

163. Which Diva beat Chyna for the WWE Women's Championship at the 2001 *Royal Rumble*?
   a) Ivory   b) Lita
   c) The Kat   d) Trish Stratus

164. Who did WWE Champion Kurt Angle beat at the 2001 *Royal Rumble*?
   a) Tazz   b) The Rock
   c) Triple H   d) Mick Foley

165. What two Divas were involved in the WWE
Championship match at the 2001 *Royal Rumble*?
a) Terri and Trish
b) Stephanie McMahon-Helmsley and Terri
c) Stephanie McMahon-Helmsley and Chyna
d) Trish and Stephanie McMahon-Helmsley

166. Who won the 2001 *Royal Rumble* match?
a) Kane   b) The Rock
c) Stone Cold Steve Austin   d) Undertaker

167. Who was the No. 1 entrant in the 2001 *Royal Rumble*
match?
a) Matt Hardy   b) Jeff Hardy
c) Bull Buchanan   d) Test

168. What Hollywood star was a part of the 2001 *Royal
Rumble* match?
a) Drew Carey
b) Michael Clarke Duncan
c) Charlie Sheen
d) Lemmy from Motörhead

169. This former Intercontinental Championship winner
was in the 2001 *Royal Rumble* match.
a) Ricky Steamboat   b) Goldust
c) Mr. Perfect   d) Honky Tonk Man

170. Who lasted more than an hour in the 2001 *Royal
Rumble* match?
a) Haku   b) Test
c) Kane   d) Raven

171. How many men were a part of the 2001 *Royal Rumble*
match?
a) 20   b) 25   c) 30   d) 40

172. What city hosted the 2001 *Royal Rumble*?
a) New York, NY   b) New Orleans, LA
c) Atlanta, GA   d) Tampa, FL

173. What submission move did Chris Jericho apply to Chris Benoit on top of the ladder in their Intercontinental Championship match at the 2001 *Royal Rumble*?
a) Crippler Crossface
b) figure-four leglock
c) Walls of Jericho
d) ankle lock submission

174. At the time of the event, what reigning WCW Hardcore Champion was a part of the 2001 *Royal Rumble* match?
a) Terry Funk   b) Haku
c) Big Boss Man   d) Raven

175. Who prodded Drew Carey into entering the 2001 *Royal Rumble* match?
a) Chyna   b) Lita
c) Mr. McMahon   d) Stephanie McMahon

176. What caused Chyna to lose the Women's Championship at the 2001 *Royal Rumble*?
a) Interference from Lita.
b) A collision of heads.
c) A chairshot.
d) Ivory beat her up.

177. What Spanish announcing team has a history of having their table destroyed at ringside?
a) Hugo Savinovich & Carlos Cabrera
b) Tito Santana & Pedro Morales
c) Joel & Jose Maximo
d) Max Mini & El Torito

178. **True or false:** Undertaker was a part of the 2001 *Royal Rumble* match.

179. Who was the first man eliminated from the 2001 *Royal Rumble* match?
a) Faarooq   b) Drew Carey
c) Jeff Hardy   d) Bull Buchanan

180. What team known as "Head Cheese" was a part of the 2001 *Royal Rumble* match?
a) Edge & Christian
b) Al Snow & Steve Blackman
c) Too Cool
d) Test and Albert

181. What city hosted the 2002 *Royal Rumble*?
a) Nashville, TN
b) Toronto, Ontario, Canada
c) Atlanta, GA
d) New Orleans, LA

182. Who eliminated Undertaker from the 2002 *Royal Rumble* match?
a) Jeff Hardy   b) Matt Hardy   c) Lita   d) Maven

183. What legendary star faced Vince McMahon at the 2002 *Royal Rumble*?
a) Ricky Steamboat
b) Shane McMahon
c) Stone Cold Steve Austin
d) Ric Flair

184. What former Intercontinental Champion was NOT in the 2002 *Royal Rumble* match?
a) Honky Tonk Man   b) Goldust
c) Mr. Perfect   d) Kurt Angle

185. Who won the 2002 *Royal Rumble* match?
a) **Kurt Angle**   b) **Triple H**
c) **Kane**   d) **Stone Cold Steve Austin**

186. Who was the last man eliminated from the 2002 *Royal Rumble* match?
a) **Stone Cold Steve Austin**   b) **Mr. Perfect**
c) **Kurt Angle**   d) **Triple H**

187. Who said "Hello ladies!" on his way to the ring for a surprise at the 2002 *Royal Rumble* match?
a) **The Godfather**   b) **Val Venis**
c) **Goldust**   d) **Mr. Perfect**

188. Which team retained the WWE Tag Team Championship at the 2002 *Royal Rumble*?
a) **the Dudley Boyz**
b) **Edge & Christian**
c) **Tazz & Spike Dudley**
d) **Billy & Chuck**

189. Who won the Intercontinental Championship at the 2002 *Royal Rumble*?
a) **Edge**   b) **Lance Storm**
c) **Christian**   d) **William Regal**

190. Who was the special referee for the Women's Championship match at the 2002 *Royal Rumble*?
a) **Ric Flair**   b) **Mick Foley**
c) **Jacqueline**   d) **Tazz**

191. Who won the WWE Championship match at the 2002 *Royal Rumble*?
a) **Chris Jericho**   b) **The Rock**
c) **Triple H**   d) **Kurt Angle**

192. Who was the No. 1 entrant in the 2002 *Royal Rumble* match?

a) Test   b) Rikishi

c) Kurt Angle   d) Jeff Hardy

193. What move did Ric Flair use to win his match against Vince McMahon at the 2002 *Royal Rumble*?

a) Flying Elbow

b) People's Elbow

c) figure-four leglock

d) ankle lock submission

194. What superhero was a part of the 2002 *Royal Rumble* match?

a) Spider-Man   b) the Incredible Hulk

c) The Hurricane   d) Underdog

195. Who entered No. 30 at the 2002 *Royal Rumble* match?

a) Test   b) Goldust

c) Rikishi   d) Booker T

196. Who retained her Women's Championship with a win at the 2002 *Royal Rumble*?

a) Jazz   b) Trish Stratus

c) Lita   d) Ivory

197. What was William Regal's secret weapon that helped him capture the Intercontinental Championship at the 2002 *Royal Rumble*?

a) lead pipe   b) steel chair

c) brass knuckles   d) wooden spike

198. Which household item did Vince McMahon use to "record" a moment in history against Ric Flair at the 2002 *Royal Rumble*?

a) VCR   b) camera

c) tape recorder   d) DVD

199. What controversial referee officiated the Edge vs.
William Regal Intercontinental Championship match
at the 2002 *Royal Rumble*?
**a) Teddy Long   b) Earl Hebner
c) Nick Patrick   d) Dave Hebner**

200. What announcers called the action from the 2002
Royal Rumble?
**a) Michael Cole and Jerry Lawler
b) Jim Ross and Paul Heyman
c) Michael Cole and Tazz
d) Jim Ross and Jerry Lawler**

The Game and I am
damn good.
Banzai Dro
Twist Of Fate
The Walls Of Jericho

Pilot Episode

1. What two members of the McMahon family headed to the ring for a promo as the pilot episode of *SmackDown!* kicked off in April 1999?

2. Where did that episode of *SmackDown!* emanate from?

3. Shane McMahon and Undertaker united their respective factions on the pilot episode of *SmackDown!* to form a new group, called what?

4. What two Superstars were in the ring when Shane and Undertaker made their announcement?

5. What Superstar returned from injury to save his former partner on the pilot episode of *SmackDown!*?
   a) Val Venis   b) Mark Henry
   c) Test   d) Road Dogg

6. What dark trio broke their silence on the pilot episode of *SmackDown!*, giving their first-ever interview to Dok Hendrix?

7. The pilot episode of *SmackDown!* planted the seeds for an alliance between Big Show, Test, Mankind and Ken Shamrock. Indeed, in the weeks following, these four would team up for a brief period. What was the name of their group?

8. After losing a Tag Team Championship match to X-Pac & Kane, what legendary tag team began to fight amongst themselves?

9. The main event of the pilot episode of *SmackDown!* pitted Undertaker and Triple H against whom?
   a) The Rock and Mankind
   b) Stone Cold and Mankind
   c) Stone Cold and The Rock
   d) The Rock and Kane

10. Whom did Undertaker nail with a chair as the pilot episode of *SmackDown!* drew to a close?

1999

11. Who was shining Chris Jericho's boots on the August 26, 1999, episode of *SmackDown!,* as he trained to become a warrior?

12. What two Superstars got engaged on that episode?

13. What former WWE Champion helped Triple H to retain his WWE Championship over The Rock on that episode?

14. On the September 4, 1999 episode of *SmackDown!,* Shane McMahon made Triple H defend his WWE Championship against a bald-headed, goateed son of a bitch. Who did Triple H defend against?

15. What two Superstars met in a tuxedo match on that episode?

16. At a local hotel, what meal did Big Boss Man serve to Al Snow on that episode?

17. What international Superstar returned to World Wrestling Entertainment on the September 9, 1999 episode of *SmackDown!,* winning the Hardcore Title in his first match back?

18. After delivering an insulting interview to women all over the world, what former WWE Women's Champion did Jeff Jarrett crack over the head with a guitar that night?

19. Undertaker and Big Show won the Tag Team Championship from The Rock and Mankind on September 9, 1999 in a _____ Match.

20. Who won the WWE Championship on the September 16, 1999 episode of *SmackDown!*?

21. Vince McMahon made Triple H compete in five different matches on the September 23, 1999 episode of *SmackDown!* Match the opponent with the type of bout.

1) Big Show	**a) Inferno match**
2) Kane	**b) Boiler Room Brawl**
3) Mideon and Viscera	**c) Casket match**
4) Mankind	**d) Brahma Bullrope match**
5) The Rock	**e) Chokeslam match**

22. What former WWE and Tag Team Champion walked out of the WWE on the September 23, 1999 episode of *SmackDown!,* not to return until the following May?

23. What legendary tag team reunited on the September 23, 1999 episode of *SmackDown!,* winning the Tag Team Championship in their first match back together?

24. What tournament began on the September 30, 1999 episode of *SmackDown!*?

25. What was the winner of that tournament to be awarded?

26. What two teams faced each other in that tournament?

27. What Superstar revealed that he'd had sex with his sister as part of a therapy session on the October 7, 1999 episode of *SmackDown!*?

28. What animal did Triple H attack with a sledgehammer on that episode of *SmackDown!*—just ten days before he was set to face Stone Cold Steve Austin at *No Mercy*?

29. One week later on *SmackDown!*, Triple H's face was bright purple at the start of the show. Although it turned out to be a ruse, why did "The Game" say his face was so swollen?

30. What Superstar portrayed Dude Love on the October 14, 1999 episode of *SmackDown!*?

31. Why did Mark Henry walk out of his therapy session on the October 14, 1999 episode of *SmackDown!*?
a) He had to meet a woman.
b) The male therapist showed a liking for "Sexual Chocolate."
c) He didn't think he needed therapy.
d) He had to use the bathroom.

32. A match on the October 21, 1999 episode of *SmackDown!* pitted two legends against each other in a bout where the combined age of the two competitors was more than 150. What two ring generals clashed on that night?

33. In February 1997, the British Bulldog defeated Owen Hart in a tournament final on *Raw* to become the first European Champion. On the October 28, 1999 episode of *SmackDown!*, the Bulldog regained that championship, defeating whom?

34. Mankind & Al Snow beat Hardcore & Crash Holly to capture the Tag Team Championship on the November 4, 1999 episode of *SmackDown!* Prior to their match, Mankind and Snow were discussing Snow's action figure, which had recently been banned by what national chain?

35. On that same night, Vince McMahon forced D-Generation X to compete in an eight-man elimination tag bout. Which of these Superstars was NOT a member of the opposing team?
**a) Shane McMahon   b) Kane   c) The Rock
d) Stone Cold Steve Austin   e) Vince McMahon**

36. What happened when Test ran to the ring to attack D-Generation X on the November 11, 1999 episode of *SmackDown!*?
**a) His pants fell down.
b) He hit the bottom rope as he leapt into the ring, breaking his nose.
c) He joined the faction.
d) They shaved his head.**

37. What box office superstar appeared on that same episode?

38. Who interviewed the movie star when he arrived to the arena?

39. The morning of November 11 was the funeral for Big Show's father. But, as seen on that night's *SmackDown!,* what instead happened?
**a) Big Boss Man popped out of the casket.
b) Big Boss Man spray-painted the casket.
c) Big Boss Man tied the casket to the back of a car and dragged it through the cemetery.
d) Big Show revealed that his father wasn't really dead.**

40. Kurt Angle made his *SmackDown!* debut on November 18, 1999. Whom did he face?
a) **Shawn Stasiak**   b) **The Godfather**
c) **Mark Henry**   d) **Gangrel**

41. On that same night, Triple H gave Stephanie McMahon a wedding gift for her upcoming nuptials to Test. What did he give her?

42. Which of the following did NOT happen in the final segment of the November 18, 1999 episode?
a) **Triple H and Stephanie McMahon joined forces.**
b) **Triple H challenged Vince McMahon to a match at** *Armageddon.*
c) **Shane McMahon fell down stairs.**
d) **Triple H called Vince McMahon a punk.**

43. D-Generation X gave Triple H some wedding gifts on the December 2, 1999 episode of *SmackDown!* What did Road Dogg give him?

44. After signing the contract to face Vince McMahon at *Armageddon,* whom did Triple H throw off the stage on the December 9, 1999 episode of *SmackDown!*?

45. What all-star shortstop appeared with The Rock on that same episode?

46. Triple H and Stephanie McMahon-Helmsley held a locker-room meeting on the December 16, 1999 episode of *SmackDown!* They said it was their time, declaring the _____ had begun in WWE.

47. On that night, Triple H and Stephanie forced two sets of brothers to battle each other—Matt Hardy vs. Jeff Hardy and Edge vs. Christian. Who won those matches?

48. Also on that night, The Rock took on Big Show. What
type of match was that?
  a) Lumberjack match
  b) "Pink-Slip-on-a-Pole" match
  c) European Championship match
  d) Arm Wrestling match

49. What Superstar stood up to Triple H and Stephanie
on the December 23, 1999 episode of *SmackDown!,*
calling their reign the "McMahon–Helmsley Error"?

50. Stephanie McMahon-Helmsley invited five Superstars
to ringside for the Mankind vs. Big Show main event
on that show. Which of the following was NOT one of
those Superstars?
  a) Test
  b) Matt Hardy
  c) Jeff Hardy
  d) Edge
  e) Christian
  f) Albert

51. The December 30, 1999 episode of *SmackDown!*
featured a number of "Classic Mick Foley moments."
Which of the following was NOT one of those
moments?
  a) Foley flies off Hell in the Cell.
  b) Foley leaps from the top of the cage at
     SummerSlam 1997.
  c) Mankind, Dude Love and Cactus Jack interview
     each other.
  d) Mick's WWE debut.

2000

52. The first *SmackDown!* match of 2000 pitted:
a) **Big Show vs. X-Pac**
b) **Billy Gunn vs. Scotty 2 Hotty**
c) **Road Dogg vs. Kane**
d) **Triple H vs. Test**

53. On that same episode of *SmackDown!,* several random drawings were held to see which Superstar would get a title shot against WWE Champion Triple H. Who won the third and final drawing?

54. The following week, Mankind informed Triple H that he would not be facing him for the WWE Championship in a Street Fight at the *Royal Rumble*—but Mankind named a suitable replacement. Who was that replacement?

55. A Triple-Threat Over-The-Top-Rope battle royal was held on the January 20, 2000 episode of *SmackDown!* Who won that bout?
a) **The Rock**   b) **Kane**
c) **Big Show**   d) **Triple H**

56. What was the name of the tavern in Providence, RI, at which the New Age Outlaws and the APA had a barroom brawl on that episode?

57. Tori turned her back on Kane and sided with X-Pac on the January 27, 2000 episode of *SmackDown!* What was the name of the story X-Pac told Kane about how the two of them had gotten together?

58. What huge announcement did Mae Young make on that same episode?

59. Triple H promised to give WWE contracts to the Radicalz if they could win two out of their three matches against D-Generation X on the February 3, 2000 episode of *SmackDown!* How many of those matches did the Radicalz win?

60. One of the Radicalz suffered a severe elbow injury on that episode. Which member was it?
a) Chris Benoit   b) Eddie Guerrero
c) Dean Malenko   d) Perry Saturn

61. Jacqueline won the Women's Championship on that same episode from a most unique champion. Who was that?

62. Kurt Angle won his first WWE title on the February 10, 2000 episode of *SmackDown!,* defeating Val Venis. What title did he win?

63. What was the name of the EMT that the Dudley Boyz put through a table on that same episode?

64. What was the name of the tour bus on which D-Generation X arrived on the February 17, 2000 episode of *SmackDown!?*

65. What "Houdini of Hardcore" won the title for the very first time on the February 24, 2000 episode of *SmackDown!?*

66. Which of the following was born on the March 2, 2000 episode of *SmackDown!?*
a) European Championship
b) the 24/7 Rule in the Hardcore Division
c) Brawl-for-All
d) the Brood

67. What former WWE Champion did Kurt Angle face on that same episode?
a) Sgt. Slaughter   b) Bob Backlund
c) Randy Savage   d) Diesel

68. On the March 16, 2000 episode of *SmackDown!,* what did Shane McMahon announce as the main event for *WrestleMania XVI,* which was just three weeks away?
a) Triple H vs. Big Show
b) Triple H vs. The Rock
c) Triple H vs. The Rock vs. Big Show
d) Triple H vs. The Rock vs. Big Show vs. Mick Foley

69. What type of farm animal did Steve Blackman attack with nunchucks on the March 23, 2000 episode of *SmackDown!?*
a) cows   b) horses
c) chickens   d) sheep

70. What shocking act did Stephanie McMahon-Helmsley do on that same episode?
a) She bought ECW.
b) She revealed her alliance with Triple H.
c) She slapped her mother.
d) She fired her husband.

71. Who defeated Jacqueline for the Women's Championship on the March 30, 2000 episode of *SmackDown!*—just three days before *WrestleMania?*

72. What Superstar made reference to a "monkey's nipple" and a "llama's anus" during an interview on the April 6, 2000 episode of *SmackDown!?*

73. What character from *Austin Powers: The Spy Who Shagged Me* did Big Show dress-up as on the April 13, 2000 episode of *SmackDown!?*

74. What was unique about the Triple H vs. Tazz match on the April 20, 2000 episode of *SmackDown!*?
a) Tazz won the WWE Championship.
b) It was a Lumberjack match.
c) Tazz was ECW Champion heading into the bout.
d) It was a Cage match.

75. What then-ECW competitor and current WWE Superstar interfered in that bout?

76. On that same show, Crash Holly was attacked at the circus by a trio of clowns. What trio of sweater vest-wearing competitors were they?

77. What WWE Superstar returned to television on the April 27, 2000 episode of *SmackDown!,* blowing up the DX Express?

78. How did Trish Stratus escape from being put through a table by Bubba Ray Dudley on that same episode?
a) She kissed him.
b) She flashed him.
c) She gave him a low blow.
d) She begged him.

79. Matt Hardy defended the Hardcore Championship against an interesting challenger that week. Who was his challenger?

80. What Superstar—who would go on to become the first-ever WWE Undisputed Champion—defeated Chris Benoit on the May 4, 2000 episode of *SmackDown!* to win the Intercontinental Championship?

81. After Essa Rios attacked his valet, Lita, on the May 25, 2000 episode of *SmackDown!,* who ran down to save her?

82. Who won a No. 1 Contender's match for the WWE
Championship on the June 1, 2000 episode of
SmackDown!?
a) The Rock   b) Undertaker
c) Kane   d) All of the above

83. Who won a Divas battle royal on the June 8, 2000
episode of *SmackDown!,* earning the first shot at
Stephanie McMahon-Helmsley's Women's
Championship?

84. The June 15, 2000 episode of *Raw* saw Crash Holly
running all over New York City, trying to elude Pat
Patterson and Gerald Brisco. Finally, he got away,
thanks to what accomplished Hollywood actor and
star of *Shaft*?

85. On that same episode, Edge & Christian argued over
whether to call it the "McMahon-Helmsley Faction"
or the "McMahon-Helmsley Regime." What name do
they finally decide on?

86. Whose arm did Kurt Angle break with a moonsault on
the following week's show?

87. Later on that show, performing artist Wyclef Jean was
shown at ringside. Wyclef had just completed a music
video with The Rock, appropriately titled what?
a) "It Doesn't Matter"
b) "Smell What I'm Cookin' "
c) "Just Bring It"
d) "Pie"

88. Val Venis won his second Intercontinental
Championship on the July 6, 2000 episode of
SmackDown!, defeating Rikishi. Who was Val's
manager at the time?

89. Shockingly, Triple H lost a Handicap match to Taka, Funaki and the Brooklyn Brawler on that episode of *SmackDown!* Which of those three men pinned "The Game"?

90. Who did The Rock make Kevin Kelly do an impression of on the August 3, 2000 episode of *SmackDown!*?
a) Chris Benoit   b) Chris Jericho
c) Edge   d) Christian

91. Who kissed Stephanie McMahon-Helmsley on the August 24, 2000 episode of *SmackDown!*—just three days before *SummerSlam*?

92. Also on that show, who proclaimed that he would fight Chris Benoit on a goat, in a boat, when the score is tied and as a blushing bride?

93. On the August 31, 2000 episode of *SmackDown!,* Triple H was arrested for spousal abuse. Who had called the cops on "The Game"?
a) Stephanie McMahon-Helmsley
b) Kurt Angle
c) Test
d) Chyna

94. What famed landmark did Eddie Guerrero storm on the September 14, 2000 episode of *SmackDown!*?
a) Graceland   b) Playboy Mansion
c) Lincoln Memorial   d) CN Tower

95. What couple got engaged on the September 21, 2000 episode of *SmackDown!*?
a) Test and Stephanie
b) Tajiri and Torrie
c) Eddie Guerrero and Chyna
d) Val Venis and Trish

96. On the October 12, 2000 episode of *SmackDown!,* Stephanie McMahon-Helmsley introduced her new business partner. Who was it?

97. T&A took over the APA's office on the October 26, 2000 episode of *SmackDown!* What did they rechristen the business?
a) APAT&A   b) T&APA
c) TAPAT   d) T&AA

98. Which of Undertaker's catch phrases was born on the November 9, 2000 episode of *SmackDown!*?
a) You're in my yard.
b) I'll make you famous.
c) Rest in peace.
d) Big Evil

99. What WWE mainstay—and former King of the Ring, Tag Team Champion and Hardcore Champion— finally won his first Intercontinental Championship on the Thanksgiving Night 2000 episode of *SmackDown!,* defeating Eddie Guerrero?

100. What couple celebrated their one-year wedding anniversary on the November 30, 2000 episode of *SmackDown!*?

101. **True or false:** Vince McMahon asked Linda McMahon for a divorce on the December 7, 2000 episode of *SmackDown!*

102. Which member of the Radicalz took Lita out on a date on that December 7 show?
a) Chris Benoit   b) Eddie Guerrero
c) Dean Malenko   d) Perry Saturn

103. On the December 14, 2000 episode of *SmackDown!,*
Vince McMahon told the world that he and his wife,
Linda, had a "real good time" on their very first date,
in the backseat of what kind of car?
a) 1966 Buick Skylark   b) 1969 Chevy Impala
c) 1964 Lincoln Towncar   d) 1963 Chrysler Imperial

104. Ivory dressed up like Chyna on the December 28,
2000 episode of *SmackDown!,* and mocked the Ninth
Wonder of the World during an interview. Which
Right to Censor member dressed up as Jim Ross for
the interview?
a) Steven Richards   b) The Godfather
c) Bull Buchanan   d) Val Venis

2001

105. What was the first *SmackDown!* match of 2001?
a) Chris Jericho vs. Chris Benoit
b) Big Show vs. Test
c) Rhyno vs. Kurt Angle
d) Spike Dudley vs. Tazz

106. Who was rubbing Vince McMahon down with oil on
the January 4, 2002 episode of *SmackDown!,* much to
Stephanie McMahon-Helmsley's chagrin?

107. A Fatal Four-Way match was held on the January 11,
2002 episode of *SmackDown!* to determine who
would enter the *Royal Rumble* at No. 30 that Sunday.
Who won the Fatal Four-Way?
a) Undertaker   b) Kane
c) Rikishi   d) The Rock

108. Also on that episode, Trish Stratus announced that she would be accompanying Kurt Angle to the ring at *Royal Rumble.* Vince was mad at her—and Trish said she'd been so bad that she deserved a _____!

109. The following week, Vince was seen talking to a mystery Superstar in a limo. That Superstar—a former Intercontinental Champion—turned out to be one of four surprise entrants in the 2001 *Royal Rumble.* Who was it?

110. In February 2001, Vince McMahon still had yet to reveal his relationship with Trish Stratus. In fact, on the February 8, 2001 episode of *SmackDown!,* he had Trish walk to the ring with another Superstar, who Vince claimed was her boyfriend. Who was that Superstar?

111. The February 15, 2002 episode of *SmackDown!* saw Triple H name the stipulations for his match with Stone Cold Steve Austin at *No Way Out.* According to "The Game," the Two-out-of-Three Falls match would be straight wrestling in the first fall, a street fight in the second fall and a _____ in the third fall.

112. That week's show emanated from Nassau Coliseum on Long Island, New York. What Long Island native did Al Snow visit during the episode?

113. What did Kevin Kelly do prior to interviewing The Rock on that episode?
a) Ate a sandwich.
b) Picked his nose.
c) Made fun of someone's mother.
d) Wrote trivia questions.

114. After Stone Cold had given Stephanie McMahon-Helmsley a Stunner that Monday on *Raw*, Triple H retaliated on the February 22, 2002 episode of *SmackDown!*, launching a vicious attack on which of Austin's close friends?

115. Which member of the Right to Censor did leader Steven Richards chastise on the March 1, 2001 episode of *SmackDown!*, after that member had a one-night stand?

116. Chris Benoit tried to run the gauntlet against his Radicalz partners on the March 8, 2001 episode of *SmackDown!* Which of his fellow Radicalz was the one who finally defeated him?
a) Eddie Guerrero   b) Perry Saturn
c) Dean Malenko   d) All of the above

117. On that same show, Vince McMahon and Trish Stratus enjoyed a major liplock in front of what wheelchair-bound WWE executive?

118. Later that night, a match was held to determine the new commissioner of WWE. Who won the bout?

119. The March 22, 2001 episode of *SmackDown!* featured a video package promoting the upcoming *WrestleMania X-Seven*. What was the name of the Limp Bizkit song to which that package was set?

120. Also on that show, Edge shoved his brother and screamed, "Christian, get the _____!"

121. Shane McMahon arrived to the March 29, 2001 episode of *SmackDown!* with what written on the license plate of his limousine?

122. Later on that show, Vince McMahon told _____ that she would no longer be the manager of The Rock.

123. Just days after turning heel at *WrestleMania X-Seven,* whom did Stone Cold Steve Austin brutally assault on the April 5, 2001 episode of *SmackDown!,* which emanated from Oklahoma City?

124. What did Vince McMahon do to The Rock on that same episode?
a) **Fired him.**
b) **Indefinitely suspended him.**
c) **Fought him.**
d) **Stripped him of the WWE Championship.**

125. Later in that episode, Chris Jericho lost his Intercontinental Championship to what Grand-Slam Winner and member of the Two-Man Power Trip?

126. One week later, that man lost the Intercontinental Championship to a Superstar who became the youngest Intercontinental Champion in history. Who was it?

127. What Superstar lost the Hardcore Championship and won the Tag Team Championship on the April 19, 2001 episode of *SmackDown!*?

128. Undertaker wrestled a Four-on-One match against what faction on the April 26, 2001 episode of *SmackDown!*—essentially putting an end to that extreme group?

129. On the May 3, 2001 episode of *SmackDown!,* Under-taker attacked Stone Cold Steve Austin as the Rattle-snake was being put into an ambulance. The scenario echoed a similar segment from 1997, when Austin did the same thing to what former WWE Champion?

130. After missing four months of action due to injury, what Superstar returned to WWE on that May 3 episode—only to be reinjured the following Monday, putting him back on the shelf for another six months?

131. What Superstar made his first move for Molly Holly on the May 10, 2001 episode of *SmackDown!*?

132. The May 24, 2001 episode of *SmackDown!* featured the TLC III match. Which of these teams did NOT take part in that bout?
a) Hardy Boyz
b) APA
c) Dudley Boyz
d) Edge & Christian
e) Chris Benoit & Chris Jericho

133. What team won that bout?

134. One week later, Chris Benoit challenged Stone Cold Steve Austin for the WWE Championship in Benoit's hometown of Edmonton, Alberta, Canada. How many German suplexes did Benoit give Austin in that bout?

135. The June 14, 2001 episode of *SmackDown!* saw Stone Cold Steve Austin asking Superstars to sign a petition that said it was unfair that he had to defend his WWE Championship against both Chris Benoit and Chris Jericho at *King of the Ring.* Who ripped up that petition?
a) Shawn Stasiak   b) Tommy Dreamer
c) Spike Dudley   d) Triple H

136. Also on that episode, what Diva made her WWE debut in her hometown of Baltimore, accompanying WCW owner Shane McMahon to the ring and helping Test to capture the Hardcore Championship?

137. WCW owner Shane McMahon got some inside scoops on the June 28, 2001 episode of *SmackDown!,* with some help from a "mole." Who did the source of that inside leak turn out to be?

138. Stone Cold Steve Austin gave Vince McMahon and Kurt Angle presents on the July 5, 2001 episode of *SmackDown!* What did he give them?
a) cowboy hats   b) crossbows
c) baseball hats   d) cheese

139. One week later, Stone Cold and Kurt Angle played some guitar for Vince McMahon. Which of these songs did they NOT play?
a) "Jimmy Crack Corn"
b) "We Are the Champions"
c) "Kumbaya"
d) "Hold on Loosely"

140. What was historic about the July 19, 2001 episode of *SmackDown!?*
a) ECW re-formed.
b) The WWE Championship changed hands twice.
c) It was the one hundredth episode of the series.
d) Brock Lesnar debuted.

141. The July 26, 2001 episode of *SmackDown!* saw the first WCW title change in the history of WWE programming. What WWE Superstar upended Booker T that night to capture the WCW Championship?

142. Also on that show, Booker T lost another title when he handed his U.S. Championship over to what WCW Superstar?

143. Undertaker vs. Steven Richards match on the September 4, 2001 episode of *SmackDown!* marked the WWE debut of what tag team, who left the company after just three weeks?

144. For the first time in history, the WWE and WCW Champions teamed up on the September 27, 2001 episode of *SmackDown!* The two Superstars who teamed were The Rock and Kurt Angle—who held which title?

145. What Superstar pinned WWE Champion Kurt Angle in a nontitle match on the October 4, 2001 episode of *SmackDown!,* earning Stone Cold Steve Austin a title shot that Monday on *Raw*?

146. After firing William Regal as WWE commissioner on the October 11, 2001 episode of *SmackDown!,* whom did Linda McMahon name as the new commissioner?

147. Maven won his first WWE match on the October 18, 2001 episode of *SmackDown!,* defeating which of his *Tough Enough* trainers?

148. On the October 25, 2001 episode of *SmackDown!,* the Alliance did a little bit of house cleaning. What Superstar was indefinitely suspended, the result of him losing the U.S. Championship to Kurt Angle the previous Monday on *Raw*?

149. Who slapped Linda McMahon on that episode of *SmackDown!,* at the request of Shane McMahon?

150. Who did Kurt Angle successfully defend his U.S. Championship against on the November 1, 2001 episode of *SmackDown!*, in what Kurt would go on to call his best *SmackDown!* match of the year?
a) Kane   b) Undertaker
c) Chris Jericho   d) The Rock

151. What WWE personality tore into Vince McMahon on the November 15, 2001 episode of *SmackDown!*, accusing him of stealing ECW's ideas and destroying wrestling, among other things?

152. The November 22, 2001 episode of *SmackDown!* featured what two Divas fighting in a "Gravy Bowl" match?

153. What Diva did Vince McMahon attempt to induct into his "Kiss My Ass" club on the November 29, 2001 episode of *SmackDown!*, only for The Rock to come down and save her?

154. Which of these Superstar's asses did Vince McMahon kiss on the December 6, 2001 episode of *SmackDown!*?
a) The Rock   b) Jim Ross
c) Trish Stratus   d) Rikishi

155. The following week, in what kind of store did Stone Cold Steve Austin and Booker T get into a huge brawl?
a) a record store   b) a grocery store
c) a clothing store   d) a furniture store

2002

156. On the January 3, 2002 episode of *SmackDown!,* Mr. McMahon announced what as his New Year's Resolution?
a) **To give up drinking.**
b) **To embarrass Ric Flair at the *Royal Rumble.***
c) **To inject WWE with a lethal dose of poison.**
d) **To become a genetic jackhammer.**

157. During an interview with The Rock on that same episode, "The Coach" revealed who his favorite singer is. Who is it?

158. On the January 10, 2002 episode of *SmackDown!,* it was announced that four Superstars would make their return to WWE in the upcoming *Royal Rumble* match. Which of the following was NOT one of those Superstars?
a) **Goldust**
b) **Val Venis**
c) **Hulk Hogan**
d) **Mr. Perfect**
e) **The Godfather**

159. Also on that episode, what did Booker T do after Rikishi gave him a Stinkface?
a) **He hit Rikishi with a steel chair.**
b) **He threw up.**
c) **He fainted.**
d) **He did a Spin-a-roonie.**

160. What Superstar—known for his pearly whites—defeated Big Boss Man on the January 17, 2002 episode of *SmackDown!* to earn a job with WWE?

161. Later that night, Triple H and Stone Cold took on Kurt Angle and Booker T. What was notable about that match?

   a) **It was Triple H's first match in eight months.**
   b) **Stone Cold and Triple H won the Tag Team Championship.**
   c) **It was the match where Triple H tore his quadriceps muscle.**
   d) **Booker T turned on Angle.**

162. Vince McMahon announced his plans to inject a "poison" into WWE on the January 24, 2002 episode of *SmackDown!* What renegade group did he say he planned to bring back to do so?

163. Also on that show, The Rock made "The Coach" dance for the fans. What kind of dance did Coach do?

164. The APA played cards with the stars of the movie *Rollerball* on the January 31, 2002 episode of *SmackDown!* Name the three stars they played with.

165. Ric Flair was about to sell his stock in WWE back to Vince McMahon on the January 31 show, until what Superstar convinced him to change his mind?

166. What recording artist—who performs Edge's theme song—was sitting at ringside at the February 7, 2002 episode of *SmackDown!*?

167. The February 7 episode was truly a star-studded show. Later in the program, Chris Jericho brought out his own Stone Cold imitator, as played by what star of *MADtv*?

168. What rookie pinned Undertaker to win the Hardcore Championship on that show?

169. After losing his Hardcore Championship, 'Taker took out his frustration on The Rock, giving him a Tombstone on top of what type of vehicle?
a) Corvette   b) truck
c) Zamboni   d) limousine

170. On the February 21, 2002 episode of *SmackDown!*, what duo defeated Spike Dudley & Tazz to capture their first Tag Team Championship—a title they would hold for the next three months?

171. Also on that show, what did Christian do after losing to his brother, Edge?
a) He attacked Edge with the ring bell.
b) He quit WWE.
c) He and Edge reunited.
d) He challenged Edge to a match at *WrestleMania X8*.

172. What two former enemies became business partners on the February 21 episode?
a) Chris Jericho and Stephanie McMahon
b) Stone Cold and Vince McMahon
c) The Rock and Triple H
d) Rob Van Dam and William Regal

173. On the February 28 episode of *SmackDown!*, Booker T was seen practicing for an audition for a shampoo commercial to air in what country?

174. One week later on *SmackDown!*, Triple H and Stephanie were arguing over who got to keep their pet bulldog in the divorce proceedings. What was the dog's name?

175. On that same episode, Stephanie presented Chris Jericho with a robe that Triple H's first wrestling trainer had given to him. That trainer is also a WWE Hall of Famer. Who is it?

176. What close ally of Ric Flair did Mr. McMahon force into a match against Undertaker on the March 14, 2001 episode of *SmackDown!*—just days before *WrestleMania X8*?
a) **Charles Robinson**   b) **Arn Anderson**
c) **David Flair**   d) **Dr. Tom Prichard**

177. March 21, 2002, marked the *SmackDown!* debut of what WWE Superstar?
a) **Randy Orton**   b) **Brock Lesnar**
c) **Rico**   d) **John Cena**

178. World Wrestling Entertainment held an historical brand extension draft on March 25, 2002. Who was Mr. McMahon's first draft pick for *SmackDown!*?

179. The APA and Dudley Boyz tag teams were both split up by the brand extension. Which members of those respective teams were taken by the *SmackDown!* brand?

180. Which of these titles were not drafted to the *SmackDown!* brand?
a) **Hardcore title**
b) **Cruiserweight title**
c) **Tag Team title**
d) **European title**

181. The Dudleys wrestled their last match as a team on that Thursday's episode of *SmackDown!* Who were their opponents?

182. What two Superstars with rhyming names battled for the Hardcore Championship that week?

183. After a six-month reign, who lost his Cruiserweight Championship to Billy Kidman on the April 4, 2002 episode of *SmackDown!*?

184. That previous Monday on *Raw,* Ric Flair had named Undertaker as the No. 1 contender to Triple H's WWE Undisputed Championship. But on the April 4 episode of *SmackDown!,* Mr. McMahon revealed that it was actually he who got to select the No. 1 contender. Who did he select?

185. The following week, who did Mr. McMahon hire as his new personal assistant?

186. What former European and Tag Team Champion suffered a serious neck injury during a match with Hardcore Holly on the April 18, 2002 episode of *SmackDown!*?

187. Kurt Angle was supposed to unveil his new T-shirt to the world on the April 25, 2002 episode of *SmackDown!,* but Edge replaced Kurt's T-shirt with a design of his own. What two-word phrase did Edge's T-shirt design sport?

188. What third-generation Superstar made his WWE debut on that same episode, upsetting Hardcore Holly?

189. On the May 9, 2002 episode of *SmackDown!,* Mr. McMahon orchestrated a seven-on-one attack on Triple H, and then told "The Game" he would face Chris Jericho at *Judgment Day 2002* in a _____ match.

190. Reverend D-Von introduced the world to his new deacon on that episode. What was his deacon's name?

191. Just one week after she and Tajiri went their separate ways, who asked out Torrie Wilson on the May 16, 2002 episode of *SmackDown!*?

192. Prior to Mr. McMahon's heading to the ring on the May 23, 2002 episode of *SmackDown!,* what had Hollywood Hulk Hogan planned on doing?
   a) retiring
   b) challenging Undertaker for the WWE Undisputed Championship
   c) calling out Edge
   d) attacking Shane McMahon

193. What newly bald Superstar showed up on that same episode wearing a wig and wrestling headgear?

194. After The Hurricane had been receiving mysterious notes, his alter ego—a reporter for *The World News*—set out to do some investigating that week. What is the name of The Hurricane's alter ego?

195. What former ECW valet made her WWE debut on the May 30, 2002 episode of *SmackDown!* as a member of Mr. McMahon's legal counsel?

196. Later that night, Edge injured his shoulder in an incredible Cage match victory over what Superstar?

197. On the June 6, 2002 episode of *SmackDown!,* who was revealed as The Hurricane's mystery stalker?

198. That show featured a battle royal to determine the No. 1 contender to the WWE Undisputed Championship. Which of these Superstars was NOT in that battle royal?
   a) Triple H   b) Chris Jericho
   c) The Rock   d) Hollywood Hulk Hogan

199. Also that week, the two *Tough Enough 2* winners made their first appearance on *SmackDown!* Name them.

200. Who was named as the new general manager on the July 18, 2002 episode of *SmackDown!*?

SURVIVOR SERIES

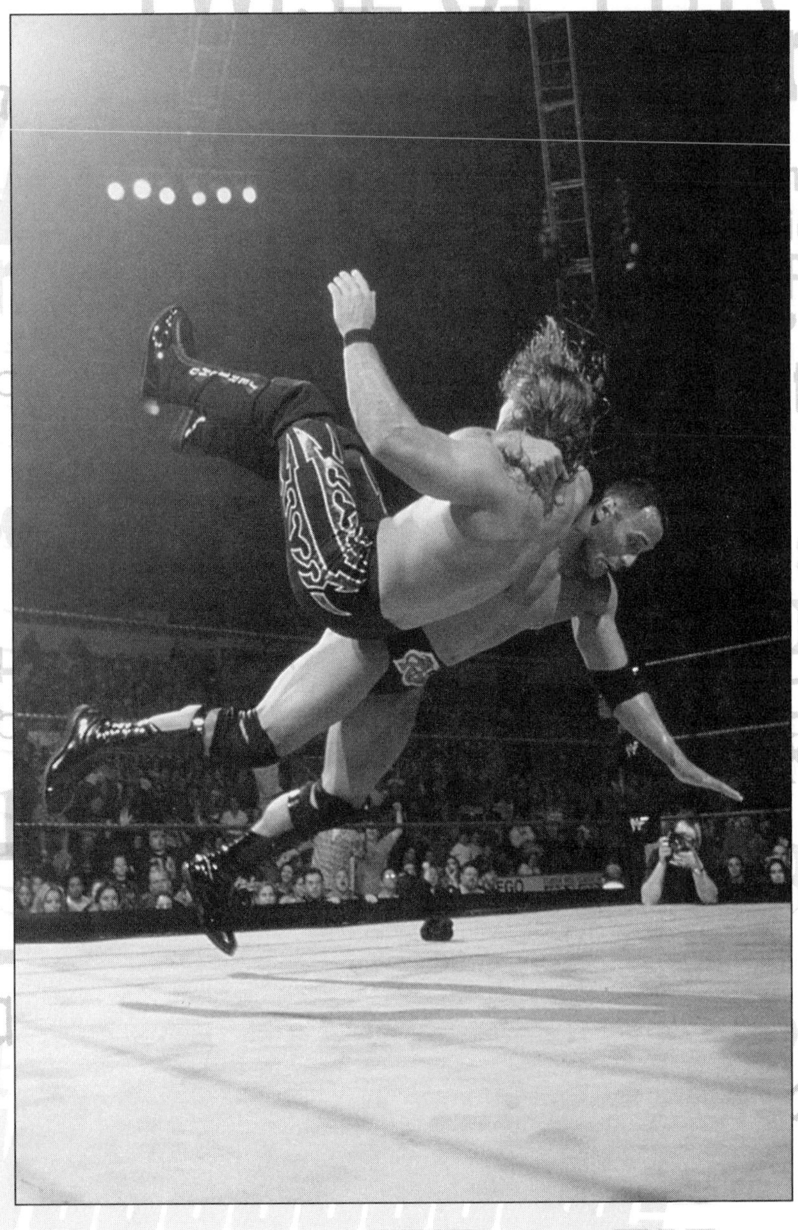

Survivor Series

In the following list, name the year each of the following Superstars made their *Survivor Series* debut.

1. Bad News Brown
2. Tatanka
3. Haku
4. Lita
5. Rocky Maivia
6. Hunter Hearst-Helmsley
7. Kurt Angle
8. Big Boss Man
9. Undertaker
10. Ultimate Warrior
11. 1-2-3 Kid
12. Diesel
13. Booker T
14. the Conquistadors
15. Jerry Lawler
16. Cheesy
17. the Fabulous Moolah
18. Sable
19. Faarooq
20. Blackjack Bradshaw
21. The Interrogator
22. Randy Savage
23. Jimmy Snuka
24. Nailz
25. Bastion Booger
26. Jacqueline
27. Tom Prichard
28. Hercules
29. The Warlord
30. Matt Hardy
31. Duane Gill
32. Chris Benoit
33. Stacy
34. Zeus
35. The Mountie
36. The Head Shrinkers
37. Adam Bomb
38. Bubba Ray Dudley
39. Noriyo Tateno
40. Aldo Montoya
41. Tajiri
42. Leif Cassidy
43. Boris Zukov
44. Mr. Perfect
45. Barry Horowitz

Survivor Series 1987

46. In what city did *Survivor Series* take place?

47. How many matches took place that night?

48. The first match featured Brutus Beefcake, Jake Roberts, Jim Duggan, Randy Savage and Ricky Steamboat vs. Danny Davis, Harley Race, Hercules, Honky Tonk Man and Ron Bass. Who were the first two men eliminated?

49. Who was the last man left in the ring for the Davis, Race, Hercules, Honky Tonk Man and Ron Bass team?

50. How many Superstars on the winning team of Beefcake, Roberts, Duggan, Savage and Steamboat ended up surviving the match?

51. The second *Survivor Series* match was a ten-woman elimination match that featured all of the following women except:
**a) Sherri Martel   b) Leilani Kai
c) Miss Elizabeth   d) Fabulous Moolah**

52. Itsuki Yamazaki and Noriyo Tateno won this match. What did they call themselves?

53. The third match featured all of the following tag teams except:
**a) the Bolsheviks   b) the New Dream Team
c) the Killer Bees   d) the Fabulous Freebirds**

54. In the main event ten-man elimination match, the first Superstar to be eliminated was:
**a) One Man Gang   b) Butch Reed
c) Don Muraco   d) Dusty Rhodes**

55. **True or false:** In this match, Bam Bam Bigelow pinned King Kong Bundy and One Man Gang.

56. The sole survivor of this match was:
a) Bam Bam Bigelow   b) Hulk Hogan
c) Andre the Giant   d) Paul Orndorff

Survivor Series 1988

57. **True or False:** *Survivor Series 1988* took place in the same venue as *Survivor Series 1987*.

58. The first two people to be eliminated in the ten-team Elimination match were:
a) the Brain Busters
b) the Rockers
c) the Fabulous Rougeau Brothers
d) Danny Davis and Jim Brunzell

59. The winners of this match were
a) Demolition   b) Conquistadors
c) British Bulldogs   d) The Powers of Pain

60. In the first ten-man Elimination match, Ultimate Warrior and what other Superstar was left?

61. **True or false:** Bad News Brown eliminated Jim Brunzell and Sam Houston.

62. The second ten-man Elimination match featured Andre the Giant, Dino Bravo, Harley Race, Mr. Perfect and Rick Rude against which five Superstars?

63. **True or false:** Andre the Giant was the sole survivor in this match.

64. Eight of the participants in the final ten-man elimination match were Hercules, Hillbilly Jim, Hulk Hogan, Randy Savage, Akeem, Big Boss Man, Haku and Ted DiBiase. The other two were:
a) **Red Rooster and Bam Bam Bigelow**
b) **Koko B. Ware and "Superfly" Jimmy Snuka**
c) **Red Rooster and Koko B. Ware**
d) **Bam Bam Bigelow and Earthquake**

65. Who eliminated Hillbilly Jim?

66. Randy Savage pinned which two Superstars?

Survivor Series 1989

67. In the first eight-man elimination match, the Dream Team squared off against the Enforcers. What four Superstars made up the Dream Team?

68. Bad News Brown was neither pinned nor did he submit. How was he eliminated from this match?

69. The second eight-man elimination match featured the 4x4's against The King's Court. Which Superstar was not on 4x4's?
a) **Jerry Lawler**   b) **Jim Duggan**
c) **Hercules**   d) **Bret Hart**

70. Three Superstars ended up surviving the match for The King's Court. Which one did not?
a) **Dino Bravo**   b) **Earthquake**
c) **Greg Valentine**   d) **Randy Savage**

71. In the Hulkamaniacs vs. The Million-Dollar Team, who ended up being the sole survivor?

72. How was Jake Roberts eliminated?

73. **True or false:** In the Roddy Rowdies vs. the Rude Brood match, the Bushwackers were on the Roddy Rowdies team.

74. The final eight-man elimination match featured what two teams?

75. **True or false:** Bobby Heenan was the first man to be eliminated.

76. Who were the final two members of The Heenan Family that Ultimate Warrior pinned to win the match?

Survivor Series 1990

77. Where did *Survivor Series 1990* take place?

78. How many matches were held?

79. In the second match of the evening, the Dream Team faced the Million-Dollar Team. What future World Champion made his debut in this match?

80. The third match featured the Vipers vs. the Visionaries. What four Superstars made up the Vipers?

81. What "first" did the Visionaries accomplish that night?

82. Which Superstar was not a member of the Natural Disasters?
a) Earthquake   b) Typhoon
c) Haku   d) Dino Bravo

83. In the Alliance vs. the Mercenaries match, which Superstars did Sgt. Slaughter not pin?
a) Nikolai Volkoff   b) Luke
c) Butch   d) Rick Martel

84. The final match was a Handicap match featuring three Superstars who had already won their matches earlier in the evening against five other Superstars. Who were the three Superstars?

85. True or false: Rick Martel was the only Superstar who was counted out in this match.

86. Who were the two Superstars to survive this match?

Survivor Series 1991

87. Where did *Survivor Series 1991* take place?

88. What future two-time WWE Champion made his *Survivor Series* debut by winning the first eight-man elimination match?

89. True or false: In the evening's second match, no one from the team of Jim Duggan, Sgt. Slaughter, Texas Tornado and Tito Santana was eliminated.

90. Who pinned Hulk Hogan to win the WWE Championship?

91. Why was there controversy surrounding the outcome of this match?

92. True or false: In the match featuring the Beverly Brothers and the Nasty Boys against the Bushwackers and the Rockers, no one who was eliminated was pinned.

93. How was Earthquake eliminated in the six-man elimination match featuring Big Boss Man and the Legion of Doom against Irwin R. Schyster and the Natural Disasters?

94. Who besides Earthquake made up the Natural Disasters?

95. Who survived this match?

96. **True or false:** *Survivor Series 1991* was the first *Survivor Series* in which the WWE Championship changed hands.

Survivor Series 1992

97. In the first match, the Head Shrinkers defeated High Energy. What two Superstars made up High Energy?

98. Big Boss Man defeated Nailz in what type of match?

99. Who won the match featuring Mr. Perfect & Randy Savage vs. Razor Ramon & Ric Flair?

100. In the four-team elimination match featuring the Nasty Boys and the Natural Disasters vs. the Beverly Brothers and Money Inc., who was the first team eliminated?

101. Which two Superstars made up the team of Money Inc.?

102. Who did Virgil lose to?

103. Undertaker fought Kamala in what type of match?

104. Who won the match between Undertaker and Kamala?

105. Bret Hart retained his WWE Championship by defeating which WWE Superstar?

106. What finishing move did Hart use to secure the victory?

Survivor Series 1993

107. Where did *Survivor Series 1993* take place?

108. In the first eight-man elimination match, all of the following were Randy Savage's partners except:
**a) Tatanka   b) Marty Jannetty
c) The 1-2-3 Kid   d) Razor Ramon**

109. The second match featured Bret Hart and his three brothers. Name them.

110. In the same match, Shawn Michaels teamed up with three "knights." What were the colors of these knights?

111. The Heavenly Bodies fought the Rock 'n' Roll Express to win what Championship?

112. Who won this match?

113. In the eight-man elimination match featuring Butch, Luke, Mabel and Mo vs. Bam Bam Bigelow, Bastion Booger, Fatu and Samu, who did Butch, Luke, Mabel and Mo paint their faces to look like?

114. The final match featured what two teams?

115. Which Superstar did not take part in this match?
**a) Ludvig Borga   b) Yokozuna
c) Lex Luger   d) Diesel**

116. Who ended up being the sole survivor in this match?
a) Yokozuna   b) Scott Steiner
c) Lex Luger   d) Ludvig Borga

Survivor Series 1994

117. The first match was a ten-man elimination match featuring the Bad Guys vs. whom?
a) Team Express   b) Running Wild
c) the Specialists   d) the Teamsters

118. Which Superstar did Diesel NOT pin in this match?
a) Fatu   b) Davey Boy Smith
c) the 1-2-3- Kid   d) Seone

119. The second match featured Clowns 'R' Us vs. The Royal Family. Who made up the Clowns 'R' Us team?
a) Dink, Doink, Zonk and Wonk
b) Dink, Zonk, Wink and Fink
c) Doink, Pink, Zonk and Wink
d) Dink, Doink, Pink and Wink

120. What Superstars made up the team of The Royal Family?
a) Jerry Lawler, Cheesy, Queasy and Sleazy
b) Jerry Lawler, Cheesy, Sleazy and Easy
c) Jerry Lawler, Queasy, Measly and Sleazy
d) Jerry Lawler, Wheezy, Cheesy and Sleazy

121. In the Bret Hart vs. Bob Backlund Championship match, who served as Bret Hart's corner man?

122. Who threw in the towel securing Backlund's victory?

123. In the ten-man elimination match featuring Guts 'n' Glory vs. the Million-Dollar Team, who was NOT a member of Guts 'n' Glory?
a) Adam Bomb   b) Billy Gunn
c) Tito Santana   d) Mabel

124. Undertaker squared off against Yokozuna in what kind of match?

125. What movie star made a special appearance as a ringside enforcer?

126. What two Superstars did this movie star prevent from interfering on Yokozuna's behalf?

Survivor Series 1995

127. In what Maryland city did the 1995 *Survivor Series* take place?

128. **True or false:** Barry Horowitz was the sole survivor of the Bodydonnas vs. the Underdogs match.

129. In the eight-woman elimination match, who did Aja Kong pin to become the sole survivor?

130. Who did Goldust beat in a singles match?

131. In the Darkside vs. the Royals match, which Superstar was NOT on The Royals?
a) Hunter Hearst-Helmsley
b) Isaac Yankem, D.D.S.
c) Mabel
d) Harley Race

132. What members of the Darkside survived this match?

133. Which one of these Superstars was not in the wild card match?
a) **Tom Prichard**   b) **Dean Douglas**
c) **Sid**   d) **Razor Ramon**

134. **True or false:** Ahmed Johnson and Davey Boy Smith were on the same team in the wild card match.

135. Who did Bret Hart pin to win the WWE Championship?

136. **True or False:** The Hart vs. Diesel match was the first *Survivor Series* singles match that lasted more than an hour.

Survivor Series 1996

137. Where did *Survivor Series 1996* take place?

138. Who was NOT on Aldo Montoya's team in the first eight-man elimination match?
a) **Bart Gunn**   b) **Savio Vega**
c) **Bob Holly**   d) **Jesse James**

139. The second eight-man elimination match featured the debut of what two Superstars?
a) **Doug Furnas and Leif Cassidy**
b) **The Rock and Mr. Y**
c) **Doug Furnas and Phil Lafon**
d) **Edge and Christian**

140. Where was Paul Bearer forced to stay during the Undertaker vs. Mankind match?

141. Who won this match?

142. **True or false:** In the third eight-man elimination match, Rocky Maivia made his WWE debut and ended up being the sole survivor.

143. **True or false:** Bret Hart kicked out of the Stone Cold Stunner and defeated Steve Austin in their singles match.

144. Who survived the eight-man elimination match featuring Diesel, Faarooq, Razor Ramon and Vader against Flash Funk, Jimmy Snuka, Savio Vega and Yokozuna.

145. In the WWE Championship match between Sycho Sid and Shawn Michaels, who came into the match as the champion?

146. What was the name of Michaels's mentor who ended up playing a role in the outcome of the match?

Survivor Series 1997

147. In what Canadian city did *Survivor Series 1997* take place?

148. Which of the following Superstars was not on Billy Gunn's team?
a) Henry O. Godwinn
b) Jesse James
c) Doug Furnas
d) Phineas I. Godwinn

149. The Disciples of Apocalypse squared off against what team?

150. Who won the Team Canada vs. Team U.S.A. match?

151. Who made his official in-ring debut by defeating Mankind?

152. Who was not a member of The Rock's team?
a) Ahmed Johnson   b) Kama Mustafa
c) D'Lo Brown   d) Faarooq

153. Who did Stone Cold Steve Austin pin to win back the Intercontinental Championship?

154. Who called for the bell during the Shawn Michaels vs. Bret Hart WWE Championship match?

155. Who was the referee for this match?

156. What was Hart's complaint after the match was over?

Survivor Series 1998

157. What was this *Survivor Series* subtitled?

158. Who did Sable beat to become the Women's Champion?

159. In the first round of the WWE title tournament, why was Big Boss Man disqualified from his match?

160. How long did it take The Rock to defeat Boss Man?

161. Why was Boss Man fighting The Rock?

162. Who did Mankind defeat in the quarter finals?

163. Who did Undertaker beat in the quarter finals?

164. Who ran in as the replacement referee during the Mankind vs. Steve Austin semifinal match?

165. Why did Undertaker get disqualified in his semifinal match with The Rock?

166. What hold did The Rock have Mankind in when Mr. McMahon called for the bell in the Championship match?

Survivor Series 1999

167. Who was not a member of D'Lo Brown's team in the first eight-man elimination match?
a) **The Godfather**   b) **Faarooq**
c) **Mosh**   d) **Thrasher**

168. Who did Kurt Angle beat?

169. **True or false:** Joey Abs, Pete Gas and Rodney were the only survivors in the second eight-man elimination match.

170. Who won the sudden death eight-woman tag match and became the Women's Champion?
a) **Mae Young**
b) **the Fabulous Moolah**
c) **Ivory**
d) **Debra**

171. In the five-man elimination match, what Superstar took on and defeated four other Superstars?

172. What woman defeated Chris Jericho to become Intercontinental Champion?

173. **True or false:** In the last eight-man elimination match of the evening, Christian and Edge were on opposing teams.

174. True or false: Al Snow and Mankind defeated the New Age Outlaws to become Tag Team Champions.

175. Why was Big Show in the WWE Championship Triple-Threat match?

176. Who were the other two competitors in the match?

177. Who won the match and the WWE Championship?

Survivor Series 2000

178. In what Florida city did *Survivor Series 2000* take place?

179. In the *Sunday Night Heat* match that preceded *Survivor Series,* who interfered in the match between Val Venis and Jeff Hardy?

180. Who did Crash and Molly Holly team with to defeat T&A and Trish Stratus?
a) Hardcore Holly
b) Steve Blackman
c) Grandmaster Sexay
d) Bubba Ray Dudley

181. Who were the four Superstars on the Radicalz team that defeated Road Dogg, K-Kwik, Chyna and Billy Gunn?

182. Who beat Chris Jericho in a singles match?

183. Who did William Regal beat to retain his European Championship?

184. True or false: The Rock made Rikishi submit to the Sharpshooter.

185. **True or false:** Lita defeated Ivory to become the Women's Champion.

186. Who did the Hardy Boyz team up with to defeat Edge, Christian and Right to Censor?

187. Who was hiding under the ring during Kurt Angle's match against Undertaker?

188. Who else interfered on Angle's behalf during this match?

189. Who won the match between Stone Cold Steve Austin and Triple H?

Survivor Series 2001

190. *Survivor Series 2001* "Winner-Take-All" format put the fate of what two organizations on the line?

191. The first match of the evening featured Al Snow and Christian fighting for what Championship?

192. Who was the Alliance commissioner who defeated Tajiri in the second match of the evening?

193. After the evening's third match between Edge and Test, what was the score between the Alliance and World Wrestling Entertainment?

194. The Hardys and Dudleys met in what type of a match?

195. Who won the Battle Royal Immunity match?
a) Scotty 2 Hotty   b) Bradshaw
c) Lance Storm   d) Test

196. The Women's Championship match was referred to as what kind of challenge?

197. Mr. McMahon's Federation team consisted of what five Superstars?

198. What five Superstars made up the Alliance team?

199. In the "Winner-Take-All" match, who were the last two Superstars left in the ring?

200. Which Superstar rushed down to the ring, interfered in the match and allowed the WWE's last remaining Superstar to secure the win and the WWE's victory?

PAY-PER-VIEW

the Game and I am
damn good.

Banzai Dr...

Twist Of Fate

The Walls Of Jericho

Name that Pay-Per-View

1. *WrestleMania X-Seven* exploded from the Reliant Astrodome at Reliant Park in Houston, Texas, on April 1, 2001. What was the last WWE Pay-Per-View presented in Houston before that? (*Hint: It was held at the Compaq Center.*)
   a) *Fully Loaded 2000*
   b) *SummerSlam '91*
   c) *No Way Out '98*

2. The red-hot feud between Triple H and The Rock lasted through most of 2000, but their enduring rivalry goes back years. At which event did they have their first one-on-one Pay-Per-View match?
   a) *In Your House: Final Four*
   b) *Survivor Series 1996*
   c) *No Way Out '98*

3. At what Pay-Per-View event was the McMahon-Helmsley Era born?
   a) *Armageddon '99*
   b) *WrestleMania XVI*
   c) *No Way Out 2000*

4. Triple H first met Stone Cold Steve Austin in the ring at which event?
   a) *In Your House: Buried Alive*
   b) *Survivor Series 1997*
   c) *In Your House: Revenge of 'Taker*

5. Mick Foley had his last match at what event?
   a) *No Way Out 2000*
   b) *Royal Rumble 2000*
   c) *WrestleMania XVI*

6. Vince McMahon made his last Pay-Per-View appearance as a TV commentator at _____ in _____ of 1997.

7. Undertaker made his return as the "American Bad Ass" at which Pay-Per-View event?
a) *King of the Ring 2000*
b) *No Way Out 2000*
c) *Judgment Day 2000*

8. Which Pay-Per-View event featured the first ground-breaking ladder match between the Hardy Boyz and Edge & Christian?
a) *Royal Rumble 2000*
b) *No Mercy '99*
c) *Fully Loaded '99*

9. Which 1999 Pay-Per-View featured the "Six-Pack Challenge"?

10. Lita made her first Pay-Per-View appearance at which event? (*Hint: She did not compete.*)
a) *WrestleMania XVI*
b) *Backlash 2000*
c) *Armageddon '99*

11. At which event did The Rock and Triple H have their first one-on-one Pay-Per-View WWE title match?
a) *1997 Royal Rumble*
b) *SummerSlam '96*
c) *Backlash 2000*

12. Val Venis's Intercontinental title victory over Rikishi in July 2000 was not the first time the former adult film star captured that belt. At which Pay-Per-View did he defeat Ken Shamrock for Intercontinental gold in 1999?
a) *King of the Ring*
b) *St. Valentine's Day Massacre*
c) *Fully Loaded*

13. Big Show made his WWE debut at what 1999 Pay-Per-View?

14. At which Pay-Per-View did Stone Cold Steve Austin coin the phrase "Austin 3:16"?

15. At which Pay-Per-View did Stone Cold Steve Austin and Undertaker win the Tag Team Championship?
a) *Fully Loaded '98*
b) *WrestleMania XV*
c) *Survivor Series '97*

16. The McMahon vs. Austin feud finished with the "End of an Era" match at which Pay-Per-View?
a) *SummerSlam '99*
b) *Judgment Day 2000*
c) *Fully Loaded '99*

17. Taka Michinoku won the Light-Heavyweight title at what Pay-Per-View?
a) *In Your House: A Cold Day in Hell*
b) *In Your House: D-Generation X*
c) *In Your House: International Incident*

18. At which Pay-Per-View did Vince McMahon fire Stone Cold Steve Austin?

19. What is the name of the WWE's February Pay-Per-View?
a) *Backlash*
b) *Judgment Day*
c) *Armageddon*

20. What Pay-Per-View featured The Rock's victory over Triple H for his fourth Heavyweight Championship?
a) *Judgment Day 2000*
b) *Backlash 2000*
c) *No Mercy '01*

No Way Out

21. February brings the Pay-Per-View spectacular *No Way Out,* one of the last steps on the road to *WrestleMania.* At the first *No Way Out,* Stone Cold Steve Austin, Owen Hart, Cactus Jack and Terry Funk faced the team of Triple H, the New Age Outlaws and...
a) Savio Vega   b) Shawn Michaels   c) Chyna

22. *No Way Out 2000* featured Triple H defending the World title against...
a) Cactus Jack   b) Mankind   c) Dude Love

23. What type of match was it?
a) Hell in the Cell
b) Ladder match
c) No Disqualification match

24. What was the name of the Pay-Per-View event held in 1999 in place of *No Way Out*?

25. What city held *No Way Out* in 1998?
a) Houston, TX   b) Austin, TX   c) San Diego, CA

26. Name the arena in which *No Way Out '98* was presented.

27. Who was the WWE Champion at the first *No Way Out*?
a) Triple H
b) Undertaker
c) Stone Cold Steve Austin

28. What was Terry Funk's nickname when he competed in the main event of *No Way Out '98*?

29. **True or false:** Mick Foley's retirement match took place at *No Way Out '01*.

30. _____ won his sixth Championship by defeating _____ at *No Way Out '01*, setting a new record.

31. The previous record holder was...
a) Hulk Hogan
b) Stone Cold Steve Austin
c) Undertaker

32. **True or false:** The WWE Championship has changed hands at every edition of *No Way Out*.

33. **True or false:** The legendary Hollywood Hulk Hogan made his return to the WWE at *No Way Out '02.*

34. The faction known as the _____ made their WWE debut at *No Way Out '02*, but they didn't wrestle. Instead, they interfered in the match of _____ _____, causing him to lose.

35. Who was the WWE Undisputed Champion at *No Way Out '02*?
a) The Rock   b) Triple H   c) Chris Jericho

36. Who challenged for the Undisputed WWE title at that event?
a) Stone Cold Steve Austin
b) Kurt Angle
c) The Rock

37. Which Superstar fought to preserve his *WrestleMania* title shot at *No Way Out 2000*?
a) Vince McMahon   b) The Rock   c) Triple H

38. **True or false:** The original *No Way Out* was held in 1998.

39. **True or false:** The original *No Way Out* was the only one that didn't take place in February.

40. **True or false:** The WWE Championship has never changed hands at *No Way Out.*

Backlash

41. Who did Stone Cold Steve Austin defend the WWE Championship against at *Backlash '99*?

42. Who was Dean Malenko's opponent at *Backlash 2000*?

43. What was the main event of the first *Backlash*?

44. In what year was the first *Backlash* held?

45. **True or false:** Hollywood Hulk Hogan's title shot against Triple H at *Backlash '02* was his first shot at the WWE title since *WrestleMania IX.*

46. Mankind had his second Boiler Room Brawl on Pay-Per-View at *Backlash '99* against whom?
a) Big Show
b) Undertaker
c) Stone Cold Steve Austin

47. True or false: The Rock was the first Superstar to win the WWE title at *Backlash.*

48. What city hosted *Backlash 2000*?
a) Denver, CO   b) Austin, TX   c) Washington, D.C.

49. True or false: *Backlash 2000* featured six title matches, but no titles changed hands.

50. The six-way Hardcore Championship match at *Backlash 2000* featured the champion Crash, the Hardy Boyz, _____, Perry Saturn and _____.

51. Who was Big Show's opponent at *Backlash 2000*?
a) Kurt Angle   b) Triple H   c) Kane

52. William Regal defeated _____ in a "Duchess of _____" match at *Backlash '01.*

53. In a Triple-Threat match at *Backlash '01*, European Champion Matt Hardy defeated Christian and who else?
a) Eddie Guerrero   b) Chris Benoit   c) Jeff Hardy

54. True or false: At *Backlash '01*, Triple H and Stone Cold Steve Austin became the first Intercontinental and WWE Champions to ever team up to win the Tag Team Championship.

55. True or false: The main event of *Backlash '01* represented the first time that all three major WWE titles were up for grabs in the same match.

56. Who was Shane McMahon's opponent in the "Last-Man-Standing" match at *Backlash '01*?
   a) Kurt Angle   b) Big Show   c) Rob Van Dam

57. **True or false:** Triple H has been in the main event of every *Backlash*.

58. **True or false:** *Backlash '02* was Hollywood Hulk Hogan's first Pay-Per-View back in the WWE.

59. What city hosted *Backlash '02*?
   a) Kansas City, MO
   b) Detroit, MI
   c) Toronto, Ontario, Canada

60. Who was the first European Champion to defend his title at *Backlash*? (*Hint: It happened in 2000.*)
   a) William Regal
   b) D'Lo Brown
   c) Eddie Guerrero

Judgment Day

61. At *Judgment Day 2000*, the WWE title was defended in what type of match?
   a) Two-out-of-Three-Falls match
   b) Iron Man match
   c) Ladder match

62. At *Judgment Day 2000*, Intercontinental Champion Chris Benoit won a submission match over...
   a) Kurt Angle   b) Chris Jericho   c) Eddie Guerrero

63. Every *Judgment Day* except the first one has been held in May. When was the first one held?

64. What year was the first *Judgment Day* held?
a) 1996   b) 1997   c) 1998

65. True or false: *Judgment Day* was not held in 1999.

66. At *Judgment Day '98*, Undertaker and _____ met for the vacant WWE Championship.

67. Who was the referee of that '98 main event?
a) Stone Cold Steve Austin
b) Ken Shamrock
c) Paul Bearer

68. Against whom did The Rock defend the WWE title at *Judgment Day 2000*?
a) Mick Foley
b) Stone Cold Steve Austin
c) Triple H

69. What type of match was the Intercontinental title bout at *Judgment Day 2000*?
a) Submission match
b) Iron Man match
c) Falls-Count-Anywhere match

70. Who was the special referee for the 2000 main event?
a) Kane
b) Stephanie McMahon-Helmsley
c) Shawn Michaels

71. Last-minute interference from _____ caused The Rock to lose his WWE title at *Judgment Day 2000*.

72. True or false: The Pay-Per-View held previously in place of *Judgment Day* was entitled *No Holds Barred*.

73. What edition of *Judgment Day* featured Vince McMahon uttering the famous line, "Austin—screw you, you're *fired!*"

74. Who was the WWE Champion at *Judgment Day '01*?
a) **The Rock**
b) **Stone Cold Steve Austin**
c) **Kurt Angle**

75. **True or false:** The WWE title changed hands at *Judgment Day '01.*

76. **True or false:** Undertaker won the WWE Championship at the first *Judgment Day.*

77. Who was the Intercontinental Champion at *Judgment Day '98*?
a) **Owen Hart**   b) **Ken Shamrock**   c) **The Rock**

78. **True or false:** Triple H made his final Pay-Per-View appearance of 2001 at *Judgment Day.*

79. Who won the Intercontinental title at *Judgment Day '01*?
a) **Kane**   b) **Jeff Hardy**   c) **Albert**

80. What type of match was held for the Intercontinental title that year?
a) **Inferno match**
b) **First Blood match**
c) **Chain match**

King of the Ring

81. By winning his fifth WWE title at *King of the Ring 2000* The Rock tied the WWE record. Who originally set the record?
a) **Bret "Hitman" Hart**
b) **Hulk Hogan**
c) **Gorilla Monsoon**

82. In what type of match did Stone Cold Steve Austin lose the WWE Championship to Kane at the *King of the Ring 1998*?
a) Iron Man   b) Inferno   c) First Blood

83. **True or false:** X-Pac has never participated in the *King of the Ring* tournament.

84. **True or false:** The Hulkster's last match before leaving the WWE was at the original *King of the Ring*.

85. Who did The Rock face in the semifinal round of the *King of the Ring 1998* tournament? (*Hint: The Rock was victorious and advanced to the finals, where he lost to Ken Shamrock.*)
a) Vader   b) D'Lo Brown   c) Dan Severn

86. Who did Ken Shamrock face in the semifinal round of the *King of the Ring 1998* tournament?
a) Billy Gunn   b) Shawn Michaels   c) Jeff Jarrett

87. Who was the opponent of WWE Champion Undertaker at the *King of the Ring 1999*?
a) The Rock   b) Kurt Angle   c) Kane

88. Who won the first *King of the Ring* tournament featured on Pay-Per-View?

89. Who did Kurt Angle defeat to win the *King of the Ring 2000*?
a) Billy Gunn   b) Rikishi   c) Test

90. Who did Mabel defeat to win the *King of the Ring* in 1995?

91. Where was the first *King of the Ring* held?

92. Who was Chyna's opponent in the first round of the *King of the Ring 1999*?

93. The only competitors to ever win the WWE title at *King of the Ring* were, in chronological order, _____, _____ and _____.

94. **True or false:** The *King of the Ring* tournament was once used to determine a new WWE Champion.

95. The only *King of the Ring* at which the WWE title was not on the line was the 1995 edition. At that event, WWE Champion Diesel teamed up with _____ to take on Sycho Sid and _____.

96. The 2001 edition of *King of the Ring* took place in what venue?
a) Continental Airlines Arena
b) Gund Arena
c) Joe Louis Arena

97. **True or false:** No Superstar has ever won more than one *King of the Ring* tournament.

98. Which one of the following never won *King of the Ring*?
a) Edge   **b) Triple H**   **c) The Rock**

99. What current Superstar made his Pay-Per-View debut at the first *King of the Ring* in 1993?
a) Billy Gunn   **b) Hardcore Holly**   **c) Goldust**

100. Who did Owen Hart defeat in the finals of the *King of the Ring 1994* tournament?
a) Mr. Perfect   **b) Razor Ramon**   **c) Savio Vega**

Fully Loaded

101. At *Fully Loaded '99,* The Rock and _____
competed in a falls-count-anywhere _____ match.

102. The Hardy Boyz and Lita joined forces at *Fully Loaded 2000* for the first time on Pay-Per-View. Who were their opponents?
a) the Radicalz
b) T&A and Trish Stratus
c) Right to Censor

103. The first *Fully Loaded* was presented in...
a) 1999   b) 2000   c) 1998

104. At the first *Fully Loaded,* Stone Cold Steve Austin and _____ joined forces to oppose Kane and _____.

105. What city hosted the first *Fully Loaded*?
a) Pittsburgh, PA   b) Syracuse, NY   c) Fresno, CA

106. At *Fully Loaded 2000,* _____ received his first of several memorable title shots against The Rock.

107. Triple H's and Chris Jericho's match at *Fully Loaded 2000* was what type of bout?
a) Falls-Count-Anywhere
b) Last Man Standing
c) Hell in the Cell

108. **True or false:** *Fully Loaded 2000* featured the first match between Kurt Angle and Undertaker.

109. At *Fully Loaded '99* Edge's first Intercontinental title reign ended after one day when he lost the gold back to...
a) Jeff Jarrett   b) Chris Jericho   c) Road Dogg

110. **True or false:** At the time Edge's one-day title reign was the shortest in Intercontinental Championship history.

111. *Fully Loaded '99* was presented in what city?
a) Buffalo, NY
b) Austin, TX
c) Winnipeg, Manitoba, Canada

112. **True or false:** The Rock defeated Triple H in a strap match at *Fully Loaded '99.*

113. Fighting for the rights to the D-Generation X name, former members X-Pac and _____ collided with Billy Gunn and _____ at *Fully Loaded '99.*

114. The dreaded "Iron Circle" match at *Fully Loaded '99* was between Ken Shamrock and whom?
a) Owen Hart   b) Steve Blackman   c) Dan Severn

115. At *Fully Loaded '98,* Stone Cold Steve Austin emerged with both the WWE and Tag Team Championships. Who was the last to do this before him?
a) Bob Backlund   b) Hulk Hogan   c) Diesel

116. Name the only year since the inception of *Fully Loaded* that the Pay-Per-View event was not held.

117. **True or false:** *Fully Loaded '99* brought an end to the legendary Austin vs. McMahon rivalry.

118. Who was Stone Cold Steve Austin's opponent at *Fully Loaded '99*?
a) Kurt Angle   b) Triple H   c) Undertaker

119. Triple H and The Rock met in a strap match at *Fully Loaded '99.* Name the other stipulation of the match.

120. **True or false:** Too Cool won the Tag Team Championship at *Fully Loaded 2000.*

Unforgiven

121. During his run as European Champion last fall, Al Snow was known to appear for each of his matches using the motif of a different European nation. At *Unforgiven,* his chosen nation was Italy. Can you name the Italian-American actor whose photograph he brought down to ringside as part of this theme?
a) Robert DeNiro   b) Al Pacino   c) Tony Danza

122. Who was Stone Cold Steve Austin's opponent at the first *Unforgiven* in 1998?
a) Undertaker   b) Kane   c) Dude Love

123. The first *Unforgiven* was not held in the month of September. In what month was it held?
a) March   b) April   c) May

124. Name the city that hosted the original *Unforgiven.*
a) Jacksonville, FL
b) Chicago, IL
c) Greensboro, NC

125. The NWA Tag Team Championship was defended at *Unforgiven '98* when the champion _____ faced off against _____.

126. In what type of match did Undertaker and Kane wrestle at *Unforgiven '98*?
a) Steel Cage   b) First Blood   c) Inferno

127. What year did *Unforgiven* debut in its customary month of September?

128. Who was Steve Blackman's opponent at *Unforgiven '99*?
a) Ken Shamrock   b) Val Venis   c) Chris Jericho

129. True or false: D'Lo Brown won his record-setting fourth European Championship at *Unforgiven '99.*

130. Against whom did Jeff Jarrett defend the Intercontinental title at *Unforgiven '99?*
a) Chyna   b) Chris Jericho   c)   Shane McMahon

131. Who was the first Women's Champion to compete at *Unforgiven?*
a) Sable   b) Luna   c) Ivory

132. Edge & Christian competed for the Tag Team Championship on Pay-Per-View for the first time at *Unforgiven '99.* Who were the champions?
a) New Age Outlaws   b) the Hardy Boyz   c) APA

133. *Unforgiven '99* featured the "Six-Pack Challenge" match, featuring British Bulldog, _____, Kane, _____, The Rock and the man who won the match, _____.

134. True or false: Tazz defeated Jerry Lawler at *Unforgiven 2000.*

135. Who won the Hardcore battle royal at *Unforgiven 2000?*
a) Steve Blackman   b) Crash   c) Hardcore Holly

136. Chris Jericho made his WWE Pay-Per-View debut at *Unforgiven 2000.* Who was his opponent?
a) Road Dogg   b) The Rock   c) X-Pac

137. True or false: Edge & Christian won the Tag Team Championship from the Hardy Boyz at *Unforgiven 2000.*

138. Who was the Intercontinental Champion at *Unforgiven 2000?*
a) Rikishi   b) Billy Gunn   c) Eddie Guerrero

139. The Fatal Four Way at *Unforgiven 2000* featured Chris Benoit, _____, Undertaker and the champion, _____.

140. True or false: Stone Cold Steve Austin's longest WWE title reign to date was brought to an end at *Unforgiven '01*.

No Mercy

141. Who did Stone Cold Steve Austin face at *No Mercy 2000*?

142. Who challenged The Rock for the title at *No Mercy 2000*?
a) Kurt Angle   b) Undertaker   c) Tazz

143. True or false: The original *No Mercy* was not held in October.

144. Who was WWE Champion at the first *No Mercy*?
a) Undertaker
b) Triple H
c) Stone Cold Steve Austin

145. At *No Mercy '99*, _____ defeated _____ for the Women's Championship to become the oldest champion in WWE history.

146. Who was the first Superstar to win the WWE Championship at *No Mercy*?
a) Kurt Angle   b) The Rock   c) Mick Foley

147. The Hardy Boyz had their first historic match with _____ at *No Mercy '99*, defeating them to win the services of _____ and a grand total of $_____.

148. Chris Jericho beat X-Pac at *No Mercy 2000*. What type of match was it?

a) steel cage   b) strap   c) Iron Man

149. True or false: Steve Austin defeated Rikishi at *No Mercy 2000*.

150. *No Mercy '01* featured a Triple-Threat main event, in which Stone Cold Steve Austin defended the title against both _____ and _____.

151. True or false: Stone Cold Steve Austin didn't compete on Pay-Per-View between *No Mercy '99* and *No Mercy 2000*.

152. What tag team won its third Tag Team Championship at *No Mercy 2000*?

a) Edge & Christian
b) New Age Outlaws
c) Hardy Boyz

153. True or false: *No Mercy '01* was the first event to feature both WWE and WCW World title matches.

154. Who defended the WCW Championship at *No Mercy '01*?

a) The Rock   b) Booker T   c) Kurt Angle

155. What tag team challenged for the WCW Tag Team Championship at *No Mercy '01*?

a) the Hardy Boyz
b) Booker T & Test
c) The Hurricane & Lance Storm

156. In what type of match did Torrie Wilson and Stacy Keibler compete at *No Mercy '01*?

a) Evening Gown   b) Lingerie   c) Mud Pit

157. What arena hosted *No Mercy 2000*?
a) Allstate Arena   b) Compaq Center   c) Pepsi Arena

158. What masked tag team did Edge & Christian dress up as at *No Mercy 2000*?
a) The Machines
b) The Conquistadors
c) The Executioners

159. True or false: *No Mercy 2000* featured the first *No Mercy* appearance of Chyna.

160. True or false: Edge was the first Superstar to win the Intercontinental title at *No Mercy*.

In Your House

161. True or false: The December 1997 Pay-Per-View event was entitled *In Your House: Mind Games*.

162. Who was Undertaker's opponent in the first-ever Hell in the Cell in 1997?
a) Shawn Michaels   b) Mankind   c) Big Boss Man

163. The first *In Your House* Pay-Per-View featured Diesel defending the WWE title against...
a) British Bulldog   b) Sycho Sid   c) King Mabel

164. Name the year in which it was held.

165. What was the last *In Your House* of 1997?
a) *Revenge of the 'Taker*
b) *A Cold Day in Hell*
c) *D-Generation X*

166. What was the name of the *In Your House* at which
Undertaker defended the title against Mankind.
a) *Buried Alive*
b) *Revenge of the 'Taker*
c) *International Incident*

167. What was the name of the first *In Your House* to have
a subtitle?
a) *Beware of Dog*
b) *Rock Bottom*
c) *Good Friends, Better Enemies*

168. How many *In Your House* Pay-Per-Views were held
in 1995?
a) 5   b) 7   c) 10

169. True or false: *In Your House: Breakdown* in 1997
featured the first match between Stone Cold Steve
Austin and Shawn Michaels—while they were both
Tag Team Champions.

170. Name the first Superstar to win the WWE Championship at an *In Your House.*
a) Shawn Michaels
b) Sycho Sid
c) Bret "Hit Man" Hart

171. Which *In Your House* was it?

172. True or false: No Superstar ever lost the WWE title at
an *In Your House.*

173. True or false: Sycho Sid once challenged for the WWE
title at two consecutive *In Your House* events.

174. Name the 1997 *In Your House* at which Stone Cold Steve Austin was arrested.
   a) *Canadian Stampede*
   b) *International Incident*
   c) *In Your House V*

175. The four Superstars involved in the main event of *In Your House: Final Four* were Bret "Hit Man" Hart, _____, Undertaker and _____.

176. Against whom did Bret Hart defend the WWE title at *In Your House V* (December 1995)?
   a) British Bulldog   b) Diesel   c) Owen Hart

177. What *In Your House* actually took place on two different nights?
   a) *In Your House IV*
   b) *Beware of Dog*
   c) *A Cold Day in Hell*

178. Who challenged Bret Hart for the WWE title in September 1997 at *In Your House: Ground Zero*?
   a) Vader   b) Kane   c) the Patriot

179. **True or false:** British Bulldog never challenged for the WWE Championship at an *In Your House* event.

180. **True or false:** Popular rock band Creed once performed at an *In Your House* show.

Other Events

181. True or false: The 1999 *St. Valentine's Day Massacre* marked the first time Stone Cold Steve Austin and Vince McMahon wrestled one-on-one.

182. Who won the elimination tournament at *The Wrestling Classic* in 1985?

183. Who defeated Stone Cold Steve Austin for the WWE title at *Over the Edge '99*?
a) Undertaker   b) Kane   c) Mankind

184. What was the name of the WWE's first UK-only Pay-Per-View, held in 1997?

185. Who won the six-way Hell in the Cell match at *Armageddon 2000*?

186. Who was Triple H's opponent at the first *Armageddon* in 1999?

187. Who did Big Show defend the WWE title against at *Armageddon '99*?

188. Who defended the WWE crown in a six-man Hell in the Cell at *Armageddon 2000*?
a) Kurt Angle   b) Rikishi   c) Undertaker

189. Who did Hulk Hogan defend the WWE title against at *The Wrestling Classic*?
a) Big John Studd
b) "Rowdy" Roddy Piper
c) Paul Orndorff

190. True or false: Undertaker defeated Hulk Hogan for the WWE title in 1991 at *Tuesday in Texas*.

191. *No Holds Barred: The Match,* held on Christmas 1989, featured Hulk Hogan and _____ against Zeus and _____ in a steel cage match.

192. Who was the special referee for the WWE title match between Stone Cold Steve Austin and Dude Love at *Over the Edge '98*?
a) Vince McMahon
b) Ken Shamrock
c) Shawn Michaels

193. What was the name of the WWE's second UK Pay-Per-View, presented in 1998?
a) *Rebellion*
b) *InsurreXtion*
c) *Capital Carnage*

194. Who was Big Boss Man's opponent at *St. Valentine's Day Massacre*?
a) Mideon   b) Al Snow   c) Ken Shamrock

195. **True or false:** A referee's match between Earl Hebner and Nick Patrick was presented at *Invasion* in July 2001.

196. Who did Nikolai Volkoff face in *The Wrestling Classic* tournament?
a) Davey Boy Smith
b) Dynamite Kid
c) Ricky Steamboat

197. What arena held 1999's *St. Valentine's Day Massacre*?
a) the Pyramid (Memphis, TN)
b) Arrowhead Pond (Anaheim, CA)
c) First Union Center (Philadelphia, PA)

198. **True or false:** In addition to the American *No Mercy*, there was also a UK *No Mercy* Pay-Per-View presented in 1999.

199. Who challenged Bret "Hit Man" Hart for the Intercontinental title at *Tuesday in Texas*?
a) Skinner   b) Papa Shango   c) Earthquake

200. **True or false:** The *No Holds Barred* Pay-Per-View match was presented along with the *No Holds Barred* movie.

OLD SCHOOL

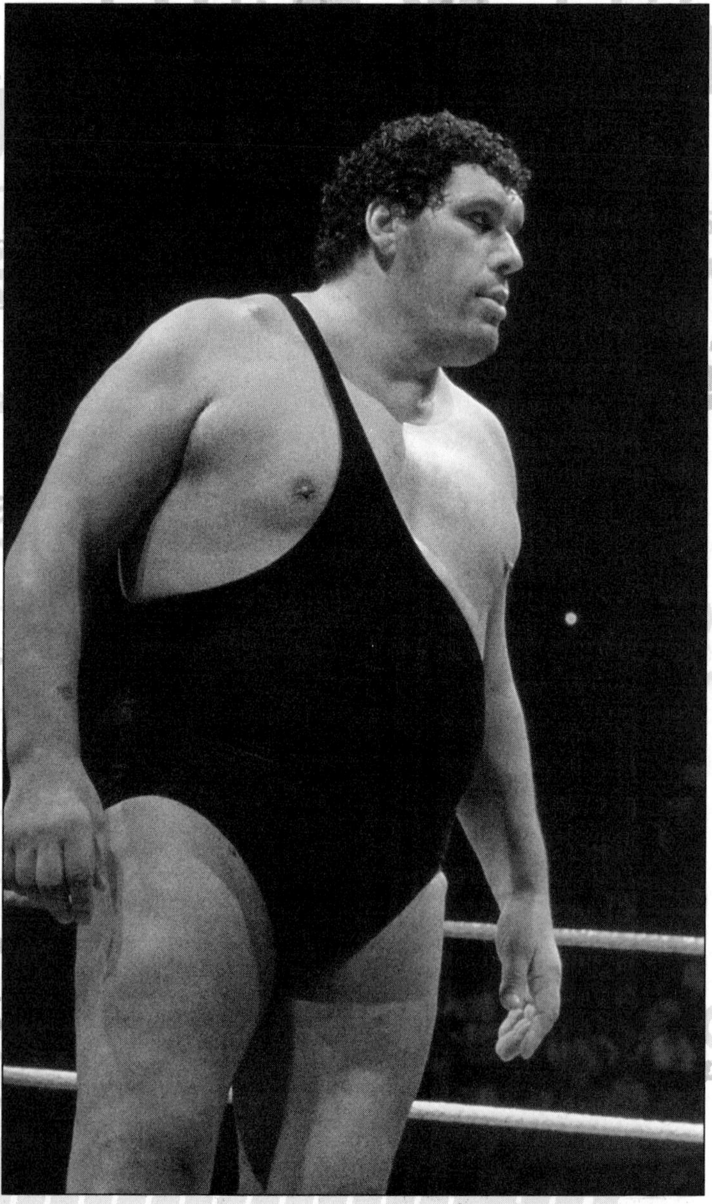

Hall of Famers

1. Vince McMahon's first role in the WWE was TV announcer. What Hall of Famer was his first broadcast partner?
   a) Pat Patterson
   b) Jesse "the Body" Ventura
   c) Antonino Rocca

2. Baron Mikel Scicluna hailed from what Mediterranean island?
   a) Sicily   b) Corsica   c) Malta

3. Captain Lou Albano managed a record seventeen tag team champions. Which one of these championship tandems did Albano NOT manage?
   a) The Head Shrinkers
   b) Strike Force
   c) Tarzan Tyler & Crazy Luke Graham

4. **True or false:** Referee Tim White was the personal assistant of the late Andre the Giant.

5. **True or false:** Ivan Putski never held a singles title in World Wrestling Entertainment.

6. **True or false:** "The Unpredictable" Johnny Rodz is a member of the World Wrestling Entertainment Hall of Fame.

7. **True or false:** Gorilla Monsoon retired from the ring in 1979.

8. Who was the first wrestler managed by Captain Lou Albano?
   a) Crusher Verdu
   b) Ivan Koloff
   c) King Curtis

9. What Pacific Island was "Superfly" Jimmy Snuka from?

10. What late Superstar was known as the "Eighth Wonder of the World"?

11. Who was Killer Kowalski's partner in The Executioners?

12. The Valiant Brothers were Jimmy, Johnny and...?

13. Who was the manager of Bobo Brazil?

Tag Teams

14. Which WWE road agent once formed a tag team with his brother?
a) Jack Lanza
b) Gerald Brisco
c) Dave Hebner

15. Killer Kowalski and Big John Studd once held the Tag Team title as a masked duo known as The Executioners. Who was their third partner?
a) George "The Animal" Steele
b) Gorilla Monsoon
c) Nikolai Volkoff

16. Edge & Christian tried to get back into the Tag Team title picture by masquerading as the Conquistadors. Longtime fans remember the real Conquistadors, who competed in the late eighties. Under the masks, they were actually Luis Rivera and what other man? (*Hint: His son was a member of Los Boricuas during the nineties.*)
a) Jose Estrada b) Johnny Rodz c) Jose Lothario

17. WWE road agent Tony Garea is a former five-time Tag Team Champion. Which one of the following did he NOT hold the title with?
a) **Rene Goulet**
b) **Haystacks Calhoun**
c) **Rick Martel**

18. During Sgt. Slaughter's days as WWE Champion, he was managed by General Adnan. Under what identity did Adnan hold the Tag Team Championship in the 1970s? (*Hint: His partner was Chief Jay Strongbow.*)
a) **Billy White Wolf**
b) **Sonny King**
c) **Jules Strongbow**

19. "Jumpin'" Jim Brunzell was a member of what WWE tag team of the eighties?
a) **the Killer Bees**
b) **The Machines**
c) **the Brain Busters**

20. At the *Royal Rumble 2001,* Haku returned to the WWE after a decade-long absence. As a member of The Islanders in the late eighties, who did Haku tag team with?
a) **Zahi Hawass**
b) **Samu**
c) **Tama**

21. Haku held the Tag Team Championship in 1990 with the legendary Andre the Giant. Who did they win the title from?
a) **Demolition**
b) **the Brain Busters**
c) **the Hart Foundation**

22. Announcer Michael Hayes was once a member of what tag team?
a) the Midnight Express
b) the Fabulous Freebirds
c) Pretty Wonderful

23. **True or false:** Tony Garea never held the Tag Team Championship with Rick Martel.

24. Warlord and Barbarian made up the tag team known as _____.

25. Former Tag Team Champion Bepo Mongol was actually _____ under a different name.

26. **True or false:** Gorilla Monsoon once held the Tag Team Championship with Waldo Von Erich.

27. Vince McMahon stooge Gerald Brisco first entered the WWE in 1984 as part of a tag team with his brother Jack. What duo did they challenge for the Tag Team Championship?
a) Adrian Adonis & Dick Murdoch
b) Tony Atlas & Rocky Johnson
c) the Wild Samoans

28. Which one of the Rougeau Brothers wore a mustache?

29. Who was the third member of Demolition?

30. Shawn Michaels was once a member of what tag team?

31. Who defeated Demolition at *WrestleMania VII*?

32. Who was Shawn Michaels's partner?

33. What tag team had their final match at *WrestleMania VII*?
a) **Legion of Doom**
b) **Nasty Boys**
c) **the Hart Foundation**

34. Who was Nikolai Volkoff's tag team partner in the Bolsheviks?

35. Who replaced Brutus Beefcake as part of the Dream Team?

36. Who was Blackjack Lanza's partner in the Blackjacks tag team?

37. Who was Roy Heffernan's partner in the Fabulous Kangaroos?

38. Which one of the following held the Tag Team title with Dean Ho?
a) **Rene Goulet**
b) **Haystacks Calhoun**
c) **Tony Garea**

39. Typhoon was a member of what WWE tag team of the nineties?

40. Which road agent once formed a tag team in WWE with Tully Blanchard?

41. In 2000, sports-entertainment lost one of its luminaries, Prof. Toru Tanaka. During the 1970s, Tanaka teamed with a fellow Japanese grappler to win a then-record three WWE Tag Team titles. Who was his partner? (*Hint: He went on to become a manager in the eighties and nineties.*)
a) **Mr. Fuji**
b) **King Curtis Iaukea**
c) **Mr. Saito**

Managers

42. Who was Undertaker's first manager?
a) **Brother Love**
b) **"The Doctor of Style" Slick**
c) **Mr. Fuji**

43. Which WWE referee was a manager earlier in his sports-entertainment career?
a) **Earl Hebner**
b) **Teddy Long**
c) **Tim White**

44. Last March, Paul Heyman became the newest member of the WWE's broadcast team. Which one of the following Superstars did he once manage early in his sports-entertainment career?
a) **Stone Cold Steve Austin**
b) **Triple H**
c) **X-Pac**

45. Who was the manager of three-time former Tag Team Champions the Fabulous Kangaroos in the 1960s?
a) **The Grand Wizard**
b) **Wild Red Berry**
c) **James Dudley**

46. Who briefly managed Undertaker after Brother Love?
a) **Mr. Fuji**
b) **"Million Dollar Man" Ted DiBiase**
c) **Paul Bearer**

47. **True or false:** Bob Backlund was once managed by Arnold Skaaland.

48. Which one of the following managers never managed a WWE Champion in the WWE?
a) "Classy" Freddie Blassie
b) "The Mouth of the South" Jimmy Hart
c) "The Doctor of Style" Slick

49. Kamala's managers in WWE were, in chronological order: _____, the Wizard, _____, Harvey Whippleman and _____.

50. **True or false:** "Superstar" Billy Graham was never managed by Bobby "The Brain" Heenan.

51. Which one of the following never managed Bam Bam Bigelow in World Wrestling Entertainment?
a) Luna Vachon
b) Frenchy Martin
c) Sir Oliver Humperdink

52. Greg "The Hammer" Valentine was managed by _____ when he beat Tito Santana for the _____ title in 1984.

53. **True or false:** Demolition was originally managed by "Luscious" Johnny Valiant.

54. Who was the manager of The Mountie?
a) Johnny V
b) Jimmy Hart
c) Slick

55. Who was the first manager of The Powers of Pain?

56. Who did Sapphire manage?

57. Who was the manager of Big Bully Busick?

58. Who was the manager of "Ravishing" Rick Rude?

59. Who managed the Fabulous Rougeau Brothers?

60. Who was King Kong Bundy's first manager in WWE?

61. Who was the manager of The Red Rooster?

62. Who was the second WWE Champion managed by the Grand Wizard?

63. Who was the manager of The Yukon Lumberjacks?

64. Who managed Stan Stasiak to the World title?

65. What was the name of "Nature Boy" Buddy Rogers's manager?

66. Who was the original manager of The Iron Sheik?

67. Who was the manager of The Moondogs?

68. Name Gorilla Monsoon's original manager in the 1960s.

Originators

69. Chris Benoit goes by the menacing nickname of the "Crippler." Who was WWE's original "Crippler"?
a) **Ron Bass**
b) **Ray Stevens**
c) **Frank Williams**

70. Kurt Angle may be the first Olympic gold medalist to compete in the World Wrestling Entertainment, but he's not the first Olympic wrestler to do so. What former Superstar represented his nation in the 1968 Olympic Games in Mexico City?
a) **Ken Patera**
b) **Iron Sheik**
c) **Chris Taylor**

71. The Rock is known worldwide for The People's Elbow, which he often uses as a finishing maneuver. What former WWE Champion used a flying elbow to vanquish his opponents?
a) **Bruno Sammartino**
b) **Randy Savage**
c) **Shawn Michaels**

72. One of Stone Cold Steve Austin's signature maneuvers is named for what old-time wrestling great who perfected it?
a) **Ed "Strangler" Lewis**
b) **Lou Thesz**
c) **Johnny Valentine**

73. **True or false:** The Rock's grandfather appeared in the James Bond movie *You Only Live Twice.*

74. **True or false:** In addition to being the site of *WrestleMania X-Seven,* the SkyDome was also the site of *WrestleMania VII.*

75. **True or false:** Arn Anderson was a member of the original Four Horsemen.

76. The Rock's dad, Rocky Johnson, held the Tag Team Championship years ago in the World Wrestling Entertainment. Who was his partner?
a) **"Special Delivery" S.D. Jones**
b) **Tony Garea**
c) **Tony Atlas**

77. Being a third-generation World Wrestling Entertainment Superstar, The Rock had a grandfather who once competed in the squared circle. What was his name?
a) **"Big Cat" Ernie Ladd**
b) **Afa the Wild Samoan**
c) **"High Chief" Peter Maivia**

78. Who is the father of Tiger Ali Singh?

79. Who was the first "King of Wrestling"?

80. Mr. Perfect's father competed in WWE under what name?

81. Who was the original manager of "Superfly" Jimmy Snuka?

82. What late Superstar was the father of Dean Malenko?

83. What sixties competitor was the father of eighties competitor Greg "The Hammer" Valentine?

84. The late Terry Gordy was a member of the Fabulous Freebirds with current WWE commentator Michael Hayes. Who was the third original member?
a) Jimmy Garvin
b) Dr. Tom Prichard
c) Buddy Roberts

85. Which legendary former wrestler trained Mick Foley for the squared circle?
a) The Great Gama
b) Ron Shaw
c) Dominic DeNucci

86. Former wrestler "Beautiful" Bobby Eaton was recently appointed to be the head trainer for WWE's developmental league in Memphis. Eaton achieved fame as one half of what legendary tag team?
a) the Rock 'n' Roll Express
b) the Fantastics
c) Midnight Express

87. **True or false:** Chris Jericho was trained in Calgary by Stu Hart.

88. Who was the longtime partner of Vincent J.
McMahon, founder of World Wrestling
Entertainment?

Famous Firsts

89. Name the only WWE title ever to change hands on the
continent of Africa. (*Hint: It was in Egypt.*)
a) **European**
b) **Women's Tag Team**
c) **Junior Heavyweight**

90. Bruno Sammartino's 1981 retirement match was
against _____, and was the first
WWE event in the venue known today as

_____.

91. Who once held the WWE's bench-press record?
a) **Dino Bravo**
b) **Ted Arcidi**
c) **Tony Atlas**

92. **True or false:** Jimmy "Superfly" Snuka was featured
on the cover of the first issue of *World Wrestling
Federation Magazine.*

93. Who was Magnificent Muraco's first manager in the
WWE?
a) **Grand Wizard**
b) **Mr. Fuji**
c) **Capt. Lou Albano**

94. Who was Big Boss Man's first tag team partner in World Wrestling Entertainment?
a) **Ken Shamrock**
b) **Akeem**
c) **Albert**

95. Mr. Perfect's first WWE manager was...
a) **the Genius**
b) **The Coach**
c) **Bobby "The Brain" Heenan**

96. Who was the first man to pin Undertaker in a televised WWE match?
a) **Ultimate Warrior**
b) **Hulk Hogan**
c) **"Rowdy" Roddy Piper**

97. Who was the first to tag up with Undertaker in a regular WWE Tag Team match?
a) **Ric Flair**
b) **Jake "The Snake" Roberts**
c) **Nailz**

98. Who opposed Bruno Sammartino in the first WWE event at the modern Madison Square Garden?

99. Who was the first member of Bobby "The Brain" Heenan's stable to win a title in the WWE?

100. Undertaker won his first WWE title at which Pay-Per-View?

101. Who was Big Boss Man's first manager in WWE?

102. Who was the first WWE competitor to appear on the cover of *Sports Illustrated*?

103. Who challenged Bruno Sammartino in the first WWE title match held in a foreign country?

104. WWE's first event in the old Madison Square Garden took place in what year?

105. Who had the longest undefeated streak in WWE history?

106. What year were the first Slammy Awards held?

107. Who did "Brooklyn Brawler" Steve Lombardi face in his WWE debut back in 1984?
a) S.D. "Special Delivery" Jones
b) "Polish Power" Ivan Putski
c) Mad Dog Vachon

108. Sid Justice made his WWE debut as the referee of Ultimate Warrior and _____ vs. Sgt. Slaughter, Gen. Adnan and _____ match that was the main event of _____ '91.

109. The Hulkster first appeared in WWE in 1979 under the management of _____.

110. What superstar originally introduced Undertaker to WWE fans?
a) "Million-Dollar Man" Ted DiBiase
b) "The American Dream" Dusty Rhodes
c) Jake "The Snake" Roberts

111. Who was the original manager of the Legion of Doom?

112. What network carried WWE's first national broadcast?

113. What former Superstar represented the U.S.A. in weightlifting at the 1972 Olympics?

Announcers and Officials

114. During his days as "the Body," Jesse Ventura hosted *Saturday Night's Main Event* along with...
a) Gorilla Monsoon
b) Lord Alfred Hayes
c) Vince McMahon

115. Who was the special main event referee at *SummerSlam '88* and *'99*?

116. *WrestleMania VI* was the last *'Mania* to be called by the broadcast team of Gorilla Monsoon and...

117. Who was WWE's first female ring announcer?

118. Who was the ring announcer for the WWE's Philadelphia events during the seventies and early eighties?

119. Who was the first president of World Wrestling Entertainment?

120. Who was Vince McMahon's cohost on *Tuesday Night Titans*?

121. Who was the broadcast partner of Antonino Rocca?

122. What ring announcer has been with WWE since the seventies?

123. Gorilla Monsoon hosted *Wrestling Challenge* along with...

Great Grudges and Matches

124. In one of the most historic grudge matches of all time, Bruno Sammartino faced his former protégé Larry Zbysko in a steel cage in 1980. What stadium housed the event?
a) **Rose Bowl**
b) **Shea Stadium**
c) **Yankee Stadium**

125. _____ turned on Hulk Hogan during a 1992 tag team match on *Saturday Night's Main Event* against Ric Flair and _____.

126. **True or false:** At *WrestleMania VII,* Jake "The Snake" Roberts faced Tito Santana in a blindfold match.

127. What Superstar once tried to run Undertaker through with a sword on an episode of *Superstars*?
a) **the Berzerker**
b) **Killer Khan**
c) **the Barbarian**

128. In 1985, Hulk Hogan vs. Roddy Piper headlined *The War to Settle the Score* on what cable channel?

129. What former ally turned on Bruno Sammartino in a violent feud in 1975?

130. High Chief Peter Maivia challenged what WWE Champion in 1978?

131. Chief Jay Strongbow was betrayed by what former tag team partner in 1974?

132. Hulk Hogan faced King Kong Bundy in a steel cage in 1986 in what arena?

133. What Texan Superstar broke Bruno Sammartino's neck in 1976?

134. Who was Pedro Morales's opponent at Shea Stadium in 1972?

135. Who did Ken Patera defend the Intercontinental title against at Shea Stadium in 1980?

136. In 1977, who became the first WWE Champion to meet the NWA Champion in a unification match?

137. By defeating Lita several years ago, Ivory became only the third person to win the Women's Championship on three occasions. Who was the first?
a) Alundra Blayze
b) Wendi Richter
c) the Fabulous Moolah

Great Champions

138. Name the only competitor to simultaneously hold WWE's World and Intercontinental Championships.
a) Ultimate Warrior
b) Bob Backlund
c) Shawn Michaels

139. Undertaker won his first WWE Championship from Hulk Hogan in 1991. At which Pay-Per-View did the win occur?
a) *Tuesday in Texas*
b) *Survivor Series*
c) *Royal Rumble*

140. **True or false:** Magnificent Muraco was a two-time Intercontinental Champion.

141. Andre the Giant defeated _____ to win the WWE title, but handed it over to _____.

142. During a match with _____, Bob Backlund once had his title belt destroyed at ringside by his hated rival _____.

143. Before *Vengeance,* who was wrestling's last undisputed World Champion?
a) Pat O'Connor
b) Ric Flair
c) Buddy Rogers

144. **True or false:** Former WWE Tag Team Champion Karl Gotch was the brother of legendary World Champion Frank Gotch.

145. Who were the heaviest Tag Team Champions in history?

146. Who won the Intercontinental Championship at the last *Saturday Night's Main Event*?

147. Who was the first to simultaneously hold the Heavyweight and Tag Team titles?

148. Name the only WWE title held by Haystacks Calhoun.

149. What hold did the Iron Sheik use to defeat Bob Backlund for the Heavyweight title?

150. What was Bob Backlund's original finishing move?

151. Who managed both Bruno Sammartino and Bob Backlund?

152. In a record four consecutive main events at Madison Square Garden, Bob Backlund defended the title against...

153. Name the only WWE title held by the late Johnny Valentine.

154. "Nature Boy" Ric Flair was fond of saying, "To _____ the man, you have to _____ the man!"

155. **True or false:** Ric Flair won his first World Championship from Harley Race.

156. Who was Ric Flair's "technical adviser"?
a) Roddy Piper
b) Vince McMahon
c) Mr. Perfect

Identities

157. Former Superstar Irwin R. Schyster also competed under what name?
a) Mike Rotundo
b) Barry Windham
c) Dan Spivey

158. When Kerry Von Erich came to the WWE in _____, he used the nickname "The Texas _____" and won the _____ title from _____ at *SummerSlam.*

159. The Superstar known as Akeem also competed under what name?

160. Big Boss Man once worked as...

161. What Superstar was known as "The American Dream"?

162. Smash of Demolition also competed under a mask as . . .

163. The Godfather first appeared in the WWE in 1992 under what persona?

164. The Iron Sheik joined forces with Sgt. Slaughter in 1991 under what name?

165. Ax of Demolition also competed under a mask as . . .

166. Who wrestled under a mask as The Executioner at the first *WrestleMania*?

167. Under what name did Tony Parisi compete during his early years in the WWE?

168. Nikolai Volkoff first won the Tag Team Championship in the sixties under what name?

Great Gimmicks

169. True or false: Kamala has never appeared at *WrestleMania*.

170. Terry Taylor once competed in the WWE as . . .
a) Nailz
b) Max Moon
c) the Red Rooster

171. The WWE's country-boy trio was composed of Hillbilly Jim, Uncle Elmer and _____.

172. True or false: Honky Tonk Man never held the Tag Team Championship.

173. What was the name of the Legion of Doom's puppet mascot?
a) Roadie
b) Rocco
c) Doomsday

174. What past Superstar is responsible for squashing Damien, pet snake of Jake Roberts?
a) Yokozuna
b) King Kong Bundy
c) Earthquake

175. Who was the host of *The Barber Shop*?

176. Who was the host of *The Funeral Parlor*?

177. Who was the host of *The Snake Pit*?

178. What Superstar was famous for wearing a kilt to the ring?

179. Who did Randy Savage defeat to become the "Macho King"?

180. Who was the host of *The Flower Shop*?

181. Who was the host of *The Body Shop*?

182. Haystacks Calhoun hailed from what Arkansas town?

183. Where was Kamala from?

184. Where was Killer Khan from?

185. Who was named "King of Wrestling" when Harley Race retired in 1988?

186. What was the name of Koko B. Ware's pet bird?

187. What was the name of "Million Dollar Man" Ted DiBiase's bodyguard?

Hollywood Hulk Hogan

188. **True or false:** Undertaker appeared in the 1991 Hulk Hogan movie *Suburban Commando*.

189. In 1980, Hogan faced _____ in a historic match at New York's _____ Stadium.

190. Who was Hogan's first manager in the World Wrestling Federation?
a) The Grand Wizard
b) "Classy" Freddie Blassie
c) Capt. Lou Albano

191. Who was the only other WWE competitor besides Andre the Giant to pin Hogan before he became World Champion?
a) Tony Atlas
b) Bob Backlund
c) Blackjack Mulligan

192. Who was the first challenger to Hogan's WWE gold?
a) Big John Studd
b) "Dr. D" David Schultz
c) Magnificent Muraco

193. What manager turned Andre the Giant against the Hulkster in 1987?
a) Jimmy Hart
b) Slick
c) Bobby "The Brain" Heenan

194. Who was Hogan's opponent on the first installment of *Saturday Night's Main Event* in 1985?
a) Cowboy Bob Orton
b) "Rowdy" Roddy Piper
c) Kamala

195. What was the name of Hogan's character in the movie *No Holds Barred*?
a) **Rip**
b) **Terry Boulder**
c) **Python**

196. Which one of these Superstars did NOT break the Hulkster's ribs?
a) **King Kong Bundy**
b) **One Man Gang**
c) **Earthquake**

197. Hogan was famous for declaring, "This is where the power lies!" and pointing to what part of his anatomy?
a) **his hand**
b) **his head**
c) **his heart**

198. Hogan's classic entrance theme "Real American" was originally intended for what tag team?
a) **Tony Atlas & Rocky Johnson**
b) **Sgt. Slaughter & Cpl. Kirschner**
c) **Barry Windham & Mike Rotundo**

199. Who did Hulk Hogan defeat for his second WWE Championship?

200. **True or false:** Hulk Hogan was the first five-time WWE Champion.

TITLES

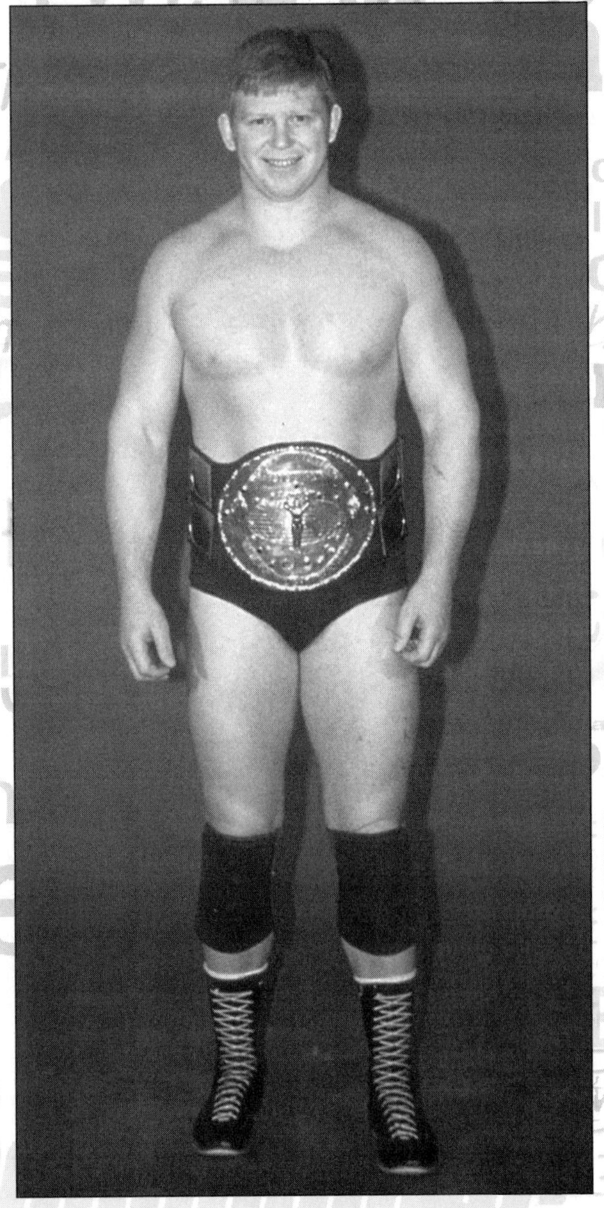

All these Federation
Superstars have worn
Championship gold.
Name them.

1. _____

2. _____

3. _____

4. _____

5. _____

6. _____

7. _____

8. _____

9. _____

10. _____

11. _____

12. _____

13. _____

14. _____

15. _____

16. _____

17. _____

18. _____

19. _____

20. _____

World Championship

21. In what city did Buddy Rogers defeat Antonino Rocca to become the first WWE World Champion?
a) New York, NY
b) London, England
c) Rio de Janeiro, Brazil
d) Albany, NY

22. The World Championship has changed hands in all these cities except:
a) Miami, FL   b) Dayton, OH
c) Nashville, TN   d) Buffalo, NY

23. Pedro Morales, the third WWE Champion, is a native of what U. S. territory?

24. The shortest reign in WWE history belongs to
a) Andre the Giant   b) Kane
c) Mankind   d) Yokozuna

25. Who did Bob Backlund defeat to win his first World Championship?

26. The first man to win the World Championship three times was:
a) Bruno Sammartino   b) Bret Hart
c) Hulk Hogan   d) Stone Cold Steve Austin

27. Which Japanese wrestler has won the World Championship?
a) Akira Maeda   b) Shinya Hashimoto
c) Antonio Inoki   d) Hiro Saito

28. The man who can claim the longest title run in history is _____.

29. **True or false:** Ivan Putski was never World Champion.

30. Randy Savage won his first World Championship at what WWE event?

31. Stone Cold Steve Austin won how many World Championships in the 1990s?
a) 3   b) 4   c) 5   d) 2

32. The name of the special empty-arena Championship match between Mankind and The Rock was called

_____.

33. How many times did The Rock beat Mankind for the World Championship?
a) 2   b) 3   c) 4   d) 1

34. The Iron Sheik defeated Bob Backlund when who threw in the towel?
a) Baron Mikel Scicluna
b) Toots Mondt
c) Sir Oliver Humperdink
d) Arnold Skaaland

35. Stan Stasiak defeated Pedro Morales to win the World Championship on December 1, 1973. Who did he lose the title to nine days later?

36. Match the following Superstars with the city in which he won his second World Championship.
a) Triple H   **1) Kansas City, MO**
b) Shawn Michaels   **2) Pittsburgh, PA**
c) Undertaker   **3) Hershey, PA**
d) Kurt Angle   **4) San Antonio, TX**
e) Ric Flair   **5) Charlotte, NC**

37. Big Show won the World Championship in a three-way match involving what other two Superstars?

38. Vince McMahon lost the World Championship to...

39. Ivan Koloff, the first man to defeat Bruno Sammartino for the World Championship was a native of what country?
a) Soviet Union   b) Ukraine
c) Slovakia   d) Poland

40. All of these Superstars won the World Championship in California except:
a) Bret Hart   b) Chris Jericho
c) The Rock   d) Hulk Hogan

Tag Team

41. The WWE Tag Team Championship was originally known as the:
a) World Wide Wrestling Federation International Tag Team Title
b) U.S. Tag Team Title
c) Collar-and-Elbow Team Title
d) Double Title

42. The first WWE Tag Team Champions were:
a) Mark Lewin & Don Curtis
b) Killer Kowalski & Gorilla Monsoon
c) Spiros Arion & Antonio Pugliese
d) Eddie & Dr. Jerry Graham

43. During the 1960s, the Tag Team Championship changed hands the most in which city?
a) New York, NY   b) Washington D.C.
c) Allentown, PA   d) New Haven, CT

44. **True or false:** Buddy Rogers never won the Tag Team Championship.

45. The first Tag Team to win the Championship four times was:
a) **the Samoans**
b) **Mr. Fuji & Mr. Saito**
c) **Billy Gunn & Road Dogg Jesse James**
d) **Demolition**

46. All of the following were Tag Team Championship partners with Tony Garea EXCEPT:
a) **Dean Ho**   b) **Rick Martel**
c) **Haystacks Calhoun**   d) **Rene Goulet**

47. Earthquake and Typhoon were also known as _____.

48. The first African-American Tag Team Champions were _____.

49. Who comprised The Executioners?

50. The Samoans were managed by:
a) **the Grand Wizard**
b) **Captain Lou Albano**
c) **"Classy" Freddie Blassie**
d) **Slick**

51. Match the decade with the number of times the tag team belts changed hands.
a) **1960s**   **1) 24**
b) **1970s**   **2) 25**
c) **1980s**   **3) 52**
d) **1990s**   **4) 21**

52. The Hart Foundation defeated whom to win their first championship?

53. How many times did The Moondogs win the Tag Team Championship?

54. Edge & Christian won their first Tag Team Championship in what city?

55. **True or false:** Cactus Jack & Terry Funk never won the Tag Team Championship.

56. Stone Cold Steve Austin has won the championship with all of the following Superstars EXCEPT:
a) **Jeff Jarrett**   b) **Undertaker**
c) **Dude Love**   d) **Triple H**

57. **True or false:** The Dudley Boyz have never beaten the Hardy Boyz for the Tag Team Championship.

58. Mankind & The Rock were also known as _____.

59. What is the name of Billy & Chuck's stylist?

60. **True or false:** No one has ever won the Tag Team Championship in three different decades.

Intercontinental

61. The tournament to decide the first Intercontinental Champion was held in which South American city?
a) **Caracas, Venezuela**
b) **Buenos Aries, Argentina**
c) **Cuzco, Peru**
d) **Rio de Janeiro, Brazil**

62. The man who won that tournament was:
a) **Pedro Morales**   b) **Pat Patterson**
c) **Mil Mascaras**   d) **Bob Backlund**

63. The first man to win the Intercontinental
Championship in the United States was:
a) **Magnificent Muraco**
b) **Greg Valentine**
c) **Pedro Morales**
d) **Ken Patera**

64. How many times did Greg Valentine win the
Intercontinental Championship?

65. True or false: Two-time Intercontinental Champion
Magnificent Muraco hailed from Waikiki Beach, Hawaii.

66. Match the following Superstars with the men they
defeated for the Intercontinental Championship.
a) **Rick Steamboat**   1) **Bret Hart**
b) **The Mountie**   2) **Razor Ramon**
c) **Jesse James**   3) **Val Venis**
d) **Diesel**   4) **Randy Savage**

67. How many men have had title runs for more than one
year?

68. The first man to win the title three times was . . .

69. True or false: Shawn Michaels was Intercontinental
Champion four times.

70. True or false: The Intercontinental Championship has
never changed hands in Europe.

71. Who did Goldust defeat to win his first
Intercontinental Championship?
a) **Savio Vega**   b) **Jeff Jarrett**
c) **Razor Ramon**   d) **Ahmed Johnson**

72. Who did Chris Jericho defeat to win his first
Intercontinental Championship?

73. Who won the Intercontinental Championship first, Edge or D'Lo Brown?

74. In which year did the Intercontinental Championship change hands the most times?
a) 2001   b) 2000   c) 1982   d) 1999

75. Triple H defeated everyone except who for the Intercontinental Championship?
a) Owen Hart   b) The Rock
c) Chris Jericho   d) Jeff Hardy

76. **True or false:** Chyna was the first woman to win the Intercontinental Championship.

77. Who was the WWE president who stripped the Ultimate Warrior of his Intercontinental Championship?

78. **True or false:** Adrian Adonis was a two-time Intercontinental Champion.

79. Edge has won the Intercontinental Championship in all these cities EXCEPT:
a) San Jose, CA
b) Toronto, Ontario, Canada
c) Jacksonville, FL
d) Greensboro, NC

80. The only Superstar listed below to win the Intercontinental Championship more than two times is:
a) Tito Santana   b) Bret Hart
c) Chris Jericho   d) Ultimate Warrior

European Championship

81. The inaugural championship match was held in what city?

82. In what year did it take place?

83. Who won that match?

84. Besides Davey Boy Smith, what other Superstar has won the championship on European soil?
a) Bradshaw   b) Crash Holly
c) Owen Hart   d) Ken Shamrock

85. All of the following Superstars have won the European Championship multiple times EXCEPT:
a) Triple H   b) X-Pac
c) Shane McMahon   d) William Regal

86. True or false: More than one European Champion has gone on to win the World Championship.

87. True or false: Matt Hardy was the first Hardy to win the European Championship.

88. D'Lo Brown defeated all the following Superstars for the European Championship EXCEPT:
a) Shawn Michaels   b) Triple H
c) X-Pac   d) Mideon

89. The first man to win the European Championship more than once was
a) X-Pac   b) D'Lo Brown
c) Davey Boy Smith   d) Triple H

90. Who is the only man to win the European
Championship by pinning his tag team partner?
a) Al Snow   b) Shane McMahon
c) Chris Jericho   d) "Iron" Mike Sharpe

91. Triple H lost the European Championship when what
Superstar impersonated him and ended up losing to
Owen Hart?
a) Billy Gunn   b) Dude Love
c) Goldust   d) Marc Mero

92. Who won the European Championship at
WrestleMania X-Seven?

93. Match the European Champion with the city in which
he won the title.
a) Owen Hart   1) Dallas, TX
b) Kurt Angle   2) Austin, TX
c) Perry Saturn   3) Davis, CA
d) Al Snow   4) Fayetteville, NC

94. True or false: Stone Cold Steve Austin has never won
the European Championship.

95. True or false: The European Championship is older
than the Light-Heavyweight Championship.

96. Which of the following Superstars is a former
European Champion?
a) Kane   b) Undertaker
c) Faarooq   d) Test

97. Who gave Mark Henry the European Championship
for helping him beat D'Lo Brown?

98. True or false: Kurt Angle lost the European Championship and Intercontinental Championship in the
same match.

99. **True or false:** Bradshaw beat The Hurricane in a cage match to win the European Championship.

100. The European Championship has been contested in all of the following cities except:
**a) Sheffield, England   b) Paris, France
c) Birmingham, England   d) Ames, IA**

Light-Heavyweight Championship

101. The first Light-Heavyweight Champion was:
**a) Brian Christopher   b) Dynamite Kid
c) 1-2-3 Kid   d) Taka Michinoku**

102. **True or false:** Christian won the Light-Heavyweight Championship in only his second televised match.

103. In what year did Duane Gill defeat Christian for the Light-Heavyweight Championship?

104. How many Light-Heavyweight Champions were there in 1997?
a) 1   b) 2   c) 3   d) 4

105. Which is older, the Light-Heavyweight Championship or the Hardcore Championship?

106. What is the most that a Superstar can weigh to be eligible for the Light-Heavyweight Championship?

107. Who unified the WWE Light-Heavyweight and WCW Cruiserweight titles by defeating Billy Kidman on July 30, 2001?

108. Who did Essa Rios defeat to win the Light-Heavyweight Championship?

109. True or false: Both members of Too Cool won the Light-Heavyweight Championship.

110. Who interfered on X-Pac's behalf and helped him defeat Tajiri at *SummerSlam 2001*?

111. Which Light-Heavyweight Champion held the title from April 25, 2000 until March 13, 2001?

112. Who is the only man ever to win the Light-Heavyweight Championship in North Dakota?

113. How many women have won the Light-Heavyweight Championship?
a) 0   b) 1   c) 2   d) 3

114. What sparked the rivalry between Dean Malenko and Crash Holly that resulted in Crash defeating Malenko for the Light-Heavyweight Championship?

115. What former ECW World Heavyweight Champion also won the Light-Heavyweight Championship?

116. Who was the tenth Light-Heavyweight Champion?

117. Who was the first Superstar to win the Light-Heavyweight Championship twice?
a) Taka Michinoku   b) X-Pac
c) Christian   d) Dean Malenko

118. Taka Michinoku first defended the Light-Heavyweight Championship at what Pay-Per-View?

119. True or false: Tajiri was the second Japanese Superstar to win the Light-Heavyweight Championship.

120. Scotty 2 Hotty won the Light-Heavyweight Championship on which "Big Ten" college campus?

Hardcore Championship

121. Mankind became the first Hardcore Champion when who presented him with the title on *Raw* in November 2, 1998?
a) **Commissioner Slaughter**   b) **Shane McMahon**
c) **Vince McMahon**   d) **The Rock**

122. Who was the first Superstar to win the Hardcore Championship in a match?

123. Who was the first Superstar to win the Hardcore Championship three times?

124. Which Superstar instituted the "24/7" rule, stating that the title would be up for grabs 24 hours a day, 7 days a week?

125. How many times did the Hardcore Championship change hands during the Hardcore battle royal at *WrestleMania XVI*?

126. Who won that battle royal?

127. Who won the Hardcore Championship first?
a) **Gerald Brisco**
b) **Pat Patterson**

128. Who was the first Superstar to win the Hardcore Championship outside the United States?
a) **Chris Jericho**   b) **Al Snow**
c) **British Bulldog**   d) **Steve Blackman**

129. Put these Superstars in the order that they won the Hardcore Championship.
a) **Billy Gunn**   b) **Bob Holly**
c) **K-Kwik**   d) **Tazz**

130. True or false: Shane McMahon was the second McMahon to win the Hardcore Championship.

131. True or false: Kurt Angle has never won the Hardcore Championship.

132. Which Hardy brother was the first to win the Hardcore Championship?

133. True or false: The Hardcore Championship has never changed hands at Madison Square Garden.

134. On which television show did Big Show defeat Rhyno to win the Hardcore Championship?
a) *Raw*
b) *SmackDown!*
c) *Sunday Night Heat*
d) *Judgment Day*

135. Which of the following WWE Champions never won the Hardcore Championship?
a) **Undertaker**   b) **Shawn Michaels**
c) **Kurt Angle**   d) **Kane**

136. Who did Test defeat to win his first Hardcore Championship?

137. What family has had three members win the Hardcore Championship?

138. True or false: Billy Gunn is the only member of DX to win the Hardcore Championship.

139. Who did Maven defeat to win his first Hardcore Championship?

140. True or false: The Hardcore Championship was Rob Van Dam's first WWE title.

Women's Championship

141. Who did the Fabulous Moolah defeat on September 18, 1956 to become the first Women's Champion?

142. In what city did this match take place?

143. How many years did Moolah's reign last?

144. Who defeated Moolah to become the second Women's Champion?

145. Who was the first woman to win the Women's Championship outside the United States?

146. The third Women's Champion was:
**a) the Fabulous Moolah   b) Sherri Martel
c) Leilani Kai   d) Wendi Richter**

147. The first Women's Champion to go by only one name was:
**a) Sable   b) Jacqueline
c) Ivory   d) Sapphire**

148. How many times did Alundra Blayze win the Women's Championship?

149. This is the only woman to have won the Women's Championship in Paris, France:
**a) Bull Nakano   b) Mon Cheri
c) Bertha Faye   d) Rockin' Robin**

150. **True or false:** The Fabulous Moolah has held the Women's Championship in five different decades.

151. The only man to win the Women's Championship is:
**a) Brooklyn Brawler   b) Harvey Whippleman
c) Goldust   d) Adrian Adonis**

152. Who did he defeat, and what was the match called?

153. List the following women in the order that they won the Women's Championship.
a) **Chyna**   b) **Debra**
c) **Lita**   d) **Ivory**

154. **True or false:** Mae Young has never won the Women's Championship.

155. Name the five women that Trish Stratus defeated to win her first Women's title.

156. **True or false:** Stephanie McMahon was the first McMahon to win the Women's title.

157. The Fabulous Moolah also competed under which following name?
a) **Super Woman**   b) **Bat Girl**
c) **Spider Lady**   d) **Feminine Mystique**

158. Jazz won her first Women's Championship in what year?

159. Debra defeated Sable for the Women's Championship in what kind of match?

160. Who declared her the winner?

Multiple Championships

161. Who was the first man to win two different WWE Championships?

162. Who was the first man to win the Tag Team Championship with two different partners?

163. Who was the first man to win the World, Intercontinental and Tag Team Championships?

164. Who's the only women to have won the Intercontinental and Women's Championships?

165. Which Superstar listed below has won the World, Tag Team, Intercontinental, Hardcore and European Championships?
a) Undertaker
b) Stone Cold Steve Austin
c) Hulk Hogan
d) Chris Jericho

166. **True or false:** Bob Backlund never won the Tag Team Championship.

167. In what order did Kane win the following Championships?
a) World Championship
b) Tag Team Championship
c) Intercontinental Championship
d) Hardcore

168. The first man to win the European and Hardcore Championships was:
a) British Bulldog   b) Val Venis
c) Kurt Angle   d) X-Pac

169. **True or false:** No McMahon has ever won more than one championship.

170. Shawn Michaels has won four different championships. Which one did he win first?

171. **True or false:** Rick Martel won two different WWE Championships.

172. Kurt Angle won both the World and Intercontinental Championships in what year?

173. How many times did Yokozuna win the World Championship?

174. **True or false:** Sgt. Slaughter has won the World and Tag Team Championships.

175. Who has won more total Championships, Billy Gunn or Andre the Giant?

176. Match the cities where The Rock first won the championship.
a) **World**   1) **Lowell, MA**
b) **Intercontinental**   2) **St. Louis, MO**
c) **Tag Team**   3) **Boston, MA**

177. Which Superstar has won the Light-Heavyweight, Tag Team, Intercontinental, European and Hardcore Championships?
a) **Christian**   b) **Edge**
c) **Rob Van Dam**   d) **Shawn Michaels**

178. **True or false:** Brutus Beefcake has won two different WWE Championships.

179. How many total championships did Tito Santana win?
a) **2**   b) **3**   c) **4**   d) **5**

180. Who won more Tag Team Championships, Tony Garea or Dominic DeNucci?

Championship Grab Bag

181. **True or false:** Swede Hanson never won a WWE Championship.

182. Who broke Billy White Wolf's neck, causing Chief Jay Strongbow and him to give up the Tag Team Championship?

183. **True or false:** Jake "The Snake" Roberts never won a WWE Championship.

184. Who did The Rock pin to win his fifth World Championship?

185. Who was the first man to win a WWE Championship outside the United States?

186. **True or false:** Both the first World and Intercontinental Championships were won in Rio de Janeiro.

187. Who did Randy Savage defeat in the finals of the World Championship Tournament at *WrestleMania IV*?

188. Who was the first WWE Undisputed Champion?

189. Multiple-time Tag Team Champion Baron Mikel Scicluna hailed from what island?

190. **True or false:** Karl Gotch, who teamed with Rene Goulet to win the Tag Team Championship, is the legendary Frank Gotch's son.

191. Who was the heaviest man ever to hold a WWE Championship?

192. Which of the following World Champions has not had a title reign last less than two weeks.
a) **Undertaker** b) **Bob Backlund**
c) **Sycho Sid** d) **Yokozuna**

193. Who was the first person to win a WWE Championship in the twenty-first century?

194. How many men did Ric Flair have to defeat in one night to win his first WWE World Championship?

195. Men on a Mission hailed from what New York City neighborhood?

196. Which of these men has never won any WWE Championships?
a) **Bad News Brown** b) **the Great Scott**
c) **Waldo Von Erich** d) **Pete Gas**

197. Which World Champion once wrestled under the name of Sterling Golden?

198. All of the following monikers have belonged to a Tag Team Champion except:
a) **Handsome** b) **Crazy**
c) **Cowboy** d) **Rawbone**

199. Who were the first two Valiant Brothers to win the Tag Team Championship?

200. Which Intercontinental Champion always told the audience, "Thank you, you've been a great audience."

OUTSIDE THE RING

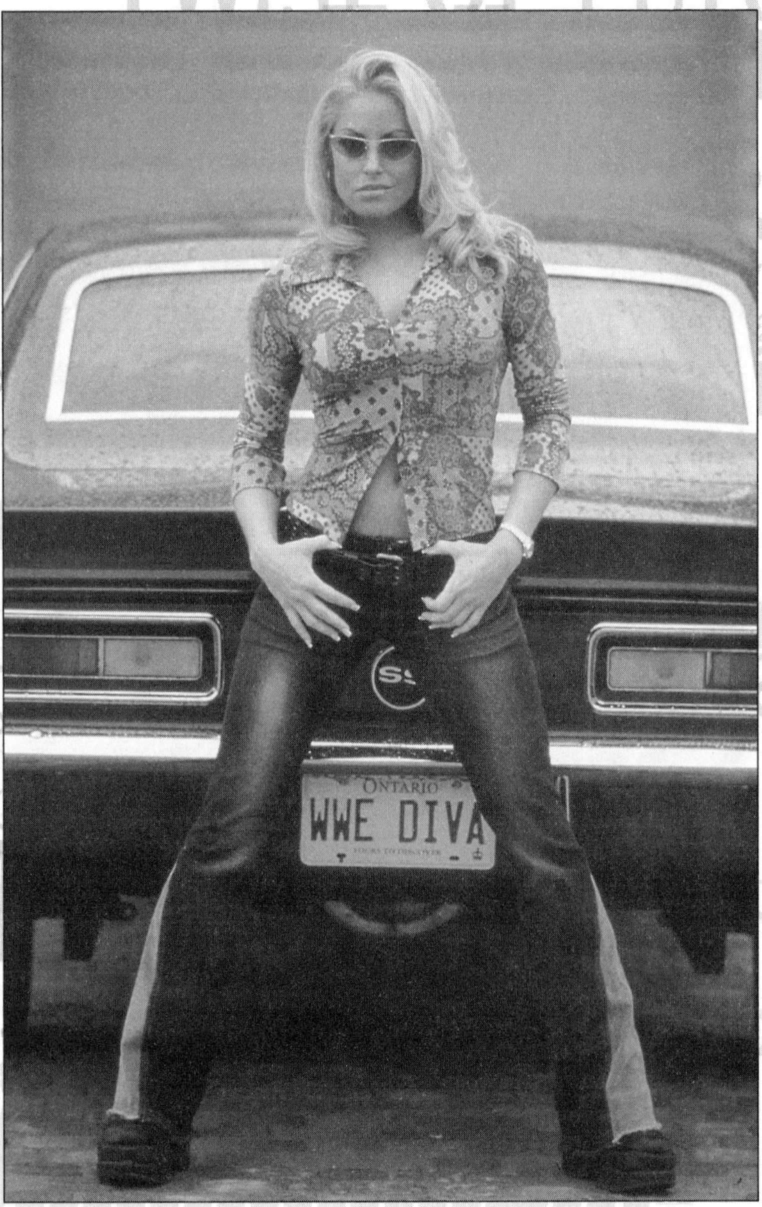
ONTARIO
WWE DIVA

Match the Superstar with his/her hometown:

a)	Maven	1)	Charlottesville, VA
b)	Brock Lesnar	2)	Minneapolis, MN
c)	Trish Stratus	3)	Dallas, GA
d)	Faarooq	4)	Dallas, TX
e)	Eddie Guerrero	5)	Toronto, Ontario, Canada
f)	Big Boss Man	6)	Yonkers, NY
g)	Jazz	7)	Point Pleasant Beach, NJ
h)	Steven Richards	8)	El Paso, TX
i)	Tommy Dreamer	9)	Mobile, AL
j)	William Regal	10)	Philadelphia, PA
k)	Chris Benoit	11)	New Orleans, LA
l)	Hardcore Holly	12)	St. Louis, MO
m)	Randy Orton	13)	Blackpool, England
n)	Diamond Dallas Page	14)	Warner Robins, GA
o)	Jacqueline	15)	Edmonton, Alberta, Canada

16. Although he didn't play organized sports in high school, Booker T was the _____.
a) drum major of the band
b) valedictorian
c) king of the pickup game
d) life of the party

17. By the time *WrestleMania X8* rolled around, Booker T's first, he had already appeared in commercials for _____ and _____.

18. In early 2002, Booker T opened _____ in Houston. The store sells music, video games and apparel.

19. Chris Jericho sings in the band Fozzy under what name?

20. What collectible item does Trish Stratus buy in every city she visits?

21. Trish Stratus once said in *WWE Magazine* that her favorite novel is _____ by Aldous Huxley.

22. In 2002, WWE had its own flavor of Slurpee at 7-Eleven stores. What was the name of the flavor?
a) **Slammin' Strawberry**
b) ***WrestleMania* Raspberry**
c) **Michael Cole Cola**
d) **Bruisin' Berry**

23. Which of the following martial arts movies did NOT feature Rob Van Dam?
a) ***Superfights***
b) ***Rush Hour***
c) ***Bloodmoon***
d) ***Black Mask 2: City of Masks***

24. Rob Vam Dam married his wife, who is named _____, on September 15, 1998.

25. Brock Lesnar was the NCAA Heavyweight Champion during his senior season at the University of _____.

26. Brock Lesnar grew up on a farm in the state of _____.

27. Kurt Angle won a gold medal in the Olympic games in _____.
a) **1992**   b) **1996**   c) **1998**   d) **2000**

28. Kurt Angle told *RAW Magazine* that, before he had to quit to concentrate on his Olympic training, he played the _____ for twenty years.
a) **drums**   b) **saxophone**
c) **bass guitar**   d) **harmonica**

29. What is the title of Kurt Angle's autobiography?

30. What does "R.E.A.L." stand for in WWE's Get R.E.A.L. program?

31. In September 2001, Bradshaw organized what kind of celebrity tournament with proceeds benefiting the North Texas Make-A-Wish Foundation?
a) pool   b) golf
c) basketball   d) fishing

32. Bradshaw was a second team All American as a junior and a consensus All American as a senior football player in college. What position did he play?

33. Stacy Keibler was once a _____ for the NFL's Baltimore Ravens.
a) radio announcer   b) cheerleader
c) quarterback   d) head coach

34. Randy Orton was in this branch of the military:
a) army   b) navy
c) air force   d) marines

35. Which of these shows did The Rock NOT appear on?
a) *That '70s Show*
b) *Saturday Night Live*
c) *The Net*
d) *Ally McBeal*

36. Chuck (a.k.a. Chuck Palumbo) was in this branch of the military:
a) army   b) navy
c) air force   d) marines

37. Perry Saturn was in this branch of the military:
a) army   b) navy
c) air force   d) marines

38. Just after winning the Olympic gold medal, Kurt
Angle had the chance to show off his instrumental
talents at which performer's concert in Pittsburgh?
a) Aerosmith   b) Ozzy Osbourne
c) Jimmy Buffett   d) Barry Manilow

39. Which of these books reached No. 1 on the *New York
Times* bestseller list?
a) *Have a Nice Day!*   b) *The Rock Says...*
c) *Foley is Good*   d) All of the above

40. In 1998, Edge flew to Bulgaria to film a role in which
feature film?

41. According to many watchers of FOX television's
America's Most Wanted, which Superstar bears a
striking resemblance to the "Civil War Bandit"?

42. Hulk Hogan was NOT featured in which of these
movies?
a) *No Holds Barred*
b) *3 Ninjas: High Noon at Mega Mountain*
c) *Mr. Nanny*
d) *Body Slam*

43. Which third-generation Superstar was born April 1,
1980?

44. Lance Storm participated in volleyball, basketball and
track and field at West Ferris Secondary School. Of
the three, which does he say he misses the most?

45. Before his days in WWE, Rico was a contestant and,
later, a cast member on which show?

46. The movie *Suburban Commando,* starring Hulk
Hogan, also featured which WWE Superstar?
a) Big Boss Man   b) Sgt. Slaughter
c) Undertaker   d) Brooklyn Brawler

47. Rico once saved a man's life while working as a police officer in _____.

48. Which Superstar won the first WWE edition of *Weakest Link*?

49. Which Superstar won the second WWE edition of *Weakest Link*?

50. Terri pens an advice column for *RAW Magazine* entitled _____.

51. Which Superstar won the first WWE edition of *Fear Factor*?

52. Jonathan "Coach" Coachman graduated from which school as its all-time leader in points, rebounds, and assists?
a) **University of Kansas**
b) **Kansas State University**
c) **McPherson College**
d) **Southwestern College**

53. During The Rock's first *Saturday Night Live* hosting gig on March 18, 2000, which other WWE Superstars appeared on the show?

54. Shawn Michaels's wife, Rebecca, was once a member of the WCW Nitro Girls. What name did she use?
a) **Whisper**   b) **Storm**   c) **Ice**   d) **Fire**

55. What is the name of the store in Miami where The Rock buys his "$500 shirts"?

56. How many new voters did the *SmackDown! Your Vote!* campaign register for the 2000 presidential election?
a) **10,000**   b) **50,000**   c) **150,000**   d) **265 million**

World Wrestling
Entertainment

57. Christian has a tattoo of a _____ on his left shoulder.

58. Undertaker's real-life wife, _____, appeared on WWE programming during the summer of 2001.

59. In 1999, Jerry "the King" Lawler ran for mayor of his hometown of _____.

60. In which movie starring Adam Sandler did Big Show appear?
a) *Big Daddy*   b) *The Waterboy*
c) *Happy Gilmore*   d) *Mr. Deeds*

61. Even though he didn't play football in college, Kurt Angle once had a tryout with the NFL's _____.

62. Chris Jericho was born in New York because his father, Ted Irvine, played for the NHL's_____.

63. Ric Flair's son _____ is a top amateur wrestler among his age group and once appeared with his father on WCW television.

64. Which of the following Superstars is NOT Canadian?
a) **Torrie Wilson**   b) **Test**
c) **Sean Morley**   d) **Lance Storm**

65. What is the name of the San Antonio, Texas-based surgeon who has operated on Stone Cold Steve Austin, Rhyno, Chris Benoit, Lita, Scotty 2 Hotty and other Superstars?

66. What is the name of the Birmingham, Alabama-based surgeon who has operated on Triple H, Kevin Nash, Kane and many other Superstars?

67. Which Superstar was the first honorary chairman of the *SmackDown! Your Vote!* campaign?
a) **Bradshaw**   b) **Ivory**
c) **Kurt Angle**   d) **Funaki**

68. What was the name of the character Triple H portrayed on *The Drew Carey Show*?

69. Which of these Superstars was NOT trained by the legendary Killer Kowalski?
a) **Hugh Morrus**   b) **Albert**
c) **Triple H**   d) **Perry Saturn**

70. Goldust and Terri have a daughter named _____.

71. What legendary competitor is Goldust's father?

72. Albert graduated from college with a degree in _____ and a minor in _____.

73. Once Lita decided that she wanted to pursue a career in sports-entertainment, she traveled to _____ to learn from the area's renowned high-flyers.

74. Which WWE referee owns the Friendly Tap in Cumberland, Rhode Island?
a) **Jack Doan**   b) **Tim White**
c) **Jim Korderas**   d) **Earl Hebner**

75. In 2002, WWE created WWE Films, naming Joel Simon president. Which movie did Simon NOT help to create?
a) *Juwanna Man*   b) *Hard to Kill*
c) *Married to the Mob*   d) *X-Men*

76. Which former member of the Radicalz became a WWE road agent in 2001?

77. How is Jamal related to Rikishi?
a) **cousin**   b) **son**
c) **nephew**   d) **brother**

78. Which United States Football League team was Ivory once a cheerleader for?

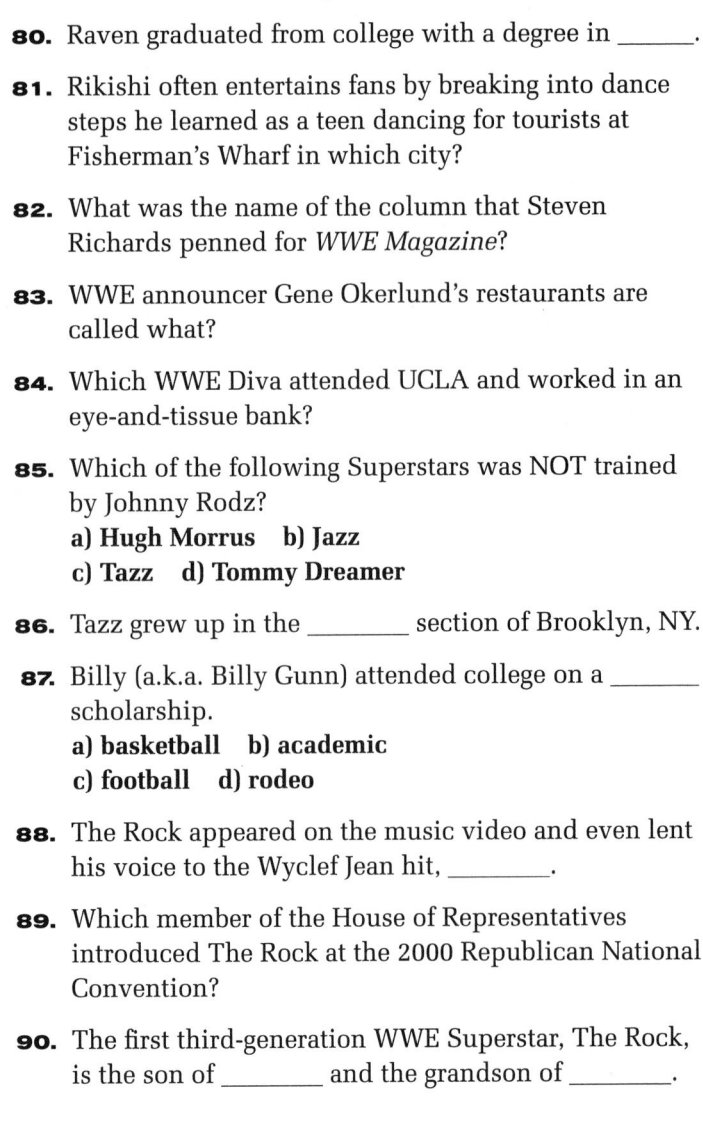
79. Which cosmetics company did Ivory once work for?

80. Raven graduated from college with a degree in _____.

81. Rikishi often entertains fans by breaking into dance steps he learned as a teen dancing for tourists at Fisherman's Wharf in which city?

82. What was the name of the column that Steven Richards penned for *WWE Magazine*?

83. WWE announcer Gene Okerlund's restaurants are called what?

84. Which WWE Diva attended UCLA and worked in an eye-and-tissue bank?

85. Which of the following Superstars was NOT trained by Johnny Rodz?
a) Hugh Morrus   b) Jazz
c) Tazz   d) Tommy Dreamer

86. Tazz grew up in the _____ section of Brooklyn, NY.

87. Billy (a.k.a. Billy Gunn) attended college on a _____ scholarship.
a) basketball   b) academic
c) football   d) rodeo

88. The Rock appeared on the music video and even lent his voice to the Wyclef Jean hit, _____.

89. Which member of the House of Representatives introduced The Rock at the 2000 Republican National Convention?

90. The first third-generation WWE Superstar, The Rock, is the son of _____ and the grandson of _____.

91. In college, The Rock played the position of ____ on the football team; he backed up future NFL great ____.

92. In 1999, which weekly publication named The Rock one of the "Sexiest Men Alive"?

93. Trish Stratus studied _____ in college.
a) political science
b) English literature
c) physics and astronomy
d) biology and kinesiology

94. Hulk Hogan starred as R. J. "Hurricane" Spencer in what syndicated action series?

95. What was the name of the Saturday morning cartoon in the mid-1980s featuring Hulk Hogan and the other WWE Superstars of that era?

96. What are the original three demandments of *Hulkamania*?

97. Which Tampa college did Hulk Hogan attend before he got into wrestling?

98. Since 1999, Chris Jericho has participated annually in "SuperSkate," a celebrity hockey game at New York's Madison Square Garden. What is the primary charity that benefits from the game?

99. Which of the following Superstars was NOT trained in the Hart Family dungeon?
a) Chris Benoit   b) Chris Jericho
c) Lance Storm   d) Trish Stratus

100. What does the K stand for in Vincent K. McMahon?

Match these Superstars with the TV show on which they appeared:

101. The Rock	a)	*The Huntress*
102. The Big Valbowski	b)	*The Strip*
103. Hulk Hogan	c)	*Suddenly Susan*
104. Rob Van Dam	d)	*Dark Angel*
105. Bradshaw	e)	*The X-Files*
106. Triple H	f)	*Grown-Ups*
107. Kevin Nash	g)	*Star Trek: Voyager*
108. Lita	h)	*Sabrina the Teenage Witch*
109. Booker T	i)	*Charmed*
110. Godfather	j)	*La Femme Nikita*

111. Kevin Nash played _____ in *Teenage Mutant Ninja Turtles 2: The Secret of the Ooze.*

112. Hulk Hogan played _____ in *Rocky III.*

113. Jim Ross played the role of Gordon Solie in the 1999 feature film _____.

114. Edge says that his one "weakness" is that he absolutely loves _____.
a) cookies   b) candy
c) cars   d) clothing

115. Terri was once the makeup artist on which television talk show?

116. Torrie Wilson grew up on a farm in which town?

117. After graduating from college, D'Lo Brown soon became a _____.
a) sportswriter
b) certified public accountant
c) lawyer
d) truck driver

118. WWE senior official Earl Hebner once played a referee in which TV series?
a) *City Guys*
b) *Sabrina, the Teenage Witch*
c) *Boy Meets World*
d) *Spin City*

119. In 2001, Scotty 2 Hotty's wife gave birth to a baby girl, who they named _____.

120. In which country did ring announcer Lilian Garcia live for eight years?
a) **England**   b) **Venezuela**
c) **Spain**   d) **Mexico**

121. Lilian Garcia graduated cum laude from the University of _____.

122. Which of the following Superstars was NOT a trainer on the first season of *Tough Enough*?
a) **Al Snow**   b) **Ivory**
c) **Jacqueline**   d) **Tazz**

123. At the season finale of the first season of *Tough Enough,* Maven won a WWE contract, beating out fellow male finalists _____ and _____.

124. Who was the female runner-up to Nidia on the first season of *Tough Enough*?

125. The trainers for *Tough Enough 2* were Al Snow, Ivory, Hardcore Holly and _____.

126. The trainers for *Tough Enough 3* were Al Snow, Ivory and _____.

127. What was the name of the 2000 made-for-TV movie featuring Hardcore Holly?

128. Shawn Stasiak is the son of former WWE Champion
_____.

129. Paul Heyman played the announcer in which 2002
feature film starring LL Cool J and Chris Klein?

130. Which cartoon character has Crash Holly often been
compared with?

131. Mark Henry was on the U.S. Olympic Team in which
years?
a) 1990 & 1994   b) 1992 & 2000
c) 1992 & 1996   d) 1996 & 1998

132. In February 2002, Mark Henry earned the distinction
of being the strongest man in the world when he won
the Arnold Strongman Challenge, which is named
after whom?

133. Released in February 2001, *WWE: The Music, Volume
5* debuted at what number on the *Billboard* Top 200?

134. Which longtime WWE ring announcer also played the
ring announcer in the 1989 feature film *No Holds
Barred*?

135. Which veteran referee has won a large handful of
humanitarian awards in his hometown of Atlanta?

136. Which legendary rap group released a remixed
version of the D-Generation X theme song entitled
"The Kings" in 2000?

137. "The Kings" was one of thirteen WWE Superstar
entrance themes remixed for what hip-hop album?

138. The World, WWE's Times Square-based restaurant
and entertainment complex, is located on the corner
of what two streets?

139. Which wrestling legend, who was once a WWE Tag Team Champion as part of The Brain Busters, is now a WWE road agent?

140. Jerry "the King" Lawler portrayed masked wrestler "the Lobotomizer" in which Michael J. Fox film?
a) *Bright Lights, Big City*
b) *Back to the Future Part II*
c) *Doc Hollywood*
d) *Life with Mikey*

141. Which former WWE Champion ran in 2000 to represent Connecticut in the U.S. House of Representatives?

142. Hulk Hogan is an accomplished _____ player who played professionally for ten years before getting into the sports-entertainment business.

143. Stacy Keibler's legs are _____ inches long.

144. Before he resigned to be a contestant on *Tough Enough,* Maven taught _____ grade at Twality Middle School in Tigard, OR.

145. Edge earned the right to attend wrestling school for free when he won an essay contest sponsored by ____.

146. Which fast-food restaurant did Molly Holly work at before she got into sports entertainment?
a) Burger King   b) Subway
c) McDonald's   d) Arby's

147. As a young teen, X-Pac decided he wanted to be a wrestler. What was his backup plan if he didn't make it?

148. Name the five men who make up wrestling's controversial "Kliq."

149. WWE had an upper hand in recruiting Brock Lesnar and Shelton Benjamin because the two men's college wrestling coach, J Robinson, was a college roommate of what WWE agent?

150. After he graduated from college, Brock Lesnar had tryouts with two NFL teams. Which were they?
a) Seattle Seahawks and Minnesota Vikings
b) Tampa Bay Buccaneers and Washington Redskins
c) San Diego Chargers and Pittsburgh Steelers
d) Denver Broncos and Oakland Raiders

151. On which CNBC financial show does Bradshaw frequently appear?

152. Trish Stratus participated in which two sports in high school?
a) basketball and tennis
b) wrestling and field hockey
c) field hockey and soccer
d) water polo and cross country

153. Long before he got into the business, Booker T took a job at what kind of company to support his young son?
a) real estate   b) fast food
c) ministorage   d) construction

154. A huge hockey fan, Ric Flair's favorite NHL team is the _____.
a) Chicago Blackhawks
b) Dallas Stars
c) Carolina Hurricanes
d) Los Angeles Kings

155. Christian is a good friend of which professional tennis player?

156. What types of animals does William Regal raise at home?
a) cows and horses   b) dogs and cats
c) pigs and chickens   d) lizards and snakes

157. Although he grew up in Toronto, Edge's favorite hockey team is the _____ because he liked the team's uniforms as a youngster.

158. On November 8, 2001, Edge married his girlfriend Alanah. Which WWE Superstar is Alanah's brother?

159. Tajiri is fluent in Japanese and what other language?

160. Hardcore Holly races cars in his spare time. What kind of cars?

161. What former WWE legend trained Jazz before his tragic death in an automobile accident?

162. What sport did The Big Valbowski participate in from age five to age eighteen?

163. What kind of jerseys does Al Snow collect?

164. Tazz and which other Superstar were the trainers at ECW's "House of Hardcore."

165. Kid Rock re-recorded the ZZ Top classic "Legs" for Stacy Keibler's entrance music. Which album did that song appear on?

166. Jacqueline was the only woman at a wrestling school run by former ring great _____.

167. Tazz is a good friend of B-Real of the rap/hip-hop group _____.

168. Although he didn't attend the school, Tazz is a big fan of which college football team?
a) **Syracuse**   b) **Texas**
c) **UCLA**   d) **Nebraska**

169. How old was Johnny Stamboli when he moved out of his parent's house?
a) **17**   b) **18**   c) **22**   d) **16**

170. Which former WWE Superstar is Rosie's father?
a) **Afa**   b) **Tonga Kid**   c) **Haku**   d) **Sika**

171. Molly Holly was a star on the high school ____ team.
a) **gymnastics**   b) **basketball**
c) **field hockey**   d) **swimming**

172. Jeff Hardy built a twenty-three-foot "aluminummy" (mummy made of aluminum) at his house. What did he name it?
a) **Matt**   b) **Lita**
c) **Hercules**   d) **Neroammmmy**

173. In February 2002, Diamond Dallas Page was invited to a "Master's Tea" at which Ivy League institution?

174. Which WWE agent approached Diamond Dallas Page several years ago at a nightclub in Florida and asked DDP why he wasn't in the wrestling business?

175. Which WWE Superstar worked as Oliver Platt's stunt double in the feature film *Ready to Rumble*?

176. Which WWE Superstar trained Jay Leno and Karl Malone as those two men prepared to wrestle on WCW Pay-Per-Views?
a) **Perry Saturn**   b) **Billy Kidman**
c) **Chris Kanyon**   d) **Raven**

177. Which current WWE agent trained Molly Holly and Jamie Noble for the ring?

178. How much money did WWE donate to the World Trade Center disaster relief effort?

179. What is the name of the official WWE cookbook, written by Jim Ross?

180. In 2000, The Rock was named Chris Grecius Celebrity Wish Granter of the Year by which children's charity?

Match these Superstars with the colleges they attended:

181. Lance Storm	a) Clarion University
182. Big Show	b) University of Pittsburgh
183. Bradshaw	c) University of Maine
184. Kevin Nash	d) Abilene Christian University
185. D'Lo Brown	e) University of Southern California
186. Raven	f) Wilfrid Laurier University
187. Trish Stratus	g) University of Nevada-Reno
188. Spike Dudley	h) University of Miami
189. John Cena	i) Red River College
190. Albert	j) Springfield College
191. Billy Gunn	k) Florida State University
192. Chris Jericho	l) Towson University
193. Christian	m) Humber College
194. Faarooq	n) Wichita State University
195. The Godfather	o) Skidmore College
196. Ivory	p) University of Tennessee
197. Maven	q) Eastern Mennonite University
198. Kurt Angle	r) University of Delaware
199. The Rock	s) York University
200. Stacy Keibler	t) Sam Houston State University

ANSWERS

WrestleMania

1. c) March 31, 1985
2. False—the first *WrestleMania* was seen by over one million people on closed circuit.
3. b) Morton Downey Jr.
4. b) Tito Santana vs. the Executioner
5. a) The Tag Team Championship
6. c) Cyndi Lauper
7. b) $15,000
8. c) Muhammad Ali and Pat Patterson
9. d) Madison Square Garden
10. b) 9 seconds
11. d) Paul Orndorff

WrestleMania 2

12. a) Jake Roberts and c) Bret Hart
13. b) 3
14. c) Cab Calloway
15. d) It was a double countout.
16. b) Cpl. Kirschner
17. b) Lawrence Taylor
18. c) Detroit
19. a) King Kong Bundy
20. c) Bruce Springsteen
21. c) Brutus Beefcake & Greg Valentine
22. b) Joan Rivers
23. a) Bobby "The Brain" Heenan
24. d) Lee Marshall

WrestleMania III

25. c) The Rolling Stones
26. b) Pontiac Silverdome
27. b) It was the first time the Intercontinental Championship changed hands at *WrestleMania.*
28. a) Little Beaver & Haiti Kid
29. d) The loser had to bow down to the winner.
30. c) Aretha Franklin
31. b) NCAA Final Four
32. a) Roddy Piper
33. d) Frankie
34. c) Dino Bravo
35. a) Joey Morella
36. b) Hercules

WrestleMania IV

37. c) What the World Is Watching
38. b) Jack Tunney
39. d) 14
40. a) Bad News Brown
41. d) Butch Reed
42. b) It was a double disqualification.
43. c) Brutus won by disqualification.
44. d) Bobby Heenan
45. b) Robin Leach
46. a) 15
47. c) Ted DiBiase
48. b) *Survivor Series 1998*

WrestleMania V

49. c) Blue Blazer
50. b) Tully Blanchard & Arn Anderson
51. a) Ultimate Warrior
52. d) Morton Downey Jr.
53. c) Brother Love
54. a) the Mega Powers
55. b) Run-DMC
56. c) Bobby Heenan
57. d) "Superfly" Jimmy Snuka
58. b) Miss Elizabeth
59. a) Shawn Michaels
60. c) Big Boss Man & Akeem

WrestleMania VI

61. b) Sapphire
62. d) Toronto, Ontario, Canada
63. c) Intercontinental Championship
64. b) Edge
65. c) 67,678
66. d) Robert Goulet
67. a) Rona Barrett
68. d) the Orient Express
69. b) Mr. Perfect
70. c) Demolition
71. b) Mary Tyler Moore
72. c) "Hacksaw"
73. a) 1
74. b) Rick Martel
75. c) The Ultimate Challenge

WrestleMania VII

76. d) Henry Winkler
77. b) Shawn Michaels
78. c) Andre the Giant
79. a) the Nasty Boys
80. c) Blindfold Match
81. d) Genichiro Tenryu & Koji Kitao
82. c) Iraq
83. a) Paul Roma & Hercules
84. b) the World Championship

85. c) Undertaker
86. d) Howard Finkel
87. d) Alex Trebek
88. b) George Steinbrenner and Paul Maguire
89. a) The Rockers
90. c) Willie Nelson
91. b) Ted DiBiase & Virgil
92. c) Regis Philbin
93. a) Macaulay Culkin
94. d) Randy Savage

WrestleMania VIII

95. b) Hoosier Dome
96. c) Ray Combs
97. d) Ultimate Warrior
98. a) Undertaker
99. c) Tatanka
100. b) Bret Hart
101. c) a spittoon

102. b) second
103. b) Smash of Demolition
104. c) El Matador
105. d) All of the above.
106. b) Reba McEntire
107. c) Papa Shango
108. c) Sweet Chin Music

WrestleMania IX

109. b) Bob Backlund
110. c) Intercontinental Championship
111. d) Rick & Scott
112. d) Finkus Maximus
113. a) 2
114. b) Jim Ross
115. c) Rikishi
116. a) It was the first

WrestleMania held outdoors.
117. b) Kona, HI
118. c) Ted DiBiase & Irwin R. Schyster
119. b) "the Narcissist"
120. c) Harvey Whippleman
121. b) Sy Sperling
122. d) Roddy Piper

WrestleMania X

123. d) Owen Hart
124. c) Hulk Hogan and Tito Santana
125. a) Doink & Dink
126. b) The Quebecers
127. c) ladder match
128. b) Marvin

129. c) Johnny Polo
130. a) Mr. Perfect
131. c) Donnie Wahlberg
132. b) 1968
133. c) Three Mile Island
134. d) Jennie Garth

WrestleMania XI

135. c) Hartford, CT
136. a) baseball
137. b) Lawrence Taylor
138. c) Jacob & Eli Blu
139. b) Yokozuna
140. d) King Kong Bundy

141. b) It was an "I Quit" match.
142. c) Lex Luger
143. b) Jenny McCarthy
144. c) chess
145. d) Nicholas Turturro

WrestleMania XII

146. c) A Hollywood Backlot Brawl
147. c) Hunter Hearst-Helmsley

148. b) Anaheim, CA
149. d) Gorilla Monsoon
150. d) None of the above
151. c) Tombstone Piledriver

WrestleMania 13

152. a) Sycho Sid
153. b) Bret Hart
154. c) Ahmed Johnson

155. d) Faarooq
156. a) the Headbangers

WrestleMania XIV

157. b) Gennifer Flowers
158. c) LOD 2000
159. b) Papi Chulo
160. c) Terry Funk
161. b) They are father and son.

162. c) 3
163. c) a defense of the European Championship at *WrestleMania*
164. b) Boston, MA
165. d) Kane

WrestleMania XV

166. b) The Ragin' Climax
167. c) Butterbean
168. c) Hardcore Holly

169. d) the Mean Street Posse
170. a) Mick Foley
171. d) Triple H

WrestleMania XVI

172. b) Fatal Four-Way
173. b) Vince McMahon
174. b) European Championship
175. d) Ice-T

176. a) Kane & Rikishi
177. c) Trish Stratus
178. b) Edge & Christian
179. c) Anaheim, CA
180. d) Hardcore Holly

WrestleMania X-Seven

181. b) *Axxess*
182. a) Chris Jericho
183. c) Iron Sheik
184. b) Tazz
185. c) Motörhead
186. c) 5

187. b) Linda McMahon
188. a) the Eighth Wonder of the World
189. c) 3–0
190. b) Right to Censor

WrestleMania X8

191. c) 10–0
192. d) Booker T
193. c) Pedigree
194. b) Nash and Hall
195. b) Intercontinental Championship

196. c) Arn Anderson
197. b) Charles Robinson
198. c) Maven
199. c) Trish Stratus
200. a) Jazz

Raw Answers

1. c) Manhattan Center
2. Koko B. Ware vs. Yokozuna
3. Vince McMahon, Randy Savage and Rob Bartlett
4. Bobby Heenan
5. Ric Flair

6. Marty Jannetty, Shawn Michaels, Intercontinental
7. Diesel
8. the Lex Express
9. Province of Quebec Rules
10. "The Model" Rick Martel

1994

11. 1-2-3 Kid & Marty Jannetty
12. Johnny Polo
13. Thurman "Sparky" Plugg
14. Dr. Tom Prichard

15. Earthquake and Yokozuna
16. Matt Hardy
17. 1-2-3 Kid (X-Pac)
18. c) Fake Undertaker
19. d) Brian Pillman
20. a) Undertaker

1995

21. the Allied Powers
22. Howard Finkel and Harvey Whippleman
23. Smokin' Gunns
24. b) Mantaur
25. Sid

26. Triple H (Hunter Hearst-Helmsley)
27. the Mall of America in Minneapolis
28. Owen Hart & Yokozuna
29. Isaac Yankem, D.D.S.
30. Owen Hart

1996

31. football
32. Smokin' Gunns
33. "Billionaire Ted's Rasslin' Warroom"
34. "The Ringmaster" Steve Austin
35. The Million-Dollar Belt
36. "The Brother Love Show"

37. Phineas I. Godwinn
38. Mankind
39. Faarooq
40. "Wildman" Marc Mero
41. Bret Hart
42. Triple H
43. Brian Pillman
44. Kevin Kelly

1997

45. Sycho Sid defeated Bret Hart
46. c) Steve Corino
47. Stone Cold Steve Austin
48. a) Madison Square Garden
49. Cactus Jack
50. Vince McMahon
51. Kane
52. Nation of Domination

53. Goldust (Dustin Runnels)
54. Butterbean
55. c) "Bret screwed Bret!"
56. New Age Outlaws
57. "Nugget"
58. strip poker
59. The Rock
60. He threw it off a bridge.
61. c) WWE would be moving in a more adult direction.

62. Shawn Michaels, Triple H, Chyna

63. Santa Claus

64. Triple H

65. Goldust

66. Chainsaw Charlie

1998

67. Jeff Jarrett

68. Stone Cold Steve Austin

69. Goldust

70. Cactus Jack & Chainsaw Charlie (Terry Funk)

71. b) suit and tie

72. Stone Cold Steve Austin vs. Mr. McMahon

73. Norfolk Scope

74. d) All of the above

75. Sam's Club

76. a) Zip

77. Patterson and Brisco

78. Parade of Human Oddities

79. Kane & Mankind

80. Edge

81. Brawl-For-All

82. "Dr. Death" Steve Williams

83. Bradshaw

84. Shamrock

85. Kane

86. Undertaker

87. The Crock

88. Mizark Henry

89. B'Lo

90. Shawn Michaels

91. Val Venis

92. Jacqueline, Sable

93. Zamboni

94. b) ring steps

95. Mr. Socko

96. Corvette

97. Ken Shamrock

98. a) The Rock won the Intercontinental Championship.

99. Hardcore

100. Mills Lane

101. c) Duane Gill

102. Shawn Michaels

103. Test

104. Mankind

1999

105. Triple H
106. Chyna
107. Mr. McMahon
108. Shane won X-Pac's European Championship
109. Ladder match
110. a beer truck
111. The Godfather
112. Big Boss Man
113. Ken Shamrock, Big Show
114. It was the most watched match in the history of Monday night wrestling, at the time.
115. Vince McMahon
116. Stone Cold Steve Austin
117. b) Road Dogg won the Intercontinental Championship.
118. Shane McMahon
119. Undertaker
120. Hardy Boyz
121. Michael Hayes
122. Ben Stiller
123. Intercontinental and European
124. "Y2J" Chris Jericho made his WWE debut
125. Jesse Ventura
126. Chyna
127. Mankind
128. Triple H, Shane McMahon
129. The Rock 'N' Sock Connection
130. Mr. Hughes
131. Jeff Jarrett
132. "This Is Your Life"
133. Al Snow
134. D-Generation X
135. Triple H
136. Vince, Shane, Stephanie
137. Mankind

2000

138. Triple H, Big Show
139. The Radicalz—Benoit, Guerrero, Malenko and Saturn
140. The Rock
141. "Hervina" Harvey Whippleman
142. Kane
143. Vince McMahon
144. Mick Foley
145. Chyna
146. Chris Jericho
147. Kurt Angle, Big Show, Chris Benoit
148. Too Cool

149. a-2) The Rock vs. T&A, b-1) Kane vs. Hardy Boyz, c-3) Undertaker vs. Bull Buchanan & Big Boss Man
150. The Rock
151. Steve Blackman, Hardcore
152. Stone Cold Steve Austin
153. ladder, Hardy Boyz, Edge and Christian
154. Ivory
155. K-Kwik

2001

156. d) Matt Hardy and Lita had their first kiss.
157. a) Kiss him.
158. Shane McMahon
159. Dudley Boyz
160. True
161. Stone Cold, Triple H
162. c) Val Venis won the Intercontinental Championship.
163. Stu Hart
164. Lance Storm
165. Jesse Ventura
166. Angle did a moonsault, Benoit did a diving headbutt
167. Mike Awesome
168. Booker T and Buff Bagwell
169. Extreme Championship Wrestling (ECW)
170. The Rock
171. Stephanie McMahon-Helmsley
172. "Stone Cold Appreciation Night"
173. "Wind Beneath Our Ring"
174. Tazz
175. a milk truck
176. Toronto—the brothers' hometown
177. Stone Cold, Kurt Angle, William Regal
178. a-3) Bradshaw—European, b-1) Tajiri—Cruiserweight, c-2) Kurt Angle—U.S., d-4) The Rock—Tag Team Championship (with Chris Jericho)
179. b) Kurt Angle
180. Street Fight
181. WCW
182. Intercontinental, Tag Team
183. Jerry "the King" Lawler, Ric Flair

184. Mick Foley

185. William Regal

186. Jim Ross

187. Triple H

188. b) *The Beverly Hillbillies*

189. c) She was pregnant.

190. Howard Finkel

191. d) All of the above

192. Brock Lesnar

193. Undertaker

194. a) Triple H won the WWE Championship.

195. Kane

196. Big Show

197. c) Get the "F" out

198. Chris Benoit

199. Rob Van Dam

200. Eric Bischoff

SummerSlam Answers

1. August

2. five

3. twice

4. *WrestleMania 2*

5. *SummerSlam 1992*

6. Edge

7. a) 28 seconds

8. Brutus "the Barber" Beefcake

9. "Outlaw" Ron Bass

10. Jimmy "Mouth of the South" Hart

11. c) 18 months

12. c) Shawn Michaels

13. Leslie Nielsen (Lt. Frank Drebin) and George Kennedy (Captain Ed Hocken)

14. Ted DiBiase

15. the Mega-Powers

16. Where the Mega-Powers . . . Meet the Mega-Bucks!

17. Regis Philbin

18. 1993

19. d) Gorilla Monsoon and "Superstar" Billy Graham

20. She tore off her skirt.

21. d) Bobby "The Brain" Heenan

22. Baron Von Raschke

23. Koko B. Ware

24. c) Marty Jannetty

25. Jesse "the Body" Ventura

26. Jake "The Snake" Roberts

27. Ghetto Blaster

28. "Hacksaw" Jim Duggan

29. d) A time-limit draw

30. Feel the Heat!

31. b) Tony Schiavone and Jesse "the Body" Ventura
32. Joey Marella
33. a) Anderson pinned Hart
34. Elvis Presley
35. b) Cage match
36. Tito Santana
37. "Rowdy" Roddy Piper
38. Barry Horowitz
39. Ronnie Garvin
40. Virgil
41. d) countout
42. Miss Elizabeth and "Sensational Queen" Sherri
43. Zeus and "Macho Man" Randy Savage
44. the Genius (a.k.a. Lanny Poffo)
45. The Red Rooster (a.k.a. Terry Taylor)
46. Demolition
47. c) Vince McMahon and "Rowdy" Roddy Piper
48. The Heat Returns!
49. a) Helsinki, Finland
50. "Texas Tornado" Kerry Von Erich
51. d) Mike Chioda
52. Sgt. Slaughter
53. Tag Team
54. Cage
55. a) pinfall
56. Earthquake
57. d) Big Boss Man

58. "God Bless America"
59. Hercules & Paul Roma
60. Big Boss Man
61. a) a cage full of sewer rats
62. Ted DiBiase
63. d) Owen Hart
64. Koko B. Ware vs. Kato
65. A Match Made in Heaven . . . A Match Made in Hell!
66. "Macho Man" Randy Savage and Elizabeth
67. Gorilla Monsoon, Bobby "The Brain" Heenan, "Rowdy" Roddy Piper
68. Mr. Perfect; first
69. the Sharpshooter
70. Jake "The Snake" Roberts, Undertaker
71. the Nation of Domination
72. Million-Dollar Championship
73. c) Tatanka joined the Corporation
74. 3—Intercontinental, Tag Team, Million Dollar
75. Hulk Hogan, Ultimate Warrior
76. Iron Sheik
77. Sid Justice
78. a) Greg "the Hammer" Valentine
79. Stone Cold Steve Austin
80. Vince McMahon, Jim

Ross, Mr. Perfect
81. Justin "Hawk" Bradshaw
82. Mankind
83. a) Sycho Sid
84. Mark Henry
85. APA
86. right arm
87. Paul Bearer
88. a) Kama
89. Vader
90. b) twice
91. Diesel and Mabel
92. Opposites Attack!
93. b) submission
94. a) Aaron Neville
95. c) 80,355
96. none
97. Hart and Soul
98. Vince McMahon, Jim Ross, Jerry "the King" Lawler
99. She slammed the cage door into his head.
100. a heart
101. c) Jimmy "Superfly" Snuka
102. Dude Love
103. Davey Boy Smith
104. He had to wear a dress
105. Dan "the Beast" Severn
106. dog food
107. d) disqualification
108. c) Spend the night in jail.
109. a broken neck
110. Kiss Owen Hart's ass.

111. Lex Express
112. Undertaker; fifth
113. He would never wrestle in the United States.
114. "O Canada" (Canadian National Anthem)
115. Paul Bearer, Owen Hart, Brian Pillman
116. d) Shawn Michaels
117. New Jersey Governor Christine Todd Whitman
118. Howard Finkel
119. a) "Highway to Hell"
120. Walter Payton
121. Insane Clown Posse
122. c) Kaientai
123. d) Jeff Jarrett
124. Shawn Michaels
125. Kane
126. a) the Godwinns
127. a) ladder match
128. Triple H
129. d) right knee
130. a) broken coccyx
131. Kane
132. Shawn Michaels vs. Razor Ramon, which was a ladder match
133. Jim Ross and Jerry "the King" Lawler
134. WWE Championship, Intercontinental Championship, European Championship, Hardcore

Championship, Tag
Team Championship

135. "An Out of Body
Experience"

136. a) John Randle

137. sixth; first

138. Mark Henry and Debra

139. Adam Bomb, Kwang

140. Lion's Den Weapons

141. Greenwich Street
Fight/Love Her or Leave
Her match

142. To stay out of Test and
Stephanie's personal
lives

143. Al Snow and Big Boss
Man

144. d) Chris Jericho

145. A Kiss My Ass match

146. a) Acolytes

147. c) Tori

148. Luna

149. Undertaker & Big
Show

150. Stone Cold Steve Austin,
Mankind, Triple H

151. Jesse "the Body" Ventura

152. Mankind

153. c) Tables, Ladders &
Chairs

154. Steven Richards

155. Steven Richards pinned
Scotty 2 Hotty

156. X-Pac

157. Crush vs. Repo Man

158. c) countout

159. b) Chyna

160. glass candy jar

161. Test and Albert

162. d) Best-of-Three Falls

163. a) Lita

164. b) Edge & Christian

165. d) Thong Stinkface
match

166. a) Vince McMahon and
Jerry "the King"
Lawler

167. Al Snow

168. Perry Saturn

169. Diana (Bret's sister;
Davey's wife)

170. The Boiler Room Brawl
vs. Mankind

171. c) his mask

172. c) severe concussion

173. United Center

174. a) The Rock retained the
WWE Championship.

175. Jim Ross and Paul
Heyman

176. a) Jazz

177. Intercontinental; second

178. Jeff Hardy and Rob Van
Dam

179. Smokin' Gunns,
Bodydonnas, New
Rockers, Godwinns

180. d) disqualification

181. a) 1993

182. Vince McMahon and

Bobby "The Brain" Heenan
183. The Rock
184. Shawn Michaels, Triple H
185. Rest in Peace match
186. Tes
187. c) countout
188. The Rock, Brock Lesnar
189. Rey Mysterio
190. Madison Square Garden

191. East Rutherford, NJ
192. Philadelphia, PA
193. London, England
194. Auburn Hills, MI
195. Chicago, IL
196. Pittsburgh, PA
197. Cleveland, OH
198. Minneapolis, MN
199. Raleigh, NC
200. San Jose, CA

Royal Rumble

1. c) "Ravishing" Rick Rude
2. b) Pat Patterson
3. False—It was seen on the USA Network.
4. d) Bret Hart
5. a) 20
6. c) "Hacksaw" Jim Duggan
7. c) "Hacksaw" Jim Duggan
8. b) Butch Reed
9. b) 715 pounds
10. d) Jesse Ventura
11. c) Ax and Smash
12. b) Big John Studd
13. d) Rockin' Robin
14. a) Haku
15. b) "Hacksaw" Jim Duggan

16. c) Ted DiBiase
17. a) Ted DiBiase
18. b) Jake Roberts's snake, Damian, spooked Andre.
19. b) 1
20. c) Tully Blanchard & Arn Anderson
21. b) Hulk Hogan
22. c) Mr. Perfect
23. d) The Bushwackers
24. c) 6—At the time, Hogan had eliminated the most of anyone in *Royal Rumble* history.
25. a) Koko B. Ware
26. b) the Genius
27. c) Akeem
28. d) Red Rooster
29. c) The Hammer

30. True—Hulk Hogan was both the WWE Champion and *Royal Rumble* winner
31. c) Randy Savage
32. d) Miami, FL
33. b) The Rockers
34. d) Dusty & Dustin Rhodes
35. c) Saba Simba
36. b) Bret Hart
37. d) Tugboat
38. b) The WWE Championship changed hands at a *Royal Rumble* event.
39. c) Big Boss Man and The Mountie
40. a) Mr. Fuji
41. b) WWE Championship
42. c) The New Foundation
43. b) Intercontinental Championship
44. c) Ric Flair
45. b) over an hour
46. c) British Bulldog
47. b) Texas Tornado
48. d) Warlord
49. b) Ted DiBiase
50. b) the Genius
51. c) Tugboat
52. a) 1
53. c) over the top rope and both feet must hit the floor

54. c) January
55. b) Sid Justice
56. c) Marty Jannetty
57. b) Yokozuna
58. d) The Steiner Brothers
59. c) Ric Flair
60. b) Damian Demento
61. c) Carlos Colon
62. a) Razor Ramon
63. d) Bob Backlund
64. b) Winner faces the WWE Champion at *WrestleMania.*
65. a) 1999
66. a) Mr. Perfect
67. c) Kato of the Orient Express
68. a) voodoo
69. b) Beau & Blake
70. c) 7
71. b) Owen Hart
72. c) Casket match
73. b) Lex Luger
74. c) 3
75. b) eliminating seven Superstars in a row
76. c) No one
77. a) Headshrinker Samu
78. b) Irwin R. Schyster
79. d) Thurman
80. d) Kwang
81. b) Oscar
82. c) Both Bret and Lex
83. b) Flames
84. d) Bam Bam Bigelow

85. a) Jeff Jarrett
86. c) draw
87. b) Shawn Michaels
88. True
89. d) Mantaur
90. a) Crush
91. b) 1-2-3- Kid & Bob Holly
92. True—Shawn Michaels and British Bulldog entered at Nos. 1 and 2 respectively.
93. b) 2
94. d) Jerry Lawler
95. c) Jeff hit Ahmed with a guitar.
96. b) Triple H
97. d) Sunny
98. a) Goldust
99. b) Billy & Bart
100. b) He won a match against Triple H.
101. c) Diesel
102. b) Isaac Yankem, D.D.S.
103. c) Diesel
104. a) Dory Funk Jr.
105. d) San Antonio, TX
106. c) Nation of Domination
107. a) Perro Aguayo
108. d) Stone Cold Steve Austin—but not without controversy; Austin was eliminated but the referees didn't see it. Austin came back in, tossed Bret Hart over the top rope and was declared the winner.
109. b) a TV camera
110. b) They were Minis.
111. a) Marlena
112. c) Vader
113. b) the Alamodome
114. d) *Survivor Series*
115. c) Terry Funk and Mankind
116. b) San Antonio, TX
117. a) PG-13
118. b) Mike Tyson
119. c) San Jose, CA
120. d) Stone Cold Steve Austin
121. b) Casket match
122. b) The Rock
123. c) 3—As Mankind, Cactus Jack and Dude Love
124. a) Stone Cold Steve Austin and The Rock
125. c) Mark Henry
126. b) Vader
127. c) Billy Gunn & Road Dogg
128. b) Salvatore Sincere
129. b) D.O.A.
130. b) He cheered wildly.
131. d) "No Chance in Hell"
132. c) $100,000
133. b) Vince McMahon
134. d) Shawn Michaels

135. c) 11
136. b) ankle lock
137. c) Strap match
138. d) Chyna
139. c) "I Quit" match
140. b) The Brood
141. c) Vince McMahon
142. d) Defeating Undertaker in a Buried Alive match in December 1998.
143. a) Dan Severn
144. b) The Oddities
145. a) Shawn Stasiak
146. b) It was a Tables match.
147. c) Mae Young
148. d) Chris Jericho
149. c) X-Pac
150. b) thumbtacks
151. d) The Rock
152. b) Big Show
153. a) Dance
154. c) D'Lo Brown
155. b) X-Pac
156. c) Chyna
157. c) Mr. Ass
158. False—The referee stopped the match and Angle, to this day, maintains that he never submitted.
159. a) A shot at the WWE Champion at *WrestleMania*.
160. b) Kaientai
161. c) the Dudley Boyz

162. b) Ladder match
163. a) Ivory
164. c) Triple H
165. d) Trish and Stephanie McMahon-Helmsley
166. c) Stone Cold Steve Austin
167. b) Jeff Hardy
168. a) Drew Carey
169. d) Honky Tonk Man
170. c) Kane
171. c) 30
172. b) New Orleans, LA
173. c) Walls of Jericho
174. b) Haku
175. c) Mr. McMahon
176. b) A collision of heads.
177. a) Hugo Savinovich & Carlos Cabrera
178. True—He entered at No. 25.
179. d) Bull Buchanan
180. b) Al Snow & Steve Blackman
181. c) Atlanta, GA
182. d) Maven
183. d) Ric Flair
184. a) Honky Tonk Man
185. b) Triple H
186. c) Kurt Angle
187. b) Val Venis
188. c) Tazz & Spike Dudley
189. d) William Regal
190. c) Jacqueline
191. a) Chris Jericho

192. b) Rikishi
193. c) figure-four leglock
194. c) The Hurricane
195. d) Booker T
196. b) Trish Stratus

197. c) brass knuckles
198. b) camera
199. c) Nick Patrick
200. d) Jim Ross and
Jerry Lawler

SmackDown!

Pilot Episode

1. Vince and Stephanie McMahon
2. Hartford, CT
3. Corporate Ministry
4. Stone Cold Steve Austin and The Rock
5. b) Mark Henry

6. The Brood (Gangrel, Edge & Christian)
7. The Union
8. New Age Outlaws
9. d) Stone Cold and The Rock
10. Vince McMahon

1999

11. Howard Finkel
12. Test and Stephanie McMahon
13. Shawn Michaels
14. Gillberg (Duane Gill)
15. Howard Finkel and Harvey Whippleman
16. "Pepper" steak
17. British Bulldog
18. the Fabulous Moolah
19. Buried Alive
20. Vince McMahon

21. 1-e) Big Show— Chokeslam match, 2-a) Kane—Inferno match, 3-c) Mideon and Viscera—Casket match, 4-b) Mankind—Boiler Room Brawl, 5-d) The Rock—Brahma Bullrope
22. Undertaker
23. New Age Outlaws
24. Terri Invitational Tournament
25. Terri's managerial services and $100,000

26. Hardy Boyz vs. Edge & Christian
27. Mark Henry
28. Rattlesnake
29. He said he'd been bitten by a snake.
30. Stevie Richards
31. b) The male therapist showed a liking for "Sexual Chocolate."
32. the Fabulous Moolah vs. Mae Young
33. D'Lo Brown
34. Wal-Mart
35. e) Vince McMahon
36. b) He hit the bottom rope as he leaped into the ring, breaking his nose.
37. Arnold Schwarzenegger
38. Marissa Mazzolla

39. c) Big Boss Man tied the casket to the back of a car and dragged it through the cemetery.
40. d) Gangrel
41. a catcher's mask
42. a) Triple H and Stephanie McMahon joined forces.
43. A front-row ticket for *Armageddon*
44. Shane McMahon
45. Nomar Garciaparra
46. McMahon–Helmsley Era
47. Matt Hardy and Christian
48. a) Lumberjack match
49. Mankind
50. f) Albert
51. d) Mick's WWE debut

2000

52. a) Big Show vs. X-Pac
53. Rikishi
54. Cactus Jack
55. b) Kane
56. the Friendly Tap
57. "The X-Pac and Tori Christmas Story"
58. She's pregnant.
59. Zero
60. b) Eddie Guerrero
61. "Hervina" Harvey Whippleman

62. European Championship
63. B.B. (Barbara Bush)
64. the DX Express
65. Crash Holly
66. b) The 24/7 rule in the Hardcore Division
67. b) Bob Backlund
68. c) Triple H vs. The Rock vs. Big Show
69. a) cows
70. c) She slapped her mother.

71. Stephanie McMahon-Helmsley
72. The Rock
73. Fat Bastard
74. c) Tazz was ECW Champion heading into the bout.
75. Tommy Dreamer
76. Mean Street Posse
77. Stone Cold Steve Austin
78. a) She kissed him.
79. his brother, Jeff Hardy
80. Chris Jericho
81. Hardy Boyz
82. d) All of the above
83. Lita
84. Samuel L. Jackson
85. The Fac-gime
86. Hardcore Holly
87. a) "It Doesn't Matter"
88. Trish Stratus
89. Brooklyn Brawler
90. a) Chris Benoit
91. Kurt Angle
92. Chris Jericho
93. c) Test
94. b) Playboy Mansion
95. c) Eddie Guerrero and Chyna
96. Kurt Angle
97. b) T&APA
98. a) You're in my yard.
99. Billy Gunn
100. Triple H and Stephanie McMahon-Helmsley
101. True
102. c) Dean Malenko
103. b) 1969 Chevy Impala
104. d) Val Venis

2001

105. a) Chris Jericho vs. Chris Benoit
106. Trish Stratus
107. c) Rikishi
108. spanking
109. Honky Tonk Man
110. William Regal
111. Cage match
112. Mick Foley
113. b) Picked his nose.
114. Jim Ross
115. Val Venis
116. a) Eddie Guerrero
117. Linda McMahon
118. William Regal
119. "My Way or the Highway"
120. Rhyno
121. WCW-1
122. Debra
123. Jim Ross
124. b) Indefinitely suspended him
125. Triple H

126. Jeff Hardy
127. Kane
128. Right to Censor
129. Bret Hart
130. Rikishi
131. Spike Dudley
132. b) APA
133. Jericho & Benoit
134. 10
135. c) Spike Dudley
136. Stacy Keibler
137. Paul Heyman
138. a) cowboy hats
139. d) "Hold on Loosely"
140. c) It was the one hundredth episode of the series.
141. Kurt Angle
142. Kanyon
143. Kronik
144. The Rock was WCW Champion, Angle was WWE Champion
145. Rob Van Dam
146. Mick Foley
147. Tazz
148. Rhyno
149. Stephanie McMahon-Helmsley
150. a) Kane
151. Paul Heyman
152. Trish Stratus and Stacy Keibler
153. Trish Stratus
154. d) Rikishi
155. b) a grocery store

2002

156. b) to embarrass Ric Flair at *Royal Rumble*
157. Barry Manilow
158. c) Hulk Hogan
159. b) He threw up.
160. DDP
161. a) it was Triplett's first match in eight months.
162. nWo (New World Order)
163. the Charleston
164. Rebecca Romijn-Stamos, LL Cool J and Chris Klein
165. Stone Cold Steve Austin
166. Rob Zombie
167. Will Sasso
168. Maven
169. d) limousine
170. Billy & Chuck
171. b) he quit WWE
172. a) Chris Jericho and Stephanie mcMahon
173. Japan
174. Lucy
175. Killer Kowalski
176. c) David Flair
177. b) Brock Lesnar
178. The Rock

179. Faarooq from APA, D-Von from the Dudley Boyz
180. d) European Title
181. Billy & Chuck
182. Maven and Raven
183. Tajiri
184. Hollywood Hulk Hogan
185. Stacy Keibler
186. DDP
187. "You Suck"
188. Randy Orton
189. Hell in the Cell
190. Deacon Batista
191. Maven
192. a) retiring
193. Kurt Angle
194. Gregory Helms
195. Dawn Marie
196. Kurt Angle
197. Nidia
198. c) The Rock
199. Linda and Jackie
200. Stephanie McMahon

Survivor Series

1. 1988
2. 1992
3. 1987
4. 2000
5. 1996
6. 1995
7. 2000
8. 1989
9. 1991
10. 1990
11. 1994
12. 1993
13. 2001
14. 1988
15. 1994

16. 1994
17. 1999
18. 1998
19. 1997
20. 1997
21. 1997
22. 1987
23. 1989
24. 1992
25. 1993
26. 1998
27. 1995
28. 1990
29. 1991
30. 1999

31. 1998
32. 2000
33. 2001
34. 1989
35. 1991
36. 1992
37. 1993
38. 1999
39. 1987
40. 1996
41. 2001
42. 1996
43. 1990
44. 1988
45. 1995

Survivor Series 1987

46. Richfield, OH

47. 4

48. Jim Duggan and Harley Race; both were counted out.

49. Honky Tonk Man

50. 3; Roberts, Savage and Steamboat

51. c) Miss Elizabeth

52. the Jumping Bomb Angels

53. d) the Fabulous Freebirds

54. b) Butch Reed

55. True

56. c) Andre the Giant

Survivor Series 1988

57. True

58. c) the Fabulous Rougeau Brothers

59. d) the Powers of Pain

60. Greg Valentine

61. False; he only eliminated Jim Brunzell.

62. Jake Roberts, Jim Duggan, Ken Patera, Scott Casey and Tito Santana

63. False; Andre was disqualified; Dino Bravo and Mr. Perfect were the only survivors.

64. c) Red Rooster and Koko B. Ware

65. Akeem by pinfall

66. Red Rooster and Ted DiBiase

Survivor Series 1989

67. Brutus Beefcake, Dusty Rhodes, the Red Rooster, Tito Santana

68. He walked out on his team and was counted out.

69. a) Jerry Lawler

70. c) Greg Valentine

71. Hulk Hogan

72. He was pinned by Ted DiBiase.

73. True

74. The Heenan Family and Ultimate Warrior

75. False; Andre the Giant was the first to be eliminated.

76. Arn Anderson and Bobby Heenan

Survivor Series 1990

77. Philadelphia, PA
78. 6
79. Undertaker
80. Jake Roberts, Jimmy Snuka, Marty Jannetty, Shawn Michaels
81. They became the first *Survivor Series* team to win without having a member eliminated.

82. b) Typhoon
83. d) Rick Martel
84. Hulk Hogan, Tito Santana, Ultimate Warrior
85. True
86. Hulk Hogan and Ultimate Warrior

Survivor Series 1991

87. Detroit, MI
88. Ric Flair
89. True
90. Undertaker
91. Ric Flair slid a chair into the ring. Undertaker used it to defeat Hogan.

92. False; everyone who was eliminated was pinned.
93. He refused to compete after Typhoon was pinned and walked out.
94. Typhoon
95. Legion of Doom
96. True

Survivor Series 1992

97. Koko B. Ware & Owen Hart
98. a Nightstick match
99. Mr. Perfect & Randy Savage
100. The Beverly Brothers

101. Irwin R. Schyster and "The Million-Dollar Man" Ted DiBiase
102. Yokozuna

103. a Casket match

104. Undertaker

105. Shawn Michaels

106. The Sharpshooter

Survivor Series 1993

107. Boston, MA

108. a) Tatanka

109. Bruce, Keith and Owen

110. Black, Blue and Red

111. the Smokey Mountain Wrestling Tag Team Championship

112. the Heavenly Bodies

113. Doink the Clown

114. the All Americans and the Foreign Fanatics

115. Diesel

116. c) Lex Luger

Survivor Series 1994

117. a) the Teamsters

118. b) Davey Boy Smith

119. d) Dink, Doink, Pink and Wink

120. a) Jerry Lawler, Cheesy, Queasy and Sleazy

121. Davey Boy Smith

122. Helen Hart

123. c) Tito Santana

124. Casket match

125. Chuck Norris

126. King Kong Bundy and Jeff Jarrett

Survivor Series 1995

127. Landover, MD

128. False

129. Alundra Blayze

130. Bam Bam Bigelow

131. Harley Race

132. All of them: Fatu, Henry O. Godwinn, Savio Vega and Undertaker

133. Tom Prichard

134. True

135. Diesel

136. False; it lasted just over twenty-four minutes.

Survivor Series 1996

137. New York, NY
138. b) Savio Vega
139. c) Doug Furnas and Phil Lafon
140. He was suspended above the ring in a cage to insure that he would not interfere in the match.
141. Undertaker
142. True
143. True
144. No one survived.
145. Shawn Michaels
146. Jose Lothario

Survivor Series 1997

147. Montreal, Quebec, Canada
148. c) Doug Furnas
149. the Truth Commission
150. Team Canada
151. Kane
152. a) Ahmed Johnson
153. Owen Hart
154. Vince McMahon
155. Earl Hebner
156. Hart claimed that he had not submitted and should still be WWE Champion.

Survivor Series 1998

157. "Deadly Game"
158. Jacqueline
159. He attacked Stone Cold Steve Austin with a nightstick.
160. 4 seconds
161. Triple H, The Rock's original opponent, no-showed and Mr. McMahon picked Big Boss Man to take his place.
162. Al Snow
163. Kane
164. Shane McMahon
165. Kane ran in and chokeslammed The Rock. The referee thus disqualified Undertaker.
166. The Sharpshooter

Survivor Series 1999

167. Faarooq
168. Sean Stasiak
169. False; none of them survived.
170. b) the Fabulous Moolah
171. Big Show
172. Chyna
173. False; they were on the same team.
174. False; the New Age Outlaws won the match.
175. Stone Cold Steve Austin was hit by a car earlier in the evening and was unable to compete.
176. Triple H and The Rock
177. Big Show

Survivor Series 2000

178. Tampa, FL
179. Steven Richards
180. b) Steve Blackman
181. Chris Benoit, Eddie Guerrero, Perry Saturn and Dean Malenko
182. Kane
183. Hardcore Holly
184. False; he pinned Rikishi.
185. False; Ivory won the match.
186. the Dudley Boyz
187. Angle's brother Eric
188. Edge & Christian
189. No one. It went to a no contest.

Survivor Series 2001

190. the Alliance and World Wrestling Entertainment
191. European Championship
192. William Regal
193. Alliance 2; World Wrestling Entertainment 1
194. a Steel Cage match
195. d) Test
196. a Six-Pack Challenge
197. Big Show, Undertaker, Kane, Chris Jericho and The Rock
198. Shane McMahon, Booker T, Rob Van Dam, Kurt Angle and Stone Cold Steve Austin
199. The Rock and Stone Cold Steve Austin
200. Kurt Angle

Pay-Per-View

Name that Pay-Per-View

1. c) *No Way Out '98*
2. a) *In Your House: Final Four*
3. a) *Armageddon '99*
4. a) *In Your House: Buried Alive*
5. c) *WrestleMania XVI*
6. *In Your House: Badd Blood; October*
7. c) *Judgment Day 2000*
8. b) *No Mercy '99*
9. *Unforgiven*
10. b) *Backlash 2000*
11. c) *Backlash 2000*
12. b) *St. Valentine's Day Massacre*
13. *St. Valentine's Day Massacre*
14. *King of the Ring 1996*
15. a) *Fully Loaded '98*
16. c) *Fully Loaded '99*
17. b) *In Your House: D-Generation X*
18. *Judgment Day '98*
19. a) *Backlash*
20. b) *Backlash 2000*

No Way Out

21. a) Savio Vega
22. a) Cactus Jack
23. a) Hell in the Cell
24. *St. Valentine's Day Massacre*
25. a) Houston, TX
26. Compaq Center
27. c) Stone Cold Steve Austin
28. Chainsaw Charlie
29. False
30. The Rock, Kurt Angle
31. a) Hulk Hogan
32. False
33. True
34. nWo, Stone Cold Steve Austin
35. c) Chris Jericho
36. a) Stone Cold Steve Austin
37. b) The Rock
38. True
39. False
40. False

Backlash

41. Dude Love
42. Scotty 2 Hotty
43. Stone Cold Steve Austin vs. Dude Love
44. 1999
45. True
46. a) Big Show
47. True
48. c) Washington, D.C.
49. False
50. Hardcore Holly, Tazz

51. a) Kurt Angle
52. Chris Jericho; Queensberry
53. a) Eddie Guerrero
54. True
55. False
56. b) Big Show
57. False
58. False
59. a) Kansas City, MO
60. c) Eddie Guerrero

Judgment Day

61. b) Iron Man match
62. a) Kurt Angle
63. October
64. c) 1998
65. True
66. Kane
67. a) Stone Cold Steve Austin
68. c) Triple H
69. a) Submission match
70. c) Shawn Michaels

71. Undertaker
72. False
73. 1998
74. b) Stone Cold Steve Austin
75. False
76. False
77. b) Ken Shamrock
78. True
79. a) Kane
80. c) Chain match

King of the Ring

81. b) Hulk Hogan
82. c) First Blood
83. True
84. True
85. c) Dan Severn

86. c) Jeff Jarrett
87. a) The Rock
88. Bret "Hit Man" Hart
89. b) Rikishi
90. Savio Vega

91. Dayton, OH
92. Road Dogg
93. Yokozuna, Kane, The Rock
94. False
95. Bam Bam Bigelow, Tatanka

96. a) Continental Airlines Arena
97. True
98. c) The Rock
99. a) Billy Gunn
100. b) Razor Ramon

Fully Loaded

101. Triple H, Strap
102. b) T&A and Trish Stratus
103. c) 1998
104. Undertaker, Mankind
105. c) Fresno, CA
106. Chris Benoit
107. b) Last Man Standing
108. True
109. a) Jeff Jarrett
110. True

111. a) Buffalo, NY
112. False
113. Road Dogg; Chyna
114. b) Steve Blackman
115. a) Bob Backlund
116. 2001
117. True
118. c) Undertaker
119. Falls Count Anywhere
120. False

Unforgiven

121. c) Tony Danza
122. c) Dude Love
123. b) April
124. c) Greensboro, NC
125. New Midnight Express, the Rock 'n' Roll Express
126. c) Inferno
127. 1999
128. b) Val Venis
129. True
130. a) Chyna

131. c) Ivory
132. a) New Age Outlaws
133. Big Show, Mankind, Triple H
134. True
135. a) Steve Blackman
136. c) X-Pac
137. False
138. c) Eddie Guerrero
139. Kane, The Rock
140. True

No Mercy

141. Rikishi
142. a) Kurt Angle
143. False
144. b) Triple H
145. the Fabulous Moolah, Ivory
146. a) Kurt Angle
147. Edge & Christian, Terri, 100,000
148. a) steel cage
149. False
150. Kurt Angle, Rob Van Dam

151. True
152. a) Edge & Christian
153. False
154. a) The Rock
155. c) The Hurricane & Lance Storm
156. b) Lingerie
157. c) Pepsi Arena
158. b) The Conquistadors
159. True
160. False

In Your House

161. False
162. a) Shawn Michaels
163. b) Sycho Sid
164. 1995
165. c) *D-Generation X*
166. b) *Revenge of the 'Taker*
167. c) *Good Friends, Better Enemies*
168. a) 5
169. False
170. c) Bret "Hit Man" Hart

171. *Final Four*
172. True
173. True
174. a) *Canadian Stampede*
175. Vader, Stone Cold Steve Austin
176. a) British Bulldog
177. b) *Beware of Dog*
178. c) The Patriot
179. False
180. False

Other Events

181. True
182. Junkyard Dog
183. a) Undertaker
184. *One Night Only*

185. Kurt Angle
186. Vince McMahon
187. Big Boss Man
188. a) Kurt Angle

189. b) "Rowdy" Roddy Piper
190. False
191. Brutus Beefcake, Randy Savage
192. a) Vince McMahon
193. c) *Captial Carnage*
194. a) Mideon

195. True
196. b) Dynamite Kid
197. a) the Pyramid
198. True
199. a) Skinner
200. True

Old School

Hall of Famers

1. c) Antonino Rocca
2. c) Malta
3. b) Strike Force
4. True
5. True
6. True
7. False

8. a) Crusher Verdu
9. Fiji
10. Andre the Giant
11. Big John Studd
12. Jerry
13. James Dudley

Tag Teams

14. b) Gerald Brisco
15. c) Nikolai Volkoff
16. a) Jose Estrada
17. a) Rene Goulet
18. a) Billy White Wolf
19. a) the Killer Bees
20. c) Tama
21. a) Demolition
22. b) the Fabulous Freebirds
23. False
24. The Powers of Pain

25. Nikolai Volkoff
26. True
27. a) Adrian Adonis & Dick Murdoch
28. Raymond
29. Crush
30. the Rockers
31. Genichiro Tenryu & Keji Kitao
32. Marty Jannetty
33. c) The Hart Foundation
34. Boris Zhukov

35. Dino Bravo
36. Blackjack Mulligan
37. Al Costello
38. c) Tony Garea

39. The Natural Disasters
40. Arn Anderson
41. Mr. Fuji

Managers

42. a) Brother Love
43. b) Teddy Long
44. a) Stone Cold Steve Austin
45. b) Wild Red Berry
46. a) Mr. Fuji
47. True
48. c) "The Doctor of Style" Slick
49. "Classy" Freddie Blassie, Mr. Fuji, Slick
50. True
51. b) Frenchy Martin
52. Lou Albano, Intercontinental
53. True

54. b) Jimmy Hart
55. Baron Von Raschke
56. Dusty Rhodes
57. Harvey Whippleman
58. Bobby Heenan
59. Jimmy Hart
60. Jimmy Hart
61. Bobby Heenan
62. "Superstar" Billy Graham
63. Lou Albano
64. the Grand Wizard
65. Bobby Davis
66. "Classy" Freddie Blassie
67. Lou Albano
68. Wild Red Berry

Originators

69. b) Ray Stevens
70. b) Iron Sheik
71. b) Randy Savage
72. b) Lou Thesz
73. True
74. False
75. True
76. c) Tony Atlas

77. c) "High Chief" Peter Maivia
78. Tiger Jeet Singh
79. Harley Race
80. Larry "the Axe" Hennig
81. Lou Albano
82. Prof. Boris Malenko
83. Johnny Valentine

84. c) Buddy Roberts
85. c) Dominic DeNucci
86. c) Midnight Express

87. True
88. Joseph "Toots" Mondt

Famous Firsts

89. b) Women's Tag Team
90. George "the Animal" Steele, Continental Airlines Arena
91. a) Dino Bravo
92. True
93. a) Grand Wizard
94. b) Akeem
95. a) the Genius
96. b) Hulk Hogan
97. b) Jake "The Snake" Roberts
98. Bull Ramos
99. Rick Rude
100. *Survivor Series 1991*
101. Slick

102. Hulk Hogan
103. Giant Baba
104. 1956
105. Andre the Giant
106. 1986
107. a) S. D. "Special Delivery" Jones
108. Hulk Hogan, Col. Mustafa, *SummerSlam '91*
109. "Classy" Freddie Blassie
110. a) "Million-Dollar Man" Ted DiBiase
111. Paul Ellering
112. Dumont Network
113. Ken Patera

Announcers and Officials

114. c) Vince McMahon
115. Jesse Ventura
116. Jesse Ventura
117. Mike McGuirk
118. Gary Michael Cappetta

119. Willy Gilzenberg
120. Lord Alfred Hayes
121. Vince McMahon
122. Howard Finkel
123. Bobby Heenan

Great Grudges and Matches

124. b) Shea Stadium
125. Sid Justice; Undertaker
126. False
127. a) the Berzerker
128. MTV
129. Spiros Arion
130. Bob Backlund
131. Johnny Valiant
132. Los Angeles Sports Arena
133. Stan Hansen
134. Bruno Sammartino
135. Tony Atlas
136. "Superstar" Billy Graham
137. c) the Fabulous Moolah

Great Champions

138. a) Ultimate Warrior
139. b) *Survivor Series*
140. True
141. Hulk Hogan, Ted DiBiase
142. Swede Hansen, "Superstar" Billy Graham
143. a) Pat O'Connor
144. False
145. the Natural Disasters
146. Shawn Michaels
147. Bob Backlund
148. Tag Team
149. Camel Clutch
150. Atomic Kneedrop
151. Arnold Skaaland
152. Pat Patterson
153. Tag Team
154. be, beat
155. False
156. c) Mr. Perfect

Identities

157. a) Mike Rotundo
158. 1990, Tornado, Intercontinental, Mr. Perfect
159. One Man Gang
160. Big Bubba Rogers
161. Dusty Rhodes
162. Repo Man
163. Papa Shango
164. Col. Mustafa
165. The Masked Superstar
166. Buddy Rose
167. Antonio Pugliese
168. Bepo Mongol

Great Gimmicks

169. False
170. c) The Red Rooster
171. Cousin Junior
172. True
173. b) Rocco
174. c) Earthquake
175. Brutus Beefcake
176. Paul Bearer
177. Jake Roberts
178. Roddy Piper

179. "Hacksaw" Jim Duggan
180. Adrian Adonis
181. Jesse Ventura
182. Morgan's Corner
183. Uganda
184. Mongolia
185. Haku
186. Frankie
187. Virgil

Hollywood Hulk Hogan

188. True
189. Andre the Giant, Shea
190. b) "Classy" Freddie Blassie
191. a) Tony Atlas
192. b) "Dr. D" David Schultz
193. c) Bobby "The Brain" Heenan

194. a) Cowboy Bob Orton
195. a) Rip
196. b) One Man Gang
197. a) his hand
198. c) Barry Windham & Mike Rotundo
199. Randy Savage
200. True

Titles

Pictures

1. Don Muraco
2. Leilani Kai
3. Hulk Hogan
4. D'Lo Brown

5. Tito Santana & Ivan Putski
6. 1-2-3- Kid & Bob Holly
7. Bertha Faye

8. Scotty 2 Hotty
9. Dudley Boyz
10. Kurt Angle
11. Greg Valentine &
   Brutus Beefcake
12. The Mountie
13. Al Snow
14. Crash Holly

15. Chief Jay Strongbow
   & Jules Strongbow
16. the Nasty Boys
17. Razor Ramon
18. Perry Saturn
19. Stone Cold Steve Austin
20. Bob Backlund

World Championship

21. c) Rio de Janeiro, Brazil
22. d) Buffalo, NY
23. Puerto Rico
24. a) Andre the Giant
25. "Superstar" Billy
   Graham
26. c) Hulk Hogan
27. c) Antonio Inoki
28. Bruno Sammartino
   (5-17-63 – 1-18-71)
29. True
30. *WrestleMania IV*
31. b) 4
32. Halftime Heat
33. b) 3

34. d) Arnold Skaaland
35. Bruno Sammartino
36. a-5) Triple H—Charlotte,
   NC, b-4) Shawn
   Michaels—San Antonio,
   TX, c-1) Undertaker—
   Kansas City, MO, d-2)
   Kurt Angle—Pittsburgh,
   PA, e-3) Ric Flair—
   Hershey, PA
37. Triple H and The Rock
38. No one; he vacated
   the belt.
39. a) Soviet Union
40. a) Bret Hart

Tag Team

41. b) U.S. Tag Team Title
42. d) Eddie & Dr. Jerry
   Graham
43. b) Washington D.C.

44. False; he won it on
   7-5-62 with Handsome
   John Barend.
45. Billy Gunn & Road Dogg
   Jesse James

46. d) Rene Goulet
47. the Natural Disasters
48. Tony Atlas & Rocky Johnson
49. Killer Kowalski & Big John Studd
50. Lou Albano
51. a-1) 1960s—24, b-2) 1970s—25, c-3) 1980s—52, d-4) 1990s—21
52. the British Bulldogs

53. once
54. Anaheim, CA
55. True
56. a) Jeff Jarrett
57. False; they beat them on 11-18-01 in Greensboro, NC.
58. The Rock 'N' Sock Connection
59. Rico
60. True

Intercontinental

61. d) Rio de Janeiro, Brazil
62. b) Pat Patterson
63. d) Ken Patera; New York, NY—4-21-80
64. Once. He beat Tito Santana on 9-24-84.
65. False. He's from Sunset Beach, HI.
66. a-4) Rick Steamboat— Randy Savage, b-1) The Mountie—Bret Hart, c-3) Jesse James—Val Venis, d-2) Diesel—Razor Ramon
67. Two—Randy Savage and Honky Tonk Man.

68. Razor Ramon
69. False; three times.
70. False; Davey Boy Smith beat Bret Hart in London on 8-29-92.
71. c) Razor Ramon
72. Chyna
73. Edge
74. a) 2001
75. a) Owen Hart
76. True
77. Jack Tunney
78. False
79. c) Jacksonville, FL
80. c) Chris Jericho

European Championship

81. Berlin, Germany

82. 1997

83. Davey Boy Smith

84. b) Crash Holly

85. c) Shane McMahon

86. True

87. True

88. a) Shawn Michaels

89. Triple H

90. b) Shane McMahon

91. c) Goldust

92. Eddie Guerrero

93. a-3) Owen Hart—Davis, CA, b-2) Kurt Angle— Austin, TX, c-1) Perry Saturn— Dallas, TX, d-4) Al Snow— Fayetteville, NC

94. True

95. True

96. d) Test

97. Jeff Jarrett

98. True—at *WrestleMania XVI*

99. False

100. d) Ames, IA

Light-Heavyweight Championship

101. d) Taka Michinoku

102. False

103. 1998

104. a) 1

105. Light-Heavyweight Championship

106. 220 pounds

107. X-Pac

108. Duane Gill

109. False. Only Scotty 2 Hotty won it.

110. Albert

111. Dean Malenko

112. Jeff Hardy

113. a) 0

114. Dean Malenko was making advances toward Molly.

115. Jerry Lynn

116. Jeff Hardy

117. d) Dean Malenko

118. *In Your House: D-Generation X*

119. True

120. Penn State University

Hardcore Championship

121. c) Vince McMahon
122. Big Boss Man
123. Big Boss Man
124. Crash Holly
125. 10
126. Hardcore Holly
127. Gerald Brisco
128. British Bulldog; London on 5-6-00
129. b) Bob Holly, a) Billy Gunn, d) Tazz, c) K-Kwik
130. False; he was the first.
131. False
132. Matt
133. False
134. a) *Raw*
135. b) Shawn Michaels
136. Big Boss Man
137. The Holly Family
138. False; Jesse James won it as well.
139. Undertaker
140. True

Women's Championship

141. Judy Grable
142. Baltimore, MD
143. 28 years
144. Wendi Richter
145. Velvet McIntyre
146. c) Leilani Kai
147. b) Jacqueline
148. 3
149. d) Rockin' Robin
150. True; fifties, sixties, seventies, eighties, nineties
151. b) Harvey Whippleman
152. The Kat in a Snow Bunny Lumberjill match.
153. b) Debra; d) Ivory; c) Lita; d) Chyna.
154. True
155. Ivory, Lita, Jazz, Mighty Molly and Jacqueline.
156. True
157. c) Spider Lady
158. 2002
159. Evening Gown match
160. Commissioner Shawn Michaels

Multiple Championship

161. Bruno Sammartino
162. Buddy Rogers; with Johnny Valentine on 11-19-60 and Handsome John Berend on 7-5-62.
163. Pedro Morales
164. Chyna
165. d) Chris Jericho
166. False; he and Pedro Morales beat the Samoans on 8-09-80.
167. a) World, b) Tag Team, d) Hardcore, c) Intercontinental
168. a) British Bulldog
169. False
170. Intercontinental
171. False; he only won the Tag Team Championship.
172. 2000
173. 2
174. False; he only won the World Championship.
175. Billy Gunn
176. a-2) World—St. Louis, MO, b-1) Intercontinental—Lowell, MA, c-3) Tag Team—Boston, MA
177. a) Christian
178. False; he only won the Tag Team Championship.
179. c) 4; two Tag Team and two Intercontinental Championships
180. Garea. He won 4. DeNucci 1.

Grab Bag Championship

181. True
182. Ken Patera
183. True
184. Vince McMahon
185. Antonio Inoki
186. True
187. Ted DiBiase
188. Chris Jericho
189. Malta
190. False
191. Haystacks Calhoun. He weighed in at 625 pounds.
192. c) Yokozuna
193. Triple H. He won the World Championship on 1-3-00.
194. 29; he won it at the *Royal Rumble 1992.*
195. Harlem

196. a) Bad News Brown

197. Hulk Hogan

198. d) Rawbone

199. Jimmy and Johnny

200. Honky Tonk Man

Outside the Ring

a) Maven—
   1) Charlottesville, VA

b) Brock Lesnar—
   2) Minneapolis, MI

c) Trish Stratus—
   5) Toronto, Ontario,
   Canada

d) Faarooq—14) Warner
   Robins, GA

e) Eddie Guerrero—
   8) El Paso, TX

f) Big Boss Man—
   3) Dallas, GA

g) Jazz—11) New Orleans,
   LA

h) Steven Richards—
   10) Philadelphia, PA

i) Tommy Dreamer—
   6) Yonkers, NY

j) William Regal—
   13) Blackpool, England

k) Chris Benoit—
   15) Edmonton, Alberta,
   Canada

l) Hardcore Holly—
   9) Mobile, AL

m) Randy Orton—
   12) St. Louis, MO

n) Diamond Dallas Page—
   7) Point Pleasant Beach,
   NJ

o) Jacqueline—4) Dallas, TX

16. a) drum major of the band

17. Hungry Man and Chef
   Boyardee

18. Jam Zone

19. Moongoose McQueen

20. shot glass

21. *Brave New World*

22. d) Bruisin' Berry

23. b) *Rush Hour*

24. Sonya

25. Minnesota

26. South Dakota

27. b) 1996

28. a) drums

29. *It's True! It's True!*

30. Respect, Education,
   Achievement, Leadership

31. b) golf

32. offensive lineman

33. b) cheerleader

34. Christian
35. d) *Ally McBeal*
36. b) navy
37. a) army
38. c) Jimmy Buffett
39. d) All of the above
40. *Highlander: Endgame*
41. Big Boss Man
42. d) *Body Slam*
43. Randy Orton
44. volleyball
45. *American Gladiators*
46. c) Undertaker
47. Las Vegas
48. Triple H
49. Kane
50. "RAW Sex"
51. Matt Hardy
52. c) McPherson College
53. Big Show, Mick Foley, Triple H, Vince McMahon
54. a) Whisper
55. Lucky's
56. c) 150,000
57. bulldog
58. Sara
59. Memphis, TN
60. b) *The Waterboy*
61. Pittsburgh Steelers
62. New York Rangers
63. Reid
64. a) Torrie Wilson
65. Dr. Lloyd Youngblood
66. Dr. James Andrews
67. c) Kurt Angle
68. The Disciplinarian
69. a) Hugh Morrus
70. Dakota
71. "American Dream" Dusty Rhodes
72. special education; sign language
73. Mexico City
74. b) Tim White
75. a) *Juwanna Man*
76. Dean Malenko
77. d) brother
78. Los Angeles Express
79. Revlon
80. criminal justice
81. San Francisco
82. Gettin' Heat
83. Mean Gene's Burgers
84. Victoria
85. b) Jazz
86. Red Hook
87. d) rodeo
88. "It Doesn't Matter"
89. Dennis Hastert of Illinois, the Speaker of the House
90. Rocky Johnson; High Chief Peter Maivia
91. defensive lineman; Warren Sapp
92. *People*
93. d) biology and kinesiology

94. *Thunder in Paradise*
95. *Hulk Hogan's Rock 'n' Wrestlin'*
96. Train, say your prayers, take your vitamins.
97. University of South Florida
98. Christopher Reeve Paralysis Foundation
99. d) Trish Stratus
100. Kennedy
101. The Rock— g) *Star Trek: Voyager*
102. Sean Morley— j) *La Femme Nikita*
103. Hulk Hogan— c) *Suddenly Susan*
104. Rob Van Dam— e) *The X-Files*
105. Bradshaw— a) *The Huntress*
106. Triple H—f) *Grown-Ups*
107. Kevin Nash—h) *Sabrina the Teenage Witch*
108. Lita—d) *Dark Angel*
109. Booker T—i) *Charmed*
110. Godfather—b) *The Strip*
111. Super Shredder
112. Thunderlips
113. *Man on the Moon*
114. a) cookies
115. *Larry King Live*
116. Boise, ID
117. b) certified public accountant

118. c) *Boy Meets World*
119. Taylor
120. c) Spain
121. South Carolina
122. b) Ivory
123. Josh and Chris (a.k.a. Harvard Chris)
124. Taylor
125. Chavo Guerrero
126. Hugh Morrus
127. *Operation Sandman*
128. Stan "the Man" Stasiak
129. *Rollerball*
130. Elroy Jetson
131. 1992 & 1996
132. Arnold Schwarzenegger
133. 2
134. Howard Finkel
135. Teddy Long
136. Run-DMC
137. *Aggression*
138. 43rd Street and Broadway
139. Arn Anderson
140. d) *Life with Mikey*
141. Bob Backlund
142. bass guitar
143. 41
144. sixth
145. the *Toronto Sun*
146. b) Subway
147. He didn't have a backup plan; he doesn't believe in them.

148. Kevin Nash, Scott Hall, X-Pac, Triple H, Shawn Michaels
149. Gerald Brisco
150. b) Tampa Bay Buccaneers and Washington Redskins
151. *Squawk Box*
152. c) field hockey and soccer
153. c) ministorage
154. a) Chicago Blackhawks
155. Tommy Haas
156. d) lizards and snakes
157. New Jersey Devils
158. The Big Valbowski
159. Spanish
160. late-model stock cars
161. Junkyard Dog
162. motocross
163. hockey jerseys
164. Perry Saturn
165. *WWE Forceable Entry*
166. Skandor Akbar
167. Cypress Hill
168. d) Nebraska
169. a) 17
170. d) Sika
171. a) gymnastics
172. d) Neroammmmy
173. Yale University
174. Blackjack Lanza
175. Chris Kanyon
176. b) Billy Kidman
177. Dean Malenko
178. $1 million

179. *Can You Take the Heat?*
180. Make-A-Wish Foundation
181. Lance Storm—f) Wilfrid Laurier University
182. Big Show—n) Wichita State University
183. Bradshaw—d) Abilene Christian University
184. Kevin Nash— p) University of Tennessee
185. D'Lo Brown— c) University of Maine
186. Raven—r) University of Delaware
187. Trish Stratus— s) York University
188. Spike Dudley— o) Skidmore College
189. John Cena—j) Springfield College
190. Albert—b) University of Pittsburgh
191. Billy Gunn—t) Sam Houston State University
192. Chris Jericho— i) Red River College
193. Christian—m) Humber College
194. Faarooq—k) Florida State University
195. Godfather—g) University of Nevada-Reno

196. Ivory—e) University of Southern California

197. Maven—q) Eastern Mennonite University

198. Kurt Angle—a) Clarion University

199. The Rock—h) University of Miami

200. Stacy Keibler— l) Towson University

Hollywood Hulk Hogan™ rules!

You want action?
You want suspense?
You want to know
everything? It's all here,
Hulkamaniacs.™
The highs. The lows.
The in-betweens. The true
story of World Wrestling
Entertainment's™ Immortal Icon—and
all in his own words,
brother.

"You think you
know Hollywood
Hulk Hogan™?
Brother, you
don't know
squat about me."